"Is email writing in light? Obviously this is a sexy book, two poets splashing around in it together while they're falling in love. It's kind of mythical and engrossing, hard not to think: 'I'm them.' *Swoon* is perfect."
—Eileen Myles

"Hesitation, escalation. Both products of a poetic education, they are at the end of youth, employed elsewhere. But what are Philip Whalen, Theodor Adorno, Tito Rodriguez, Lester Bangs, Elizabeth Barrett Browning, Pablo Neruda and the entire Japanese language good for, unless there is someone else to talk about them to? *Swoon* is fabulous, compulsive reading: proof of the ability of love and need and even writing to trump the crappiness of daily life."
—Chris Kraus

"In a compelling, intelligent and sensual *pas de deux* culminating in unstoppable flows of torrid cyber-rapture, two *kunstler-roman*tics generate an epistolary avalanche that sweeps the reader into a real-life world of romantic [emotional?] approach, detente, and (happy ending pending) resolution in the realtime of real life. 'I think all writing is a form of love, or desire,' writes Gary Sullivan early on in his relationship with Nada Gordon, the epistolary contents of which comprise the present book. This volume of letters explores the cofoundational nature, the poeisis, of writing and love, giving credence to Jean Genet's dictum, 'We cannot suppose a creation which does not spring from love' and its putative converse: that creativity and imagination beget love, birthing it into the everyday world of time (two poets who had vaguely known of each other ten years previous to the correspondence's beginning), space (the distance between Brooklyn and Tokyo, the memory of San Francisco), and the logistics that separate us and bring us together (other relationships, fear, projection, desire, etc). "i love thee because thy gaze is the loveliest thermometer of our dual being ... i love thee as i love writing, as composition. is healing," writes Nada Gordon toward the end of the book, when the two lovers are finally living together but continue to write to each other. A magnificent achievement, these 300 pages were culled from over 5,000 of email and hard-mail correspondence generated within a year between two sharp-minded poets, ranging in genre from mutually consoling letters, lyricalanguage poetry of a very high order of accomplishment, erotic fantasy-vignettes, and physical descriptions of place and everyday life. At every moment, they make for a captivating and illuminating reading experience."
—Maria Damon

Swoon

NADA GORDON

&

GARY SULLIVAN

with an Afterword
by Chris Stroffolino

GRANARY BOOKS
NEW YORK
2001

Book and cover design by Gordon and Sullivan.

With the exception of the Postscript and Afterword, the material in this book was culled from approximately 5,000 pages of electronic and paper correspondence written between March 1998 and March 1999. Some of this material was originally published in the following anthologies, journals, listserves and online magazines: *The Alterran Poetry Assemblage*; *Buffalo Poetics List*; *Cello Entry*; *Central Park*; *Duration*; *The East Village*; *The Gertrude Stein Awards for 1994-95*; *If*; *Jacket*; *Long News: In the Short Century*; *The Poetry Project Website*; *The Portable Boog Reader*; *Printed Matter*; *Readme*; *RealPoetik*; *Subsubpoetics*; *Talisman*; and *The World*.

"Anime," a rewrite of George Albon's *Empire Life*, was published as *Anime* by Voces Puerulae. "2/1" and "2/18" were published as *Two Letters to Nada* by Stephen Ellis's OASiA: Broadside Series, Boston Poetry Conference Special, no. 70(f). "Ravel" was published in *Foriegnn Bodie* by Detour Press. Most of the month of January was published as "from Correspondence" by Jack Kimball's Fauxpress.com. Thanks to Robert Creeley for kind permission to print his poem "The Conspiracy."

In the spirit of the original exchange, the authors have allowed many punctuation and other inconsistencies to be left intact. Some standardization and other changes have been made where clarity was an issue.

Thanks to the following for their attentive reading, encouragement and constructive suggestions: David Bromige; Steve Clay; Maria Damon; Jordan Davis; Johanna Fuhrman; Drew Gardner; Ruthie Goldberg; Julie Harrison; Mitch Highfill; Kent Johnson; Adeena Karasick; Jack Kimball; Kimberly Lyons; Sheila Murphy; and Chris Stroffolino.

Library of Congress Cataloging-in-Publication Data

Gordon, Nada, 1964-
    Swoon / Nada Gordon & Gary Sullivan ; with an afterword by Chris
Stroffolino.
        p. cm.
    ISBN 1-887123-54-7 (pbk. : alk. paper)
    1. Gordon, Nada, 1964—Correspondence. 2. Sullivan, Gary,
1962—Correspondence. 3. Poets, American–20th
century–Correspondence. 4. Cartoonists–United States–Correspondence.
5. Americans–Japan–Correspondence. 6. Love-letters. I. Sullivan,
Gary, 1962- II. Title.
    PS3557.O6698 Z493 2001
    811'.6–dc21   2001004707

	Distributed to the trade by:	Also available from:
Granary Books, Inc.	Distributed Art Publishers	Small Press Distribution
307 Seventh Ave., Ste 1401	155 Avenue of the Americas	1341 Seventh Street
New York, NY 10001	New York, NY 10013-1507	Berkeley, CA 94710
Tel: (212) 337-9979	Tel: (212) 627-1999	Tel: (510) 524-1668
www.granarybooks.com	Fax: (212) 627-9484	Fax: (510) 524-0582
orders@granarybooks.com	Orders: (800) 338-BOOK	Orders: (800) 869-7553

The Conspiracy

You send me your poems,
I'll send you mine.

Things tend to awaken
even through random communication.

Let us suddenly
proclaim spring. And jeer

at the others,
all the others.

I will send a picture too
if you will send me one of you.

                    —Robert Creeley

MARCH

From: nada gordon
To: POETICS@LISTSERVE.ACSU.BUFFALO.EDU
Date: March 17
Subject: fake metaphors, similes, equivalences

... a couple of questions about metaphors & analogies: they are means by which we understand or conceive of something in terms of something else, right? is there anything we understand in itself and not by any analogy whatsoever? would that be *enlightenment*?

nada

∞

From: Gary Sullivan
To: nada gordon
Date: March 17
Subject: Hello

Hi, Nada:

Understanding is translation. Literally!

Yours,
Gary Sullivan

PS: Did you used to go by "gordon" and live in San Francisco? If so, you gave a wonderful reading many years ago at the Lab I was fortunate enough to have been dragged to by Brent Sunderland.

∞

From: nada gordon
Date: March 18
Subject: Re: Hello

hi gary

yes, that was me, one and the same. i adopted nada (an anagram of my real first name) when i came to tokyo ten years ago. i'm glad you found my reading wonderful. i still, i think, give wonderful readings (maybe my forté?—i almost like the performance part better than the actual writing because of the connectedness with other humans). i think i read at the lab a couple of times. was this one an arts festival with performances both upstairs and downstairs? was i wearing a t-shirt that had "YOU" written on it?

i'm not sure i remember brent sunderland. no, i remember the name and i probably remember his face but can't stick them together just now.

i guess you were at sf state just after i was. i was thrilled to notice that you included the poems we published in *if* in dan davidson's bibliography. also i think you mentioned my name in another post about sf women poets—thanks. i do feel alienated sometimes in my self-imposed exile here.

did you and i ever actually meet? do you still live in sf? i go back once a year. the writing scene has seemed to me, on my visits back, rather politicized and fractured (what else is new).

thanks also for noting that metaphor is translation. caught daily in the interstices between two languages, that makes a lot of sense to me.

best,
nada

∞

From: Gary Sullivan
Date: March 19
Subject: Dana?

Hello, Nada:

        I'm not sure what the circumstances were with respect to your reading, though I think I would have remembered if your

T-shirt said "YOU" on it. What I remember is that you sang (in retrospect, very middle eastern sounding) in between poems (or maybe as part of a longer poem?). Unless I saw you read twice, and the singing is from a subsequent reading. Hmmm. Well, definitely, at the reading at the Lab, you passed out treats & prizes prior to the reading, I remember that much. I remember getting, right after that, your e.g. book, *rodomontade*, even though I didn't know (then) what the word meant. That was at David Highsmith's bookstore—he also had some books, maybe two or three, that you hand-made. I wanted them but for some reason didn't pick them up. I think they intimidated me, for two reasons: (a) they were so "serious" looking; and (b) they were remarkably intimate things. (By "intimate" I don't probably mean what most would mean here. I mean, the way they were made seemed very much the product of the human hand & a particular sensibility.) I was very easily intimidated then.

We may very well have been at SF State at the same time: I was there from 1983–1986. I always thought of you—accurate or not—as kind of being connected with a group of women who (that word again) intimidated me at the time: Claire Phillips, Laura Brun, Jenni Currie, and I'm sure there were one or two others. Brent actually turned me on to that whole crowd: The first time I saw Claire read was across the street from State on Holloway with Brent and one other. Laura and Jenni I first saw read, or perform really, at a reading with me. I had done a performance, too: "Writing Degree James Brown," which I think embarrassed them. I "became" James Brown for the performance, which—believe me—was easier to do in your twenties than in your thirties. Many many months after that reading, Laura and I wound up becoming—for like a year, maybe—close friends & confidantes.

I wonder if you were working at *iF Magazine* when I sent some poems in—it's sort of a long story. I had a HUGE crush on Lori Lubeski! And my roommate, Brent, told me that she co-edited *iF*. I couldn't even look at Lori without my heart pounding, whole body sweating, mouth dry, etc. I found it completely impossible to talk to her. So my plan was to write some poems that would impress her enough to publish them in *iF* ... and if she published them, I'd have an excuse to talk to her. I had never written a poem before that. But I remember looking at all the poems in *iF* and thinking that the kind of poetry they published was a sort of game you played, fitting together words, arranging, like flower arranging, words loved by the arranger, and arranging might be like remembering all your past lovers simultaneously. I thought: "I can do this!" and decided to take definitions from the crossword puzzle of the San Francisco *Chronicle* and combine them with brief passages, two- and three-word clusters, from Ann Landers, Herb Caen, etc., all of which I strung together like magnetized beads along an invisible, polarized string. The result seemed to me just like the poems in *iF*:

PRINT

Breathing sound of yarn. The Gershwin of birds. An indefinite amount of a city in Oklahoma. Heretofore, the muscatel clench of an African antelope.
    And then: there were chemical compound wings— carol or canzonet—capable of face the day; with one promise, sign, in music; tough stuff, heavy, with a mystical meaning like the power of films; a haberdashery offering; positive; blessing; a harem room or a kind of wire; pixieish, in a tranquil way.

I showed the results to Brent and he said "Yeah, they'll love this." We had a mini-argument about it because Brent was adamant about it being "real" poetry, that really worked as poetry, and at the time I thought that (a) I was faking it and (b) that anyway poems were ultimately worthless except as you might use them to move, physically and emotionally and otherwise move, through the world. Brent seemed to believe a poem was something unto itself, autonomous, and that my intention had nothing to do with it, finally, at least nothing to do with its not being poetry. To me, it didn't register that something human-made might be autonomous. But, with Brent's encouragement, I sent the stuff in. And, lo & behold, two poems I'd written this way were published in the next issue of *iF*. But, I found out soon after that—I don't remember how or from whom—that Lori was gay. I was depressed for a long time after that. The fact that my poems had been published meant nothing to me. Anyway, years later, now, thinking about it, I think all writing is a form of love, or desire. Not necessarily in the sense that it's written for the object of desire, or out of love, but that it is a FORM of love, and/or desire.

The idea that understanding is translation comes from George Steiner, specifically his book *After Babel*.

It occurs to me that you might want to participate in this memorial project I'm putting together observing Dan Davidson's life and work. I'm looking for poetry, essays, memoirs & the like. Would love to get something from you, if you're at all interested.

Well, I don't live in San Francisco anymore—I live in New York. If you're ever out here, please let me know—especially if you're going to be reading. & I'd love to read more of your work, if you have any you'd like to send.

Okay, Nada. Talk with you sooner or later, I hope,

Yours,

Gary

∞

From: nada gordon
To: Gary Sullivan
Date: March 20
Subject: Re: Dana?

yes, dana is my unfortunate misnomer-handle. clever you for figuring it out.

i loved your e-mail, especially the part about lori. isn't she swell? i still talk to her now and then when i go back to the states. she and her girlfriend have a little boy, ben—but maybe you knew that (if you didn't i hope the news isn't too devastating). apparently he does bob dylan impressions and is ridiculously intelligent.

by the way lori was never not into boys. sometimes, when we were riding around the mission on her scooter, she'd say to me, "i want a boyfriend."

of course i knew claire, beautiful claire (lori's ex!), but i don't know the other women you mentioned. i left state in 1983 and started at berkeley. lori took over *if* from me and jessica grim at around that time.

i also remember the lab reading, i wore a white cotton 50s dress and had a fake red bird (a cardinal?) on my hand. my ex-boyfriend, a—, perhaps backed me up on effected guitar? or there were effects on the mike when i sang. i have forgotten about the treats and prizes, but i still hum that tune sometimes. i think i'm starting to remember brent, too—he was not so tall but a bit muscular, with a nice-looking face? wasn't he married or about to get married at that time? am i thinking of the right person?

those were halcyon days for me—great friends, great teachers, great community. somehow sf started feeling small and confining though. i lived right at 24th and mission across from the bart station— and i guess that's ok when you're nineteen but after a while i just couldn't take it anymore.

i really do love japan although life here has its frustrations. there's so much refinement and quirkiness and the force of the clash of the ancient & hyper-modern here—it never stops fascinating me. i live with a haiku poet, m—, in a beautiful house with tatami and *shoji* and wood carvings in the wall—i find i'm very attached to the aesthetics of this place. it's perhaps not the best place for my writing. i do have some writer friends here but most not on the same wavelength as me. however as i said i do readings now and then and they are very satisfying, usually.

i agree wholeheartedly with this statement of yours:

> I think all writing is a form of love, or desire

and wonder, can't "writing" be substituted with any creative act here. i will read *after babel*.

i'll keep in mind writing something about dan. i'm sure you posted it to the list, but what's the deadline?

i may actually be in new york in august but my plans have yet to solidify. i'll contact you if i go there. before then i'll send you some writing of mine, and will hope for some of yours as well.

yoroshiku,

nada

JUNE

From: nada
Date: June 23
Subject: hello again

hi gary!

i think of you almost daily when i remember i need to send you
some poems. now my life is still so hectic i feel like i'm about to fall
down, that plus anemia, low blood pressure, the rainy season ...
    all excuses for being afraid to look again at my small pile of
weird poems that don't quite make it to perfection
    but i haven't forgotten, really really
    i hope you're well and happy.
    nada

∞

From: Gary
Date: June 24
Subject: Re: hello again

Nada! Please-to-not think of me daily, if to do so means the stomach-
wince of guilt. You know, Brent struggled with anemia for quite a while
when I was living with him. I can't remember what finally helped him
... maybe changing his diet? Well, anyway, New York has all this extra
iron lying around everywhere—if I could reduce some of it to tablet form
and ship it off to you with the knowledge it would do anything at all ...
    I'm torn between begging you for poems and wanting your
stomach to de-knot ... so I'll go, for the moment, with the latter ...
    Soon, soon,
    Gary

OCTOBER

From: nada
Date: October 4
Subject: hi again, *hisashiburi*

hi gary

sorry for the long hiatus
    i haven't forgotten your request for work and finally i am ready to send you a big hunk o' stuff which is very uneven but please do read it anyway
    my summer was too eventful
    two weeks in england where i did a course called "group dynamics in practice"—excellent—might be interesting to apply what i learned to the dynamics of the poetics list
    then two weeks in france where i collapsed with a kind of seizure— remember the anemia i told you about—turned out to be a hypoglycemic/stress thing, but led to panic attacks that somewhat reduced the pleasure i was able to take in the lavender fields and the marais
    then a week back in japan, then two weeks in the usa spent mostly seeing doctors for the body and therapists for the mind
    i got hypnotherapized, changed my diet, now eat no sugar, take no stimulants, eat protein many times a day and am utterly virtuous, and i was just starting to feel an equilibrium like i had never felt before ...
    when i discovered that my live-in "partner" of many years had been scouring the internet for women and found one, a lovely 23-year old
    so, yes, great upheavals!
    i am in a weird kind of shock
    and how are you? (wicked, ironic grin)
    nada

From: Gary
Date: October 5
Subject: many kind hellos in reply

Good morning, Nada,

Wow, it sounds like you've had an eventful summer, have gone through very very much, have had your sense of reality (existence w/in your body, existence w/in your primary relationship) tested, reshaped by experience. No apologies for hiatus, please: distance between instances feels less significant to me than the instances themselves. I'm moved mostly that you have written, and that you'll be sending along some of your work. I am only sorry that things have not been easier for you in the last several months.

I don't know what, if anything, I told you about my own life since moving to New York. It has only now, after a little more than a year, evened out such that I can actually relax, and take pleasure in relaxing. My wife & I (we'd been together for 8 years) split up, under very bad circumstances. Our relationship had really become rote, we both resented each other (for very different reasons), and while I think it's true we loved each other (& I still love her), we were not in love. Anyway. I fell in love with someone else here in NYC, and she said she was in love with me too, though she, as well, was married. But, we really fucked things up. We stayed out all night one night and when we each returned to our homes, well, in her case her husband would not let her back and she had to stay with her sister for a week. My wife asked me to leave the next day. This other woman returned, after a difficult week, to her husband. I moved from sublet to sublet for many months until this last June, when I finally got on a lease. I moved nine times in as many months. All of the money I had saved prior to coming out here is gone.

For a long time I had double-feelings about all of this: great remorse at having ended my marriage in this way, and equal, but differently felt, remorse at having lost the woman I was in love with, & who I had believed was in love with me.

More soon, I'm being kicked off my computer ...

∞

From: nada
Date: October 7
Subject: Re: many kind hellos in reply

gary, thanks for your empathetic reply.

it sounds like your life hasn't been exactly cake either. does the double loss ever make you want to become totally ascetic? i sometimes feel that way, for maybe three-minute stretches, and then i am back inside my skin with all my memories and longings.

i am looking forward to a calmer time when i can remember bemusedly all the melodrama. it's the being still embroiled that is so taxing.

hoping you're well ...
nada

∞

From: Gary
Date: October 9
Subject: asceticism

I totally understand how much energy being embroiled, in anything, can take: in both of these relationships, I was embroiled for months, months afterward. Counseling sessions, long talks, arguments, & so on. I'm still sort of embroiled in one of them, against my will, if not necessarily against my desire. I've been trying to avoid it, but what do you do? I can't be an ascetic. That's actually more taxing for me. Besides, it's impossible to be an ascetic in New York. Having no money helps, but not entirely. Everything tempts.

What was the fallout of your situation? Are you still together? Are you trying to work together to save the relationship? Did it just end, suddenly?

I really look forward to reading your new work, Nada. And I hope that whatever happens, you are able to keep your head above water and your life, desires & energies more or less focused.

Many kind thoughts,
Gary

∞

From: nada
Date: October 9
Subject: Re: acesticism

hi gary—i was happy to get your catalytic questions. you know the brokenhearted want nothing more than to talk about it.

m—and i are still living together. since my discovery of his affair, the mood has been mostly rage and threats. there has also been some intimacy, as there often is in breakups, which confuses the issue. our communication had gotten very bad, not just remote but resentful, before this happened, and the affair acted as a catalyst for truth-telling, and we are talking now. as far as working on staying together though, my primary question is, is it worth it. the relationship with the other woman is still continuing. although she has cut off their sexual connection, i sense he is still romantically longing for her in an unclean avuncular sort of way. the sex he and i have been having is classic breakup sex, charged and emotional but somehow unhealthy. example of our sunday plans this fine autumn weekend: i am going to go house hunting; he is going to go to a movie with the girlie, with whom he says he won't sleep.

i too am seeing a therapist and having long talks with m—. i am really wanting to do what's best for myself here. terrified that if i lapse back into the relationship it will have not only its old flaws but these new awful jealous wounds to deal with all the time, and that my self-esteem will fit into a thimble—but also terrified that if i cut the relationship i will be thrown into the lonely pit of tokyo which is a morass of super-geeky white guys and doll-like japanese girls and japanese guys who are mostly scared of white girls. i suppose i could go back to america, but i don't want to be forced back by something like this. i have a good but problematic job which rewards me professionally and financially. at the moment i live in a beautiful house, which is my sanctuary, or was until he fucked it all up, but i understand why he did.

there are moments when i feel a beautiful distance from all this. i wonder if leaving the relationship wouldn't give me that at least, a clear head even if i have to be lonely for a while. it's just that he and i have been acting so reactively, it isn't spiritually or physically healthy, i want to make sure i don't act overly reactively in leaving

too, because it has been seven and a half years, and people do make
mistakes, and forgiveness is possible and a virtue.
    and that's where i'm at.
    happy for this cyber therapy
    and how are you?
    nada

                            ∞

From: Gary
Date: October 12
Subject: Re: asceticism

Dear Nada,

Asceticism ... is definitely a kind of drama ... there is, in attempting
to live "the ascetic life," that conflict between what the body & heart
longs for vs. the peace the mind "needs." Or at least seems, occasionally, to beg for. Because, well, we don't stop thinking when we
sleep, it goes on, all of it, or at least our experience of it is such that
it seems to. ... I did not, I have to admit, not willingly, pursue an
ascetic life after everything that happened. I mean, I had it. Given to
me. But I didn't really live it.
    It's Friday night, I'm home after work, typing this into my lap-
top (which doesn't have a modem, but I'll bring this on a disc with
me to work on Monday). I'm smoking cigarettes, drinking white
wine (free, excess from a work party), my two new plants on either
side of me (palm-like with serrated leaves, near-thorns, semi-dan-
gerous things I carried home from work on the subway, holding the
leaves back from grown people's legs & children's necks & faces), listening now to Tito Rodriguez, *Mama Guela*, recordings made in New
York 1949–1951, admittedly not terrifically calming or otherwise "at-
peace-with-the-okay-pretty-much-mostly-fucked-up-world" ...
    At one point, Nada, after leaving my wife's place in SoHo, I was
subletting a huge but really depressing apartment in the Kingsbridge
area of the Bronx, home of one G—, Russian poet & translator of
Lewis Carroll, Yeats, Wallace Stevens & John Ashbery, who'd gone
back to Moscow for a month to try & convince his estranged wife to

move to the U.S. with him while he finished a degree at Columbia. (He was unsuccessful. This letter is all about failure.) This was last January. I had two CDs, Tito Rodriguez *Mama Guela* and the Raincoats *Odyshape*. I listened to them incessantly.

My wife was understandably upset with me and pretty much refused to talk, except to ask, over & over, a very legitimate question, which I couldn't really answer: "Why?" Not that I had anything better to ask of D—, the woman I thought I was in love with. D— had just gone back with her husband and one night, after a really bad e-mail exchange, I called her up, desperately begging her to tell me "what happened?!?" ... I don't know, I think I had to hear her say she'd fallen in love with me, which she wouldn't do. I told her I couldn't talk with her anymore unless she explained what, for her part, had happened. She said she couldn't deal with an ultimatum like that. So, she hung up on me. Two days later, I get a call from my mother telling me my grandmother had died. My grandmother! This was the woman my mother had sent me to live with when my father left her & she was too broke to raise me. My grandmother taught me, at like age 3, to begin to read, to listen to poetry, to listen to music, to play the piano ... And the really awful part, for me, was that, I don't know why, but D— really reminded me of her for some reason. I spent the whole month drinking, writing very bitter poems, listening to the same two CDs over & over again. It was awful. &, of course, it got worse. (I'll spare you details.)

Why tell you all this? Well, okay. In part, hearing about what happened with your partner, I feel guilty, like, "Oh, dear, that's just the sort of thing I did to my wife." Also, well, my heart aches cuz also, so recently having found myself totally alone when I'd thought I was really connected with someone, and then hearing this about you, because, well, you lived with this person for so long and, then, what happened? So, I don't know, there is this Older Brother in me maybe, that wants to write you some stupid boring long letter & basically commiserate. Except, I don't know, maybe this is a male thing, I don't know, I want to "make it all better," which is I realize ludicrous, presumptuous, & insert whatever epitaph works for you here, I'm sure it's valid. But also: Aiii! We're all human beings, & I remember, you know, the worst thing about My Month at G—'s was that I was completely & utterly alone. Almost everyone who knew me &

my wife, together, as a couple, hated my guts for what I'd done. & let me know it. I couldn't really talk with anyone about it, and it drove me crazy.

Oh, I don't know.

If you could hear "Besame la Bembita" (now playing) maybe you'd understand my motivation in listening to it over & over every night. Cuz, okay, how are you going to live in a world where such a thing as this mid-century recording of Tito Rodriguez's "Besame La Bembita" exists ... and give up all hope? Sure, we're told that, for instance, all of Ella Fitzgerald's relationships ended tragically ... but, please, listen to her! That voice! You're gonna tell me her fucked-up relationships didn't fuel her, spiritually as well as artistically? No, you're not going to tell me that. Because it's obvious they, or SOMEthing, did, but probably they were not insignificant. I mean, it doesn't take much. Someone looks at you on the subway &, okay, I'm gonna betray my California roots here, some kinda "energy" is released as you lock eyes, sure, only for a moment, & then one of you is too chicken-shit to keep staring, well ... human beings! How can you resist them? &, admittedly not a great thing for the con- tinued health of this planet, but we're EVERYwhere. & we, all of us, Nada, long to be with each other. I mean, okay, I'm not naive, I mean, we do have our preferences, and some of us are idealistic to the point of, well, how many people on the planet will ever satisfy us but that One we feel, when we look into their eyes, our will is snapped like a dry twig, our legs give ... we have No Choice. & maybe our friends & our parents hate him/her, don't understand how we can "fall" or whatever for that person, but, what the fuck? We know our own hearts well enough, our bodies well enough, our souls (assuming we believe such a thing exists) well enough ... so ... I know without even asking, or am so presumptuous I'm gonna assume, from what you've told me, whoever this person was, you were, at some point, In Love. & I know that's not an easy thing to be in. & an even more difficult thing to be wrenched out of. "Difficult," like that even describes it. Like anything could. Lester Bangs writing about death (Bangs') wrenching him from his beloved soundtrack. (I'm from California. Did I tell you that yet?) What else? Elizabeth Barrett Browning's "Consolation," maybe:

All are not taken; there are left behind
Living Beloveds, tender looks bring
And make the daylight still a happy thing,
And tender voices to make soft the wind:
But if it were not so—if I could find
No love in all the world for comforting,
Nor any path but hollowly did ring
Where 'dust to dust' the love from life disjoined,
And if, before those sepulchres unmoving
I stood alone, (as some forsaken lamb
Goes bleating up the moors in weary dearth,)
Crying 'Where are ye, O my loved and loving?'—
I know a Voice would sound, 'Daughter, I AM.
Can I suffice for HEAVEN and not for earth?'

* * *

Nada, it's Monday, I'm back at work, drinking coffee. Re-reading your last e-mail, I can't imagine what it must be like to still live together, and to be going through all of this, and trying to decide, from within that situation, "is this something I want to continue working on? is it worth it?"

Anyway ... I look forward to reading your work. I don't know if this will mean anything to you or not, but the couple times I saw you read I thought, "wow," and then, and then you were gone. So, I'm really glad you're there, even "here," now, & that I'll get to read what you've done in the years since we were both much younger, & no doubt more naive, but equally no doubt probably happier, in San Francisco.

Please write down the thoughts & emotions & events you experience in the next 24 hours and send them to me.

Gary

∞

From: nada
Date: October 14
Subject: Re: RE asceticism

i can't drink coffee anymore now that i am so pure. actually i've never dealt with coffee well at all. before my health conversion though i drank three to five cups of sweet milky tea a day and would choose chai over any other beverage. now i drink only water and occasionally chamomile tea and my personality is different. we are so very porous and easily influenced by any substance—just think what another human can do.

i am relying a great deal now on the i-ching and various usually inapplicable internet horoscopes, no matter how much adorno sneered at such things. i have got to wrench some sense out of what's going on is all.

m— actually came to counseling with me a couple of days ago, a novel experience for him. it was interesting to see his articulate-ness in a language not his own in action, and afterwards i felt closer to him—not so much that i feel i want to prolong the relationship, but that margin of confusion lingers.

it was his voice and way of communicating that i found so intriguing to begin with, this man with a foot in two languages, two cultures. i don't think i was in love with him after the first six months except sporadically. as he said, it turned into "power politics." i stayed with him out of convenience, affection, fear, hope that it would get better. and because i was trying to heal a broken heart (isn't it always like that? we just keep opening up the same wound).

i've decided i really do not want to leave this house. last night i went to wander in my potential new neighborhood and felt horrified by its busy-ness, the big streets. i want to stay in this house and puri-fy it too along with my body.

i want to sit here and write lots more but i have to get ready for my university job today, have to try to patch my nervous system together. my homeopathic calm pills and dr. bach's rescue remedy aren't totally working. my doctor said i'm doing well though! happy news in the maelstrom. more words where these came from ...
nada

From: Gary
Date: October 16
Subject: Purity

Nada, I'm amazed to know someone who only drinks water &
chamomile tea. Do you think if I limited myself like that, I'd be able
to quit smoking? I hate smoking. No, I mean, I love smoking. But,
you know. How did your personality change? Did you find you had
more energy? Or that things became more clear? Were emotions
more crisply felt, ideas more intensely held? I'm suddenly flashing
on this cartoon Zippy the Pinhead creator Bill Griffith did, two veg-
ans sitting opposite each other at a table, one goes, "I've been so
HIGH since I gave up lettuce!" Then, come to find out (Laurie Price
tells me) lettuce is actually the most difficult vegetable for your body
to digest.

I know how seductive people w/feet in two cultures are. Well,
that's a whole other story. It's a long one & very romantic, but I can't
type it up now because I'm at work. I'll write you about that this
weekend.

Did you send your work yet? Please-to-say you have. If you get
a chance, Nada, I'd love to read about what you read, what's been
influencing you, your work, why you write in the first place.
Remember those groovy handmade books you made when you lived
in San Francisco? Do you still do stuff like that?

Now, I need to go smoke. I will send two or three new poems
later today.

Gary

∞

From: nada
Date: October 17
Subject: Re: Purity

i did send my work. you should be getting it soon.

i smoked for a while, about two years—only garam, clove cigarettes. it was a vice i picked up in bali, that sweet spicy languid fiery
island of sweet spicy languid fiery smoke. i didn't smoke more than

3 cigarettes a day but they were very strong and with 35 mg of tar *each*. i know that death wish and that seduction. prefer purity.

when i went into purification mode, my personality changed into someone more even and focused; my brain seemed to start working a little better and my mood swings cleared up—until the relationship crisis happened. i fatalistically think, i think i've said, that that was part of the necessary purification, but i'm not pure yet. i mean, i saw him washing dishes downstairs at about 6:30 this morning and thought, yes, i hate him, i love him.

i don't think i told you that i did something very dramatic last weekend, that is, i presented myself at their meeting place for their date. the scene was fellini-esque, a bright day in shinjuku (one of tokyo's many hubs), people milling about in a pedestrian daze. i hung out and watched my friend's husband's andean band perform on the street for a while, then when the time came zeroed in. when m— saw me standing next to her he looked pretty uncomfortable, told me, "we're just going to see a movie." he then greeted her, she kind of pawed his chest coyly, still unaware of my presence, and i stepped forward and introduced myself to her rather formally. she looked, how can i say, evasive, evil, triumphant, crumpling, complicated, confused? i told m— that this was a very delicate point in our relationship and that this was unacceptable, platonic or not, and (here i switched into japanese to ensure she'd understand) it was very painful. since he seemed to be leaning toward protecting her feelings rather than mine, i stormed off in tears saying "enjoy your movie."

i thought he would come back furious that i'd spied on him again. or that he'd at least call me and find out if i'd done anything else dramatic. but no, he came back past midnight. he was solemn and calm and said he wanted to be with me. i wonder if he would have said that if i hadn't freaked her out and she hadn't cut things completely (?) with him. i anyway feel i can't wholly believe anything he says. isn't that a scene? i do feel i'm tuned into some melodrama which just happens to impact my life. not quite real.

you asked about my writing. i don't write very much these days. there's a cable connected from my creativity to my teaching, and i only occasionally reconnect the cable to the writing. i feel very bad about this, but i know i am a great teacher.

you asked about what i read. lately i am reading books about education and empowerment. i'm going to give a workshop on that topic at a big teachers' conference in november. it's very inspiring stuff but not so much for writing. what makes me write in the first place is emotion and (sometimes thwarted) desire. i know that's not postmodernistically p.c. it just gets me high and in flow and when i do it it feels like the right thing to do and sometimes i like what comes out, i like manipulating words and letting them manipulate me. it's just that for the past decade my writing hasn't had, i haven't sought or allowed it to have, much of a context. i do give readings and performances sometimes but it's not like being in the states and hanging out with writer friends and being caught up in the writing world, the gossip and push-pulls and controversies and new books and readings. that world felt problematic to me anyway, too kind of solemn most of the time (i mistyped most of the rime). and too full of power plays and positionings, or people just showing off how clever they were. real intellectual passion spurted out sometimes, but there was so much to wade through, like the poetics list, there's also so much blah blah blah.

i don't know why i'm so alienated from my writing really. i think it has to do partly with this relationship i'm still kind of in. he's a careerist poet to the point of being unable to really be in a committed relationship (the writing always comes first), and he has never been interested in my writing at all, although our connection started when he gave me a book of english poems he had written and i responded enthusiastically, with cogent commentary. he seemed amazed by that attention but never ever reciprocated. i think my writing is just too hard for him to understand. but it's not just that, it comes down to that lack of curiosity, that selfishness. out of the 15 or so readings/performances i've done during the time i've been with him i think he's been to two. what does that say? one blames one's job, one's relationships. ultimately it's an evasion of authenticity, i know that.

(rubbing snow on a rash)

there is evidence that my eye
is slipping down

this is known by the carved mask
to the right of the food
horns on the mask
horns in the distance
exactly full moon
my father left me when
i was five years old
rubbing snow on a rash

nada

∞

From: Gary
Date: October 19
Subject: hello, hello

Dear Nada,

You know, I wrote you a whole long letter this weekend, but destroyed it. I wrote you Friday night, and Saturday morning, read it over, and just rolled my eyes & hit "delete." I'm sure I'd do it with this one, too, but I'm not going to allow myself to read it before sending it.

I have a thing about names. Now, what about "Nada" (nothing). And, how you describe the relationship, admittedly colored by M—'s recent betrayal, sounds, well, it sounds like he thinks very highly of his contribution to poetry, and doesn't think much of yours. I would last in that relationship for like, maybe two months.

Which is not to say I pick perfect partners. Okay, a story. Saturday morning I woke very early, made a full breakfast & coffee and sat down to seriously begin my comic book. I've done strips all my life, or more than 2/3rds of it, except for a long period of time when I quit, out of spite, for, okay, ten years. I mean, I gave it entirely up. In part because I wanted to be a poet "instead"; but, really, the truth was ... do you remember W—? Well, she was an SF State person, we met there, had kind of a fiery relationship, lived together for about a year. She helped get me a job as cartoonist at the weekly paper where she worked. Anyway, when we broke up, a year or so later, that was the end of my cartoon job. (Surprise, surprise.) I was replaced by Tom Tomorrow, who has since gone on to become incredibly successful. I think I was so saddened by that betrayal, you know, I gave up cartoons altogether for 10 years. Despite having done them since I was, like, the moment I could read & write (which, thanks to my grandma, was very early on). Anyway. So, obviously, W—, if she respected my work, which I think she actually did, didn't, you know, ultimately respect me. I mean, she pulled this great opportunity out from under me, out of spite.

I admire your resolve to be pure. Someday, time & other factors will no doubt conspire to convince me, okay, there are certain things I just have to quit doing to my body. It's not a death wish. Not for me. Paz talks about drugs & vice, Baudelaire's sense of it, & relates it to "our love for the infinite." I've thought about that one a long time, because it seems like a paradox. I mean, it is a paradox. But then, all the most profound religious ideas are expressed as paradoxes. No? Okay, maybe not.

I want to tell you more, I want to go on & on, I want to hear more & more from you. Yes, that sounded very "dramatic," what you did. Those things never work how we want or imagine. Which is not to say they necessarily backfire. But we so often sniff out others' intent, subvert it. It's odd because we love plot. I mean, who doesn't? But, intention (upon which plot is predicated?) we despise or are at least suspicious of. One of the most hilarious & true things Laurie Price ever told me was, when I asked her, "Well, you were working at Maelstrom Books when you lived in San Francisco; didn't lots of guys ask you out?" and she said, no, only people she didn't wanna go out with, and I asked, how come she didn't wanna go out with those guys, and she said: "Oh, I don't know, it just seemed like they had a PLAN, you know?"

I'm looking forward to getting & reading your work. I promise full engagement & reply. Let me know how it's going. All emotions, speculations, & other -ions will be indulged.

Very,
Gary

∞

From: nada
Date: October 20
Subject: more funny stories from the far east

i can't believe you wrote a long e-mail and then destroyed it. isn't that violating the basic rule of the spontaneity of this medium? i'm rarely offended by spontaneity or impulsiveness. the only things that really offend me are cruelty and sarcasm and logic that it is in love with its own force (buddha said some wise things about the beguiling trap of logic and the intellect). so i guess what i'm saying is don't constrain yourself worrying about what i might think. i need all the language i can get right now and i'm not ashamed to ask for it.

a word on names. my name may seem to mean only nothing, but if you look at other etymologies besides the spanish you'll find

indonesian: pitch or melody

russian: hope

arabic: morning dew

japanese: the name of a sake-producing area that was devasted by the kobe quake ... it also has some connection to peacefulness and the pacific ocean

i don't remember the nationality for sure but i think there's a famous israeli transsexual singer named nada

and best of all

sanskrit: the roaring sound of the universe (the sound of nothing; nada brahma; of course sanskrit/indo-european is behind the spanish and probably the indonesian too)

i'm really proud of my name, the sound of it and the clever anagram, so there.

i do remember w— but i don't know if i ever actually met her. i noticed all the redheads on campus (as potential friends? rivals? copycats? idols?). about the betrayal: a catholic lady i work with told me, "sooner or later everyone will disappoint you" which is awfully pessimistic unless you're convinced there's an afterlife. ...

m— thinks himself a genius, i find this really funny. once we were on our way to see *shine* (which i told him was about a genius) and i asked him if he thought he was a genius and he said yes. i told him that most people who think they're geniuses just believe that in order to avoid responsibility, that it's usually a kind of adolescent delusion. i mean hell, i used to think i was a genius too, and then i got a job. so he started asking me about various poets, composers, etc., "do you think so and so's a genius? how about so and so?" and i said, "well it's not really for me to say. i can only say my own opinion. it seems to me that a genius is someone who breaks new ground in a field or form. i've read some of your haiku and they don't seem to be radically new or special. they're *competent* though." well as you can guess he didn't like that very much. we were sitting in the first row of the movie theater and he wasn't talking to me. i could feel him sitting there getting madder and madder. just as the credits started, he got up and walked out! isn't that stupid? i mean, i at least would have sat in another seat. as it was he lost the entire ticket price—about 12 bucks here in tokyo. is that the action of a genius?

anyway i'm still in inertia with this genius. wishing i could just push the eject button and he'd be gone. in the meantime, in the muck, thanks for your empathy, and i hope you are somehow amused by the story too!

sleepy ...

nada

∞

From: Gary
Date: October 21
Subject: Your wacky western correspondent

Dear Nada,

I finally got your poems, the first of which, "my penis," is wonderful & which I remember you posting to the poetics list a month or so back ... & "Absence" is gorgeous, too, something about the way it halts. "White ape." And, please, "and the metal walls are/ washed over/ in green light//ARA" ... I don't know what "ARA" means, but that, you know, in a way, really doesn't matter to me (though of course I'd love for you to tell me). It's beautiful. And, dang, "Naigo," also great, I wonder, is "Naigo" a section of Tokyo maybe, where you'd find people like in the tableau of your final stanza? "Japan, what is Japan, what are they doing there," you don't really ask (no question mark), in "The Grebe," but do question. I like that. Sometimes to question is not to ask at all. Or is but not really. (Do you really think so.) Who (or what) is "Marunouchi"? This poem is odd, funny, though I don't know why, like hearing a joke told in a bar in the next booth over, some details of it crisp, the punch line there, but info missing. Ah, and here's "the gender continuum" where "Maybe if I don't shave/ I'll become a man." Hee hee. Though, of course, we don't know if this is male or female speaking. Did I mention Julie Doucet? A cartoonist-hero of mine. I'm going to photocopy her great page of herself shaving ("If I Was a Man") for you & send it, soon, soon, I promise. Okay, you know what Chris said to me two nights ago? Well, it was part of a longer conversation (we stay up some nights until 3–4 a.m. talking) & so arrives, here, out of context, but he said, "you know, poetry has always had this element of ..." well, I forget the word he said, but he was talking about the epigrammatical quality some lines have, and that, you know, a lot of poetry doesn't really have, but, okay, you go back, and it's there, prior to the 20th century. (Though actually lots of 20th century poetry has it too. I think it's too easy to make sweeping generalized statements that sound great in the middle of conversations & arguments, but maybe disintegrate, later, with experience.) Anyway, "Only love has the fury to make peace," and wow, thank you for writing that. And for "irritation/ is a form of pleasure," which of course it is. (I'm not going to give you any personal examples.) I don't know, this is great, "I'm not really here/ except for the glowing red light/ under my arm ..." wow. I mean, wow. This whole poem is so, I don't know, it's sensual (as is so much of what you do) and really eerie, but also erotic. How is it erotic? Is it in part that the poem is called "Nothing"? This isn't something I want to think about right now. I mean, because it's disturbing. At least to me at the moment. I'm going to dream about this image. & it's not like I'm happy about it.

"Columns" is equally as erotic as it is disturbing, the human imaged as column (of light? energy? how the human is a line vertical to the horizon: a column)? There is such an odd giving over to I don't know what to call it, to the situation of being I guess, in "Our brains/ make us do things.// We make each other/ do things." I don't know what to tell you, reading this, after having read that M— doesn't really get involved in your work. Did you show him this poem? How could he not love you reading this poem? This is incredible, Nada, I don't feel like I have any skin reading this. I don't know. I mean, I don't know about the first stanza, how this works with the rest, but by the end, you know, I'm lost. I can't read any more. I'm gonna have to wait, set this aside for tonight. My feeling is, probably I should really sit with your work for a while before writing anything. It's not that I care how I sound or come off, but that I think you really deserve some very considered reply.

As I type I'm staring off at Manhattan, the World Trade Center & sprawl beyond it, the lights glowing, some flickering (effect of the window screen?), a mostly black horizon occasionally dotted with lights … I can even see the Statue of Liberty, off beyond the BQE, a never-ending stream of traffic moving purposefully, though to no discernable purpose …

Your story about M— and "genius" was funny. It was also sad, like, well, the point not being that he blew 12 bucks. I'm imagining the two of you there in the theater. I don't know what he looks like. I vaguely remember what you look like. But I'm imagining it, and there you are, and you're sort of goading him, "are you a genius?" and this could be fun, or this could be something, it could be anything, it's a question. A question means "I'm allowing anything to follow." No? But, it becomes personal, and not even personal, but contentious. I need some music, hold on. *Astral Weeks*. Don't laugh. My mother was a hippie. My father, being absent, was replaced (by me) by Lester Bangs. Not the ideal role model, but he did give me *Astral Weeks*, so, well, so there you go. Anyway. Now, I'm kind of distracted. If I was a woman I'd be like all over Van Morrison. Right after recording this stuff. I'd case the studio. You think I'm kidding. He never did anything as great as this again, I don't know what happened to him, how he got there, why he didn't or couldn't stay there, or "here," as I listen to it. "To never, never, never wonder why … I'm beside you …" Uhn. Okay, to type out the words, the lyrics, okay, no big deal. I mean, John Dowland, for instance, isn't maybe a great poet or anything, but, wow, those songs. It pisses me off I wasn't given to do something like this sometimes. I mean, cuz all the hairs on my neck now are raised. Even "Cypress Avenue" (on now) is great, and it's a song about failure. ("Conquered in a carseat.") Sometimes, he gets this sound in his voice, I don't know to describe it, like a sheep bleating. Really. Uhn!

So, we're alive, and at all times we're alive, and it's not like we don't have nerve endings & it's not like we don't have, you know, the capacity to feel everything if we want ... so ... when someone poses a question, anything, "how are you?" "are you a genius?" anything, I mean, you can go anywhere with that. So, you are sitting in a movie theater, the woman you love asks "Are you a genius?" and what do you say. I don't even need to think about that one. I'd kiss her. I mean, I wouldn't say anything, I'd look into her eyes, I'd wait for that moment ... Because it's the same question as "how are you doing?" & how I was doing, if someone was asking me, & if her asking me, anything, meant anything, well ...

"My withers are foamy" ... well, of course they are, Nada, you've read Neruda, & even if you haven't, well, you know the ocean is more than "ocean," as who doesn't? I went out to Coney Island this weekend, it was closed, desolate, wonderfully baroque edifice perched on the shore of the Atlantic. This is the human response to the ocean? Wow. I mean, in a way, it was kind of great. The Nathan's Hot Dog place can't be described. I mean, it really would take a genius to do it. (Know any?)

I don't know how you deal with loneliness in Tokyo, I don't know if loneliness in Tokyo is the same thing as loneliness in New York, but here's a partial description: Imagine the most beautiful people on the street, in the subway, everywhere everywhere, literally gorgeous people, people who if you had no other desire in life but I don't know some kind of total sensual overload, all you'd be thinking about is I want her her & him & her & him & so on, it's ever-present, I mean it's like all of the beautiful people were just dropped onto the island of Manhattan & told, "Okay, do whatever you want, just walk around & make everyone uneasy" & there they are, & it's awful, there isn't a single subway ride I don't completely crush out on someone, & all for nothing, & not even for nothing, but really, for this feeling of utter worthlessness, I'm not beautiful, I'm average, I'm boring, I read books all night I work all day I write things no one cares about, I make no money, I'm totally passionate & though we're told this counts it really doesn't until you're dead what counts is how much you make how beautiful you are and what are you wearing this season?

It's not like I haven't tried. My favorite book title is Philip Whalen's *You Didn't Even Try*.

Gary

∞

From: Nada
Date: October 23
Subject: Re: Your wacky western correspondent

gary

suddenly just a few days after a distinctly summery sultry typhoon
it's cold here again, and i'm thinking if everything were normal i'd
plant bulbs. i like the daffodils whose outer petals are cream-colored
and whose trumpet is the color of lox. it's a brunch flower! a deli-
catessen flower! a grandma flower! i also like the really deep purple
tulips that look like an isabella rosselini lipstick ad. i'm afraid to
plant anything though because the situation is so unstable.

    it's interesting to have someone paying attention to my poems.
i don't offer them to much of anyone anymore. it seems that you are
reading them vividly. i like what you like about "absence." that one's
in *chain* this time. i explain the meaning of *ara* there—it's an exclamation that marvels, a very feminine and refined kind of "wow".
naigo has no meaning—i mean it's a neologism. i was too lazy to look
up the word for "code" (which is something i feel many of my poems
are written in) so i tried to think of a creative new japanese word to
mean code. i came up with *nai* (inner) *go* (words). no japanese person would understand what i meant, neither would anybody else.
my inner word. "marunouchi" is a section of and a train line in
tokyo. i chose the title after a poem by nakahara chuya (the japanese rimbaud) in *the penguin book of japanese verse*. that poem is called
"the marunouchi building." the marunouchi is one of the many
downtown centers of tokyo (there are about twelve). it goes like this:

> ah! lunch and
> there goes the siren,
> there goes the siren,
> out they stream,
> out they stream.
> salarymen out for lunch,
> aimlessly swinging arms.
> and still out they stream,
> out they stream.

vast building,
coal black tiny
tiny exit.
thin cloud filming the sky,
thin cloud and
dust blowing up.
comical salarymen
looking up,
looking down.
why should i be
the great man that
i know i am?

i haven't read this poem in japanese but i love it here in the english—esp. the environmental clouds and dust and the verb *blowing up*. this really is the post-hiroshima nightmare. the last stanza brings me to tears almost every time, partly from identification, partly from empathy. i also like the nursery rhyme rhythm and repetitions and parallels, even in translation, i tend to remember this poem.

   i know what you mean by liking epigrams. i call them axioms, what's the difference. i've always liked that device. i remember talking to larry price at the poetry center about that—he liked them too. that's one reason i like alan davies' writing so much. it is full of little words to live by, that just intuitively feel true even if they're illogical. i mean, "only love has the fury to make peace" sounds somehow right even though it's not strictly true. i mean some people make peace just in order to survive or to bear their existence. and of course irritation *is* a form of pleasure—even physical pleasure, a caress, say, is just on the other end of the continuum from a blow. but that could just be my masochistic notion.

   the glowing red light. yes, it is weirdly erotic in the way that the first butoh performance i ever saw was. that performance opened up my perceptions of the world in ways i had never expected. it was a solo dance by a male dancer, masaki iwana. he wore only a loincloth, and strapped to his thigh was a kind of glowing florescent tube. during the over-an-hour performance he made no sudden moves. he began reclining and later stood but the sequence of movements altogether was so slow you almost never perceived him as moving at all. mostly the stage was dark or partially dark but the tube glowed throughout. he seemed like a man alone in his room. the soundtrack was chance radio—i remember it sounded so urban and alienating and lonely, a man listening to the radio in his dark room. by the time he stood up, something remarkable started to happen. he had a cold, but he couldn't make any broad movement like nose-wiping, so snot started to flow out of his nose. but get this—it wasn't disgusting. it got really long, the line of snot, but it looked like a luminescent thread of life glittering in the spotlight. it was a precious bodily fluid and it was an emblem of intense aesthetic integrity. he was so beautiful, with a chiseled face and very slight, delicately muscled body, and longish hair. i was converted to butoh by that performance. i even studied for a while, but it was a big challenge for me as i had never really done anything physical before (yeah, i mean except *that*)— always shunned sports and dance lessons and so on. what an experience. all of "dolor core recede sanpo" is connected to my experience studying it. it namedrops the great dancers. the title is an anagram of a translation of the the the title of a famous collaboration between hijikata tatsumi, kazuo ono and yoshito ono called "rose-colored dance." *sanpo* means a stroll or walk, so the poem is the walk that makes the core of dolor recede.

you asked if i showed "columns" to m—. no! i don't bother to show him anything. that is an old poem i wrote with another guy in mind, before i met m—. actually only one of those poems was written thinking of him—"nothing"—that is, "devotion doesn't pour from your nose or throat" and it was probably seven years ago i wrote that. all of the other poems that seem to have some other in mind are not for or about him. he hasn't earned that kind of attention. or is it that i haven't felt it. or both.

did you say your mom was a hippie? hey, so was mine. i played in the jefferson airplane's swimming pool when i was nine, the same year i got to sing backups for a band called ONE that made a record called *come* on the grateful dead's "grunt" label. we lived in bolinas (there's the inspiration for "the grebe"), for a time in tents, on welfare. i was dragged along to a million yoga and meditation retreats. i used to get brown rice vegetarian sushi in my lunchbox instead of the bologna and mustard sandwiches i so craved. i was into embroidery. my mom used to listen to van morrison excessively (shangalangalangashangalangalang) and i remember her and my ex-quasi-step-father making love to *dark side of the moon*, which seemed like such a cliché and drove me into hardcore punkdom at age fourteen. but by that time i'd already taken lsd (i was twelve the first time) and to this day i can sing just about all of donovan, joni mitchell, jimi hendrix, janis, csny, and lots of others. we lived in fairfax for a few years, the same town where van morrison bought his parents a little record store. i saw van morrison walking on the main drag a few times. lester bangs! i haven't heard that name for years. you know, i actually had a letter published in *creem* magazine when i was 14 or so. that magazine changed my life! the ramones! patti smith! wow.

>I don't know how you deal with loneliness in Tokyo,
>i don't know if loneliness in Tokyo is the same thing
>as loneliness in New York,

no it isn't! i might argue (but i don't know because i've never experienced loneliness in new york) that at least there you feel like you are part of the organism of the city. here i am always separate. also in new york you have culture flowing out everywhere and whirling around you and you can understand it. i would certainly have to have been born japanese to understand all that surrounds me here, and i have a hunch a lot of it isn't really "culture" but rather neon stimulation. i saw these fantastic white shooting neon lights dripping down the length of a skyscraper from the window of a high-rise indian restaurant the other day and i thought how fabulous but what's the point.

it may be different here for guys but as for me i feel kind of invisible here. my friends say that people stare at me but i rarely notice it. tokyoites walk more quickly than the citizens of any other city in the world. they rarely make eye contact and if they do it's furtive and they quickly look away. from the men there is rarely a sense of, oh, testosterone approaching, although some, especially the surfer-type boys, are certainly beautiful. m— is not particularly beautiful. he has a modicum of charm, mostly verbal, and a well-shaped nose. he looks kind of intelligent; someone said he looks a little like john lennon, but only in his later etiolated phase, and with short hair. otherwise he's not my type at all, kind of elongated in body, short in legs and lacking in grace. i feel a little guilty saying that.

> completely crush out on someone, & all for nothing

no, it isn't for nothing, you're lucky to feel that way even if it's not gratified desire (which usually doesn't turn out to be as interesting or rewarding anway, does it?). i almost never feel that way about anyone here, because perhaps although there are plenty of beauties it is so very surface. this is the land of grooming and image. i love that actually, and when i go to the usa i can't believe how many people wear sweatpants or gap uniforms. still, the ever creative and refined style of the japanese does not set my heart a-pounding; nor do their full lips or soft skins even. be glad you are so responsive!

> what counts is how much you make how beautiful you are

i think these things do count in the absence of true connection. i'm kind of beautiful (when i'm not so distressed); i've got great clothes and make a ton of money for someone who majored in creative writing, ho ho. and look how happy i am. not. what counts? total passion, like you said, and true connection.

> "Well, you gonna raise my kids?" or, worse, "buy me things?"

i have never thought to make these demands on anyone but now that i'm aging i wonder if i should have, if somehow i've done it all wrong by choosing (twice) penniless creative guys and now having neither children nor presents to show for it, not that i particularly long for children and i can buy my own presents thank you. still, these women sound to me very practical, if not exactly what you were looking for.

brr. i'm so freezing. i've got to eat breakfast and take a shower and try to figure out what on earth i should do about this stupid situation i'm in.

i'm totally enjoying this e-mail exchange.

nada

∞

From: Gary
Date: October 26
Subject: Monday

Nada,

Your letter was great, and you know what I did? I wrote you back and neglected to put the file onto a disc to bring to work today so I could send it to you via e-mail this morning. So, tomorrow for that. A couple of things, though: *Creem*! I had two letters published in *Creem* (I was very proud!). One was about having long hair (justifying it because I had big ears) and one was a bizarre hero-worship letter about Robert Fripp, who I was really into at the time. I don't understand my fascination with him because I was in a band then, Submission, and while most of the songs were our own (always about sexual frustration, naturally), our models were the Ramones, Sex Pistols (I think we even did a cover of "Bodies" because it was so amazingly hideous) and the Clash, who if I hadn't overplayed them in highschool & college I'd probably still listen to now. I miss those days. I mean, sometimes.

This is not a real e-mail, Nada, I'm at work and am always either distracted, sleepy or whatnot, at the very least looking over my shoulder. But, I couldn't not say hello today. What can I tell you? It's cold here, finally, though only cold enough one day for the radiator to actually kick in. I love the smell of the radiator. I'm sure it's doing awful things to my skin & scalp, but ahhhh, you have to admit, it's so reassuring when you start to hear that *Hssssssss-hssssssssssssssss*, this smell I can't describe but which feels "brown" somehow or no, no, "amber" ... and then, ahhhh ... warmth ...

Tonight I'm going to see Bernadette Mayer read at No Moore and then off to see John McNally at the Poetry Project. John, who used to live in San Francisco & who worked at Small Press Traffic for many years, is just one of the nicest people in the poetry world ...

It's too hard to write you at work. I wanna be as bright as you or at least as much me as you are you & I need my own space in order to fully pull it off. Anyway, like I said, I wrote something this weekend, which I'll bring in for you tomorrow.

I hope things are, oh, I don't know, I don't know. I mean, I know they suck. And saying "I wish you well!" just seems so cheesy, even though I of course do wish you well. Mostly, I wish you clarity.

The only thing I enjoy reading more than your e-mails right now is your poems.

I wish I'd known you in SF.

Many kindnesses,

Gary

∞

From: nada
Date: October 27
Subject: Re: Monday

hey gary

i wish i could remember what my letter to *creem* was about. i'll bet i've got it in a file somewhere. how do you feel about long hair now? i think hair is as powerful and important as anything, and although i have had mine shorter than an inch and dyed orange, i much prefer it to be long and massive no matter what the current styles may be. as a student said once when asked why she wore her hair so (gorgeously) long, "i hate to waste material."

i miss those days hugely. first of all they were such a political and artistic turn-on, and it helped to be fourteen and precocious; i really soaked it all up. i never went to highschool because i took the calif. proficiency exam when i was thirteen and then enrolled sporadically in jr. colleges, so i had tons of free time to roam the streets of san francisco, cavorting with the likes of flipper, negative trend, the dils, the avengers (do you know these bands?), watching various friends shoot up or get ready to go to their stripper or bike messenger jobs. i used to spraypaint my jacket and spike-heeled boots silver, and once my friends and i actually set a trash bin on fire. at the same time, i was reading the surrealists, a little marx, existentialists, and feeling so cutting edge revolutionary. of course i know now i wasn't but it was all very thrilling. i remember going to some punk show up north—maybe cotati?—and steve jones was there and there was this girl in a transparent shirt who spirited him off for some fellatio. i remember our crowd (under the rubric "new youth productions"—sounds kind of scary, huh) put together a show at the people's temple—the clash headlined. i very very occasionally, like once every year and a half, put on some of the music from that era and just wallow in it, want to, not experience it again, but see a movie of my experiences.

did i tell you i wrote my thesis at berkeley on bernadette mayer? i've only seen her read once and i've never met her, although i corresponded with her a little when i was writing my thesis. i'm totally jealous that she's right there and you can just pop off and go see her. what is this "devotionals" i heard mentioned? didn't john donne write an incredible book with a similar title? yes, *devotions*. i think i have it somewhere.

i met john mcnally a few years ago when i was back one summer. i remember him being very unassuming, but not lacking in humor, and very gentle, and certainly very nice.

> The only thing I enjoy reading more than your e-mails
> right now is your poems. I wish I'd known you in SF.

yeah, ditto. but we probably have met. i thought i knew everyone in that town!
ciao for now
nada

∞

From: Gary
Date: October 28
Subject: Tuesday

Hello Nada,

Well, yet again I've neglected to bring the file in. I have a good excuse: I was out pretty late last night. The Mayer reading was okay, lots of epigrams, a few odd-formed poems, and one really wonderful poem about what her landlord was doing to try & get everyone to move out of the giant building she lived in (& still rents an apartment in) at 4th Street & Avenue A, written in like 1980.

John McNally was great, and looks exactly as he did the last time I saw him (7 years ago). Anyway, so I stayed out after the reading talking with John & Jeff Conant, another poet I knew out in San Francisco, and a bunch of their friends, some of whom I've met since I moved out here. I got back at about 2 a.m., crashed immediately, and overslept.

I saw D— at the Mayer reading. She waved hi, but I don't think we're talking at all anymore. It was very weird. But I was okay with it. That I was okay with it is what's most weird, cuz here I thought I was madly in love with the woman. I think emotions can become exhausted, even those that seem to come from somewhere not wholly of "you"—if that makes sense.

I'm yammering. My mind's mush. Tonight, I hope to get lots of sleep. Nada, how are things going? Did you guys go to a counselor again? Are you planning to? Tell me tell me tell me about your job, how it fulfills you, what you really love about it. Describe the trip to work. (I'll describe mine. But, when I've had more sleep.)

Okay. Hope this finds you well,
Gary

∞

From: nada
Date: October 29
Subject: Re: Tuesday

well, i've just got back from a night of karaoke with some of my students. the english songs i sang were "like a rolling stone" and "both sides now" and, on (by? prepositions are the first thing to go) request, the stupid whitney houston version of "i will always love you" with the stupid stupid key changes. i love dolly parton (who wrote the song)—she's got a voice like a bell or an angel and radiates instead of showing off. whitney houston has to climb around octaves to prove something, and uses so many grace notes they turn downright awkward, don't you think?

before karaoke we went to a japanese pub (*nomiya*), which is a culinary experience as well as a place to get shitfaced (of course i didn't, i just watched all their alcohol-allergic faces turn bright red).

i remember eating okra in soy sauce and rice vinegar, a kind of grated vegetable salad with raw tuna and yellowtail and boiled shrimp, a hotpot of duck and tofu and chrysanthemum leaves and chinese cabbage and carrots and shiitake mushrooms in a lovely broth (duck soup!), skewer-grilled squid, and a few other nice things.

it was my second party of the day. another class had a fantastic halloween party. they had a mummy contest. groups of three had to wrap one of their members (sounds funny) in toilet paper; the group that used the most toilet paper in the time limit was the winner. then we told a round robin ghost story. it was great! it was about a family, a mother, father and daughter. the daughter wanted a piano. one day the father went out to the graveyard and found a bone and brought it home. the bone told the girl she could have a piano if she collected some more bones. i don't remember exactly what happened next, but a piano tuner came to the house and was angry that there was no piano, so he stabbed the father. then the daughter brought the father to the graveyard and ate him (!) and brought the bones back home, so she had a piano. somehow everyone died. i had to end the story. i said that one student was walking in the village years later and found the house. she went in and found only a piano. suddenly the house, which was totally dark, turned light, and she started to play the piano. then she looked down at her body and her hands and realized she had become a skeleton. aaaagh!

you can maybe get an inkling of why i like this job. it's nice to get paid to encourage others to tell ghost stories. plus what else is good about it ...

mostly i like, no, love, the students. at their best they are so responsive and grateful to learn how to express themselves. the poor babies have spent so many years in the worst kinds of rigidities, hierarchies and manipulations. maybe that's what awaits them after they graduate, i don't know. at least in my class they get to make up recipes, tell ghost stories, write descriptions of japanese objects, give speeches on hiphop, sing rounds—i mean sure, they have to do some boring things too, but i even give them the option of writing a journal to me and i give them long responses—2 or 3 pages. i have always refused to treat this job as just a job. which is a main reason i'm always tired; the job requires a lot of soul, a lot of creativity, to keep it worthwhile.

i'm not crazy about the trip to work. i walk to the train station overly quickly because i usually leave the house just in the nick of time to get the last train that will get me to work in time to punch the clock, yes i have to punch a clock. on the way to work i see the garbage waiting for pickup on the curb, all tied up in nice plastic bags and covered with green nets to keep the crows from tearing it up (tokyo is rife with crows), assorted cats, sometimes a mother walking her child in a wheelchair, sometimes a highschool girl in a navy blazer and a ponytail so tight it looks like she's had a facelift, some nice bamboo and other plants depending on the season, and lots of houses, lots of concrete. i ride the train for about ten minutes to shinjuku, which is the busiest train station in the world. i don't know the stats but i read that somewhere. very often someone pushes me and i say, hey don't you fuckin push me and no one ever ever scowls or beats me up for saying that because i say it in english. it's fun to check out what people are wearing, especially now in the fall people are wearing such cool stuff. not the salarymen or "office ladies" but the young people and alternative types or the very fashionable city women. i somehow maneuver my way through the crowd to get to the platform for the chuo line, which goes along the kanda river. i always try to stand right at the train window so as not to feel too claustrophobic. sometimes the salarymen get what i call "miso mouth"—a not-very-nice smell at any time, especially in the morning. from the train window i see buildings and more buildings, but my favorite part of the trip is looking at the river. i have a superstition. the condition of the river tells me about my day. if it's clear and unrippled, my day will be calm. if it's filled with schmutz or dead leaves, my day will be disturbed/disturbing. one lovely thing about the river is that it's filled with carp. i always like to think they belong to the emperor. if i see a dead carp it's bad luck. if i see carp swimming (saw lots today, big fat ones!) it's good luck. there's also a beautiful effect when the light bouncing off the water reflects on the underside of an arched concrete bridge. i love that. i notice lots more things on the way to work, but i'm feeling like you must be drowning in description here. one more thing. when the train doors open and close, a little tune plays, eight notes, to me it's the sound of progress and of time passing.

they like sounds like that here (do you know about *mono no aware*?). there's also a five o'clock whistle in every neighborhood. i call it the mortality bell (well, another day gone). and at my school we've got bells ringing at the start and finish of every class. everything's so delineated. there's comfort in that, as well as negative restraint.

and you asked:

> how are things going? did you guys go to a counselor again?

things are not going (*ça ne va pas, pas du tout*). i said to my therapist (quite solo) that i felt caught in entropy and was so bummed about it. she said no, think about how things were and how things are. things are cetainly moving you just don't know where they're moving to exactly. and i think she's right. m— and i had yet another rage-filled confrontation the other night when i found (while he was out at a restaurant) a whole cache of photos of her in his schedule book, and the photos of me removed. he had forgotten his keys so i talked to him through the window for a while, no, interrogated him. he was furious that i spied on him again but what the hell am i supposed to do. he had some excuse that he had inserted the pictures at a time when i had done something really terrible, he swore he isn't infatuated with her (but why else carry pictures unless you're going to moon over them?). anyway it just felt like, yuck, i want out of this mess, i'm so tired of this. his back was out for two days and then mysteriously got better when i started being nice to him and then yesterday he said it was bothering him again (i reminded him i'm still househunting). the fact is he just doesn't have it in him to be ardent enough to say darling darling stay with me forgive me—for cultural reasons, for personality defect reasons and also because of our mutual ambivalence.

oh gary, sorry, i know this is an excessive answer to a few polite little questions. in fact i'm worn out from huddling over my powerbook. it's just like i said, i'm really enjoying having someone to narrate all this too, all this stuff in my life and in my head.

now i'm going to go have a bath. i've got to get up early and go househunting. then i've got an invitation to a halloween art opening. tomorrow i'm going to see some butoh. and the international film festival is coming to town. i want to see bulworth. is it worth seeing?

be really well.
be
really
well
        nada

∞

From: Gary
Date: October 29
Subject: Thursday

Nada, Nada, Nada,

Augh! I brought in the now near-mythical-proportioned disc with the letter I wrote you last weekend, and THE FILE WAS "CORRUPTED"!!!
Which thoroughly bums me out, especially cuz there was lots of stuff
about all this groovy afro-cuban music I was listening to while writing it.
So, I promise you promise you, I will write in the cracks & crannies of
the day today, & sew you together a patch-work e-mail. I wanna tell you
everything. & of course, that's an impossibility. I don't know, I don't
know ... where to start? Okay, I know for a fact (okay, a "fact") we never
met in SF cuz I was cognizant of your doings & person, very early on. I
have a funny story, about you, Brent (who I mentioned a long time ago,
I think) and Dan Davidson. Brent was really great about dragging me to
various readings & things, introducing me to everyone (not literally, but
as in, "Oh, here's this person, let's check them out, what they're doing").
So, he convinced me to go see "gordon" read at the Lab. Now, as you'll
remember, Dan lived on Haight, just below Divisadero, within walking
distance (5–10 minutes) from the Lab. So, I'd never met Dan, but Brent
said, "Let's pick up Dan, first, and go from there." This was my intro to
Dan, who later became really one of my best friends in San Francisco.
So, we ring his bell, we're let in, walk up to his apartment. But, he
doesn't open the door. Brent calls through the door, "Hey, we're gonna go
see gordon read at the Lab," and Dan goes immediately into this word-
soup parody of your writing, which he obviously wasn't yet into. (I know
he liked your work later. I think, though, at this time, he was still very
much invested in the Beats & really wasn't interested in much else,
poetry-wise.) The parody was hilarious, in retrospective it was like
Jackson Mac Low's "Twenties" or something, something extravagant &
with odd juxtapositions. But, Dan didn't show his face. Nor did he say he
didn't wanna go. (We were to assume from his parody that the answer
was "no.") So, me & Brent finally left and walked to the Lab. Now, probably I described this to you already, your reading, where you handed out
toys I think, and maybe mementos of some kind or other, maybe scraps
with writing on them. I don't remember, specifically. I do know that the

whole thing was so much an EVENT, & I was very taken with it. And, also, let's be honest, you were very very groovy, or had this very sort of Hipster air, which always made me intimidated. So, there was no way I was gonna like go up & talk with you, unless someone introduced us first, which no one did. Anyway, I remember not too long after that going in to David Highsmith's Talking Leaves bookstore and buying a copy of your book *rodomontade*. (Those line drawings! And how did it open? "I am Henry James. I am bigger than everyone else." Something like that.) I think I saw your other books there, or maybe that was later. Anyway, your reading made enough of an impression on me that I went to a second one, this time where you were singing in between lines or stanzas (well, according to my memory you were). Did I tell you all this stuff already? So, I knew you, but didn't know you. I doubt you were cognizant of me. I was horribly shy, though I did read a number of times.

You mentioned the power of hair. I don't know maybe I said this already but you know at one of the holocaust museums one of the most controversial exhibits was a huge display of human hair from Auschwitz victims. Braids, locks, etc. And what was at issue was the sense that this was just too personal, too personal a thing to put on display in a museum. Very moving, of course, to see this huge mass of hair. But probably just too much for many people. It's awful, and wonderful, what hair can do, how it makes you feel, wearer or seer.

Now, it's the end of the day. & I've said NOTHING. Arrrgh. I'm gonna write you again tonight from home.

Meanwhile, tell me, Nada, what love is. Seriously. For you.

Yours,

Gary

∞

From: nada
Date: October 31
Subject: Re: Tuesday

so, you asked me a very provocative question, gary, and i've been tossing the question around in my head. well, for one answer i'm going to have to send you a tape i made in 1989 called *koi maneuver*. "koi" has a triple meaning: *carp, coy,* and *passionate love*. i do a lot of "love is ..." exploration on there. this was the major cathartic work that came from my breakup with a—, who was my love between the ages of 16 and 24 (when i came to japan). i never actually meant to break up with him, did i tell you? although it was perhaps inevitable. he started having an affair two weeks before i left for japan.

anyway some of the "love is" sentence completions on that tape are

love is the thumping you hear in a race
love is a dog that you send into space
love is a trump card i hold at my waste
love is a corkscrew i twist into space
and so on
but these are aesthetic answers, not serious answers.

whenever i'm faced with this question i start parsing love into the different kinds of love, don't you? i think i actually had to do a freshman english essay on this once. but if we are talking about sexual love and passionate love, and i guess we are, rather than the magnanimous selfless spiritual kind, i think it is largely adrenaline and cultural illusion and a biological force far more powerful than anything i can begin to analyze.

one thing i think about love is that it is the attempt to heal a wound called birth. just because we don't remember the awfulness of that initial separation doesn't mean that it doesn't inform everything we do, trying always to get inside each other. i think that my "dolor core recede sanpo" poem gets at this notion a little bit, and that's why it starts out heartbroken.

other than that, what is it? physiologically, it's something that happens around the solar plexus, the heart of course, the thymus gland. it creates a quickening of all responses. it makes all nerves more sensitive. "whenever you are near, i hear a symphony ..." just barely touching the hand of someone you have that feeling for, is, you know, incredible. "why do birds, suddenly appear, every time, you are near"

i think i have an unreasonably literary sense of love as grand passion although i don't think i've ever experienced that in a fully reciprocated way. as you can see, i'm a very epistolary kind of person. i was once dangerously infatuated with a san francisco boy named j— (did you know him? he was in a band for a while called the 3 mouse guitars and then got into performance art, drumming and dancing) and really he was such a self-involved arrogant insufferable boy, and i was with the abovementioned a—!, but j— seeped instantly into my consciousness, i saw his face everywhere, until my idea of him loomed much larger than his actual person (kind of like the phenomenon one often finds in, um, e-mail romances), and i used to write him intense letters. i don't think he really knew what to make of them, in fact i think he was terrified (kind of a common male response to me). i don't think women are supposed to have muses, they're, i mean we're, supposed to be muses.

conflict is important to passionate love. that's what keeps it alive. passionate love is uncomfortable, but nothing makes you feel as vivid. or maybe instead of or as well as conflict i mean fear, fear of loss; disappointment is always a built-in danger of that kind of love. it's enough to make a person stay for years and years in a stagnant relationship to avoid having to feel that kind of disappointment. sometimes bringing conflict into a stagnant relationship makes it passionate again, as you know, if only for a little while. like yesterday i was cleaning out the refrigerator and m— came out of his room and started fucking me, there in front of the kitchen sink (how much more domestic can you get?). i asked him, are you trying to get rid of me or are you trying to keep me? and he said he didn't know.

i have no clear idea what i want. that's the problem. or i'm just too wimpy to eliminate what i don't want, for fear there will only be a vacuum awaiting me. there are so many options. today, for example, i found a potential living space. it's not as beautiful as the place i live in now, but from every window you can see green, and the landlord, who lives downstairs, has this lovely japanese garden with a little stone well which i'd be able to see from the veranda. it's not in so groovy an area as the one i live in now either, but part of me thinks it might be interesting to live in another part of the city. i could move there very easily if i were clear about what i want. all my friends and relatives keep saying, oh, get free, get free, it doesn't matter where you live, he'll just do it again and he'll never be really right for you. but when i am faced with his actual being i feel something, not love exactly, but a kind of warmth.

i'm not betting my life on that "kind of warmth," don't worry. i'm just sort of being hamlet right now, do i kill my uncle in the chapel at prayer. i know i'm driving my friends crazy with my dithering, no my shilly-shallying, no, what's the word, my endless deliberations on this, but you for example said it was ok.

i realize i've strayed from the question of what love is. really i dunno, but at my therapist's i made a list of the things i want from a relationship. ten things:

1) resonance
2) mutual adoration
3) mutual respect (to include trust)
4) levity
5) shared time
6) shared tasks (some concept of our common good/common goals?)
7) world expansion
8) stimulation (intellectual, physical)
9) mutual curiosity
10) freshness

my friend ewan laughed, said i had awfully high standards. i do think my list turned out pretty adult, not all raging infatuation but rather showing desire for someone who can sweep the floor while telling a joke and gazing at me adoringly. i don't know. do these criteria sound unreasonable? maybe a tad.

the dan story of his parody of me is pretty funny esp. when you consider that he turned out to be way more language poet-y than me, don't you think?

oh this has been quite a day what with househunting and butoh and other confusions. i'm going to have to stop writing now as my head is pounding, i think i need to lie down or eat or something.

tell me, gary, what love is. seriously. for you.

(doesn't that question feel like a kind of gauntlet? but it's fun to answer.)

nada

NOVEMBER

From: Gary
Date: November 2
Subject: First answer ("explained" in later e-mail)

Among the Living

1

The aim of constructive uncertainty
lies in the corner between two windows. Such that
we, welcoming the indistinct, unlocks the door
because it likes the sound.
We abstracts the whistled body
of the word. The hazards of this opposition
become clear: the ear listens to what
becomes it, to the blood flowing through it.
Your hand on the paper doesn't belong to me;
the mysterious invisible placed on the tongue,
I, has a thing in its throat.
The air is colder than the room.
To have no place in it flattens perception
to the usual table; your hand on it can't stop talking,
is grammatically correct. Is this the way writing looks
looking back? The dignity of the road,
the hazards of water. I, aspiring to the dignity
of one who may not be brilliant
but upon whom you can rely,
rolls the thick word, the mouthful of light.

2

So great is the influence of language,
we can speak only for itself. If we is a manifesto,
I wields a deliberate response
to the aesthetic problem of simple communication.
This idea unfolds into two equal parts:
a spaciousness filled by the vernacular
that feels it, I, passing unnoticed
in the wake watching is.
We lay awake watching television
while we and our children slept.
So great is the hatred of others that they
placed itself there so that we couldn't sit down.
If the menace of numbers is only so many stones,
so many teeth, we sounds a ledge to lean from,
is grammatically correct. Sound is never enough.
I looks for what she really is, if there is such a thing.
We share nothing but space: the space you occupies
long after you is gone. Thus, you is renamed
for what I am, whom I love: what's left
unfolds, that we placed itself there.

3

Rubbed raw by the world's noise
we buries itself into focus. This picture
is porous; not only water conceals
what it shows. Where we lives becomes insolvent.
What you likes is there, in that sound, flattened
against the world. Not one another, not you
sits down, buries the first stone.
"Unseen I sees it all," walks
because it is its nature
to be coming towards. What speaks
breaks. With this rope, we cannot tell
if we are going to pull ourselves to safety

or simply hang there.
Is this a case of unconscious
distortion? "Hope is resurrected upon loss,"
so as to look more like you
than your reflection. Only this room,
a cloak to wrap around you,
warms itself. Is what we warms, a vow?
Enough to hold what focused, veers.

4

Because words mention each other
they are literally true: "I stole words and lines
from magazines," that line, that's just me,
for instance: "to make me seem more
calm." Because I reads your absence
in the space you haven't yet filled.
"So calm it could be a photograph of you."
I measures the house in this room, places
itself on its shelf. Love, beloved,
is what makes me, takes you; your tongue
is my heart in what speaking subsides.
If it's boring, that's just me. The dead
should have known better. Each line returns
to its quiet exterior, our origin.
Once spoken, we enters, is grammatically correct.
How it is that you can see this
is a mystery to me. The lights go out,
brushing against the bruised blue books.
Whatever is a possibility is therefore a necessity,
save these few minutes.

5

I, any want, wants to take your place,
lies in wait, awake for you everywhere.

Tall grass waving you on, the tug of this system
must be willing to subside into it, too.
The music comes straight through the forehead.
To the extent this is poetry,
it occludes translation;
to the extent this must be read
I lies down in your mouth;
puts his hands upon her head and disappears.
Disappears into those spare moments of inspiration,
we: "need something lovely" or: "kill our selves
to propagate our kind." A picture always leads you
to someone else, and we eat everything. Certain chewed up words
wiped from the face, face down in the river
drawing you forward. "Murder me, too." Language
claps its lid on the "when" of seeing you in bed.
Looking again at the photograph, the river
slides under our hands; the closer we look
the greater the distance from where we look back.

6

We arms itself against our invasion;
not by the noise, but by the illustration.
The telephone rings, the mailbox
is empty. It rests, it calms,
it placed a chair in the room and then went far away.
Everything in this room is covered with white dust,
as close or as thin as you. How long have you been down
where my speech is? We bear its shame,
its disfigurement; those days are in a thousand pieces.
"We haven't a prayer" is merely silence,
though perfectly white.
As recognition of reluctance begins to lapse,
sense of self begins to show: a single tear,
a silver airplane. "You are" and its audience,
strewn; the many, a form of order.
The vernacular that sheds it,

sheds itself. We curves beyond reach,
careless of index and anticipation.
This sentence driven deep into the grooves
of its shoulders, bent, as though they were true.

∞

From: Gary
Date: November 2
Subject: Second answer

Love's Oscillating

Fond of absolutes & swarming in
The musical parts unwind. Veering eye-
Level, hones no better pair of lips
Than these. Look at me, mon élé-
Phant & I will be your man. Men
Attend & men stagger off, desiring exe-
Mption, teeth, trembling hollow
To suggest. From the coff of eve
Some bell whorling thru the leaves
Leaves in looser order to wash each
Wretched other out. We are complete,
Corrupt out of bed, abruptly home, ere-
Ct. Evening drivels distant waves on
Whom we lie, we love to know away.

∞

From: Gary
Date: November 2
Subject: Okay,

Nada, I sent along two poems, in answer to the, okay, admittedly
"gauntlet" question of love. I mean, these were both written a long
time ago. The longer one was when I had first met my wife (the
poem mentions "our children"; we had none), and the second, short-

er one, was written a year or two after we'd moved from San Francisco to Minneapolis, right after a particularly wonderful day together, studying French, & having made love very passionately. My whole body was singing & I knew, or thought I knew, or at least believed, "this is the state you're supposed to be in." & I wanted to get it down on paper. The first poem is more "intellectual"; I was really thinking, how can you talk about something so commonly referred to as "love," which everyone talks about as being this very powerful thing, but which is after all abstract. I realized how difficult it was to use language to describe this. I wanted my wife to know what I felt, a constant desire on my part, mainly because she was so mistrustful. I never felt she really believed I loved her. The poem, such as it was, didn't seem to help. (The shorter one kinda did, though.)

But, sending long-ago-written poems in answer is, okay, a bit elusive. Atually, I really like your list of 10 items and no, no I don't think that, as criteria, they're unreasonable. I mean, I think, yeah, it is an "adult" list, and by that I don't mean that it also doesn't account for, you know, infatuation (you do say "mutual adoration"), cuz are you gonna be stimulated & curious, and is your relationship gonna resonate w/out that? Well, maybe, maybe, but I don't think so.

Okay. I'm gonna write more today. It's an academic holiday (tomorrow is a university-wide holiday, so I get to stay at home), so I'm gonna spend the first half of the day thinking, the second half writing to you,

Soon,
Gary

∞

From: Gary
Date: November 5
Subject: I was out for a couple days

one a holiday and one a sick day. I've been feverish since Monday … and every time I've tried to answer the question, I've wondered: Am I describing love or infatuation or obsession or brokenheartedness or mere ego-bruise? I don't know. I want to write about love, but I realize, sitting here, I have no clue what it is. I mean, I know it's some form of connection. I know it involves intimacy. I know it involves physiological things that really can't be understood, or even well described.

But I go back to something you said in one of your e-mails:

> it's as if the rupture i experienced with m— suddenly
> allowed me to see a number of beautifully colored
> ropes hanging from the sky, attached to objects i
> can't see yet. they are rescue ropes, and i'm going to
> choose one as soon as i get a better view of the objects.
> for now i am examining the colors, the threads of the
> ropes, and admiring the ways the colors weave in and
> out of each other and combine. they are all options.

& this, you know, is quite beautiful, like that instant you realize, playing an instrument in harmony with another, that it is not what you are playing, it isn't what they're playing, & it isn't, necessarily the simple fact of your playing together, but that, suddenly, you hear overtones, those sounds generated way up on the register, above what is physically being done, literally the waves of sound, as they meet, making disturbance elsewhere, shaping aural space, do you know this phenomenon, Paul Hindemith wrote whole pieces based entirely on overtone production, created melodies heard only in overtones, & I think there are two connections with this idea, here, one being, yes, when something opens up, or when your focus on the thing directly in front of you fades off, as it does, staring at it, and other things, "peripheral," become radiant, present, there, real, and also of course a kind of cheesy-but-meant metaphor for, okay, you asked me, or turned my question back on me, what is love, that's it, not just the playing together, and not just the fact of overtones (which, metaphorically speaking, are everywhere, generating by all things moving in some way together, sharing space), but that quality of attention or awareness, or how you're suddenly awake, & it takes two, both, to know this, in simultaneity, of these "overtones," and hearing them, responding to them, and beginning, as you do in dreams you're suddenly aware you're having, shaping them as you go, so that it feels like being swept away, but you're still participant the rush itself a product of you, & the other ...

I guess you know that I have all of Dan's poems, drafts & letters. He didn't keep a journal, but he did keep notebooks, which were titled for the pieces he was working on (one for "product," "transit" and so on), and include actual early drafts, but also lots of "daily life" notes, and reminders, phone numbers, etc. His stuff was fairly well ordered & kept, but you know he'd gotten this old electric typewriter on the street one day, about six months before he killed himself, and he left it on all night one night, and it caught on fire while he was asleep. Consequently, his whole room still reeked of smoke, there were smoke smudges on the walls, and his manuscripts, journals and letters, many are blackened with smoke, too. It's an odd experience going through all of his things. I've read some of his notebooks, try-ing to figure out how he made these leaps from draft to draft (they tend to be significantly different), but mostly tend to stay away from it all; it makes me feel morbid. But, I've gone through some of the letters, a very odd feeling, to be reading someone else's mail. I haven't read them all by any stretch. But, I've read a few, including a couple of mine to him, which is sort of like dipping in to an old journal. I mean, it was weird, and I don't think I could stomach read-ing more than one or two letters. Why is that? If it was someone else's letters I wouldn't be so judgmental. I'd probably go, "Oh, cool, a human being," unless of course they were very mean-spirited or something, or I don't know. If the person was being condescending. The letter to Dan I read was a response to a poem he had sent me, and it was a bit long, like 3 or 4 pages, and it just seemed like idiocy to me. And, reading it, I thought, "You know, the guy deserved bet-ter than this!" And I think I felt two things, one being a kind of remorse, that you know I try, I try, but I was never really trained very well to read things, and certainly not to respond to them. I mean, what I was saying was not wholly off the map or completely irrelevant, but even a year or two later I could tell, you know, would I say that now? I always felt inadequate writing to Dan, which you couldn't tell if you looked at his letters, cuz I wrote him a lot. (It's, embarrassingly, the biggest file among his papers.) I mean, he read mountains of theory, very little of which I could ever connect with. & he knew it, seemed to know that stuff, backwards & forwards. Yes, it is funny that Dan would make fun of your writing for the very things he later became much more invested in. He went through four writing phases that I know of. Beat, New York School (he introduced me to Kenneth Koch's writing one night, reading aloud to me from "The Art of Love" at some cafe on Haight Street, and he & I loved to go to Berkeley to the rare books room to check out copies of *Fuck You, C Comics* and other NY School journals—I remember getting kicked out once cuz we couldn't stop laughing at this one issue of *C Comics*, a Koch/Brainard collaboration, a fake advertisement, "No sad old man will come knocking at your door" is the line that I remember sending me off (funny in context)). And then suddenly language poetry, which he really took to. But, he actually stopped reading a lot of it, for a good-sized period near the end. He'd also gotten rid of all of his theory books. "I can't believe I wasted all those years reading that stuff," he told me once. I said, "Yeah, but you used it! It fed you!" Which didn't seem to convince him. He started reading the Tao. & just prior to that, Heraclitus. I remember him telling me once, "every time I reach for Olson, I grab O'Hara instead." So, I don't know, I don't know. Was he ultimately that invested in the language "project"? There were times it seemed yeah, but I was just as often amazed by the things he was reading, cuz as you'll remember, or at least my experience of San Francisco was, it was a very divided place as far as poetry groups or cliques went. If you admitted publicly you liked X you couldn't admit you liked Z. I mean, it felt like that sometimes. A lot of the time, actually.

Now, it is many hours later, the sun has set, the clouds low-slung over the horizon glowing brilliant pollution orange, black silhouettes of buildings & trees in contrast, and the sky, as you gaze further up, becoming increasingly purple. What a weird coincidence. As I finished that last sentence, Laurie Price, with whom I was out most of the day toodling around the neighborhood, just called me up and said, "Gary, you have got to go look at the moon!" But, I couldn't see it out the window, so I just now went up one flight to the roof (we have a spectacular view from there), but still couldn't see it. I think I know where it is, what building it's behind. I don't know that it'll still look as fantastic when it finally does peek over, but I'm gonna keep looking out the window to my left (east) to see.

I'm drinking chamomile tea, now. I can feel I still have a fever. You said you were exhausted in your last letter. I hope you're getting rest. (Am I responding to damsel-in-distress—"Here, miss, let me help you with that"—or just being a caring e-pal?) God. Self-consciousness! Who needs it!

Love,
Gary

∞

From: nada
Date: November 7
Subject: out of the heart

dearest gary

it is very difficult for me to be as demonstrative as this salutation suggests, especially to men i, well, don't even know. i've been called armored, unapproachable ... but i don't know what it is

   probably the cloak of e-mail
      probably accelerated cyber-intimacy
         maybe a little exhibitionism
            certainly my hyperemotional state
that's making me want to unwrap more and more, disclose more and more

   mostly because i am so grateful for all your disclosures
   your e-mails are like camellias—open, inviting, pinkish, dewy
   all this verbal energy i am getting from you right now is precisely what i need, no, LONG FOR, while we're being honest ...
   i think that in one of the pop psych books i ordered from amazon on how to break up what we're having is described as a growing relationship, that is, a relationship that helps you grow, the kind of relationship you often reach out for in times of transition and loss
   isn't it good to know that you're doing something psychologically predictable that makes you less accountable somehow, even if you find yourself running naked through telephone lines
   i read an article on flirtation somewhere
   it described the stages of courtship
   how it begins with eye contact, circling, maybe repartée
   then there is a certain point in the process where the woman

has to show a clear sign of at least potential willingness, even just the gift of a phone number or the touch on the shoulder

and that's precisely where i've so often chickened out

mostly because i've twice had the excuse of loooong relationships to protect me from new intimacies

like once i was in this bar with a dashing australian guy

this just a few years ago

i remember it was winter and i was wearing my grandmother's mink coat

and he was a little boring but super-handsome

and he very boldly bent down to kiss me

(he was very tall, i'm just over five feet)

and do you know what i did, i RAN OUT OF THE BAR

i didn't even say goodbye

and he and i were kind of co-workers

i felt so embarassed by my coyness,

i left him a note the next day kind of hoping we could strike something up after that but no way, i'm sure he thought i was just too silly and capricious.

i think the coyness and protectiveness come from a sense of being so damn porous ... people think they can just put their face on yours and it won't really mean much, just nerve endings brushing nerve endings, but really, some of their CELLS come off on yours. They absorb some of YOUR CELLS TOO. All kinds of things can result. DEPENDENCIES. BABIES. RIPPING PAIN. SIRENS GOING OFF. with these alarmist thoughts i have in my life been virtually unable to have casual sex, instead i get with guys and stay with them for small eternities, even way past the expiry dates.

speaking of expiry dates, i'm 34 (you asked). what does that age mean in america? here in japan it means, "well on your way to losing sexual currency." here in japan it means "christmas cake" (that which can't be sold after the 25th.) i'm beautiful, tho, kind of, didn't i tell you? not like drop dead sexy vavavoom, but exotic, delicate (and just stick with me while i have a little fit of narcissism here):

(ok i admit, i edited this self-description out. it felt gauche, but had possibilities as a literary exercise, or maybe soft porn-anyway suffice it to say that i am embodied, and yeah, this is coy) ...

you know i noticed the moon the other night too, and you know what, it was the very same moon, except that i saw it earlier than you did, because i'm on the other side of the world ...

autumn is moon-viewing season—there are even lots of moon-viewing haiku season words. here in japan the moon is composed of rabbits and not green cheese or a man. the image is often *susuki* (like a kind of pampas grass) in reverse silhouette against a black sky in which a round moon shines, this seen out of *shoji* on an autumn evening. and haiku are duly written in homage.

it's waning now, that ol' moon, at the time i am getting around to writing this. did i already tell you my eyes hurt, i think i did. it's late for me, very late. approaching two in the morning ...

hey, you know what, i'm going to be in the states this winter ... i'm arriving in sf on december 19, leaving back to the grind of work and domestic hell on january 4. I hadn't planned to leave the bay area, but ...

ellipses
nada

∞

From: Gary
Date: November 12
Subject: photo op

Nada,

First, yesterday, in part cuz I had no clean "casual" clothes, and in part to impress you, I wore my grooviest near-olive plaid(ish) "slacks," a white shirt, groovy vest (again, in the "olive" spectrum), & beautiful soft pinkish thin 40s paisley tie, to work, hoping the "groove factor" would be evident as I wrote you. (Was it?)

Last night, doing laundry, still in my tie, etc., I bopped kitty corner to this new bar, a thoroughly hilarious obvious yuppie pick-up place, ordered a brandy, cuz brandy's supposed to be good for colds & flus, & mine's lingering. What a fiasco. The bartender didn't know which bottles above her were brandy. Neither did her helper. So, finally, I sighed and just ordered a shot of Old Bushmills. I sat there for a few moments at the bar. The whole place was empty save for one woman sitting near the front on a couch, drinking & reading some fashion magazine. She was kinda cute & oh, if it had been two three months ago I'd have gone over & started to flirt. Or at least eyed her from the bar. Neither of which I did, I asked the bartender for a paper & pen and went over to a booth, sat down, & started writing you a letter. It was pretty bogus as letters go. I mean, cuz I hadda be back to pick up my laundry. It was an excuse to send you another photo. I have a dearth of photos. So, this one will have to do. I sent it cuz it's probably the most "attractive," except that, you know, I was sort of shitfaced when it was taken, and it shows. I'm not sure that's terrifically attractive. Anyway, so that's on its way.

I said, in the letter, I was gonna write you a love letter today. Now, I'm torn between that and wanting just to open up & tell you everything, confess everything, which you know is, as far as I'm concerned, the same thing. Except it wasn't what I had in mind. So, maybe this is a little of both ...

You're a beautiful person, Nada, your writing gorgeous, completely compelling, whether your poems or your letters. (I can't believe M— doesn't read your work, considering that you seem familiar with his.) Your aesthetic sensibility, made manifest in how you send things, wrapped in interesting paper, funny but also rather sweet Swan bag, fetching rubber stamps. And, physically attractive, very much so, of famous people I would say, maybe, less Cher and more Annie Lennox. Who the woman to my left (I'm writing this at work) is listening to. And your voice, at least on that wonderful tape you sent me, sounds like Liz Phair. Whose voice I have a super-huge crush on, melt every time I listen to her. Oh, before I forget, speaking of Cher: Do you know that Tubes song where they say "She's more beautiful than Cher!" Haw haw. I always loved that line. Like Cher was the, like, Ultimate in Beauty. (Not that she couldn't be of course. But I just loved how it was seemingly cut-&-dried "decided" like that.) (I love obvious subjective p.o.v. vigorously asserted as Objective Truth.)

I want to tell you about two women I've been seeing, or in one's case, "seeing," both of whom I think I could be with. One who doesn't call me anymore after a couple times sleeping together (she couldn't bring herself to kiss me, tho we fucked, "it's easier for me to fuck than kiss," she said—she was pining, actually, when I met her, for someone else), and someone I still talk with, but who doesn't live in New York. The first was P—, a filmmaker who studied with my hero George Kuchar at the SF Art Institute, and no longer makes movies, though she paints. She lives in my neighborhood. I met her months ago. We started hanging out, riding bikes together, talking, and of course she brought me back to her place to see the movie she "starred" in that Kuchar made. It was hilarious. She played a nun. Some guy comes in for confession. Cut to her, straddling him, about midriff, shoving a microphone down his throat (literally) screaming at him: TELL ME TELL ME TELL ME ... We would get together, watch films, eat, hang out, talk, draw. One night, I just go over to her bed, lie back, lean out her window a bit, see the moon, & exclaim, "Oh, wow, look at that!" So, she crawls over & looks out. The obvious happens, we hold hands, compare fingers. Is this like required? "My thumb is bigger." God, what a cliché. Now, I'm stuck with the image of a million thumbs floating in space, comparing themselves to each other ... uh-oh ... please-to-excuse me, I just got handed work to do, so you will have to sit with this image for a bit. & then I'll be back with "the rest of the story."

    Love,
    Gary

∞

From: nada
Date: November 13
Subject: Re: photo op

no, wait, stop, i've read m—'s english work, which he did a long time ago, but most of his haiku i simply can't read. sometimes i ask him to read them to me, and i ask about words i don't know. i can read japanese well enough to read comic books, as i said, but not haiku. i do know, however, what his sensibility is, and it's very different from mine. he aims always, as haiku is supposed to, for a kind of wistful, still, emptiness. i have nothing against this aesthetic, but it seems contrived and monotonous to try to aim for this every time, there are so many different kinds of mental states to trace in writing, and anyway with a hamster brain like mine it's hard to stay patient enough to be wistful, still and empty all the time. he and i have different base rhythms. but to be very truthful, his patience is exactly what i like about him sexually ...

ok, two cher stories. first of all, i liked cher a lot when i was, i don't know, 9 or 10. my friend melia and i used to write fan letters to our favorite famous people. i wrote one to cher (in which i think i told her she didn't have to show her bellybutton all the time) and still have, in storage, the autographed postcard she sent me.

secondly, i don't really look much like cher (although she's one of the few people i can do an impression of—i stick my tongue in one cheek, let one hand go limp, flip my hair back with the other, and start singing "gypsies tramps and thieves"), but near where my mom lives in oakland there's this great israeli restaurant called the holy land. the waitress there looks EXACTLY like cher, tall, with the pre-op bumpy nose, but with lighter-colored hair. well, the funniest thing happened, i'm laughing as i type this, she came up to me in the restaurant and said, to me, "you really look like cher."

oh phooey, i want to write more, but it's 7:07 and i have to go take a shower and eat protein and go to work. but i loved the thumbs stuff in the last para of your e-mail ... and i didn't get to any of the stories i had planned to tell you.

nada

∞

From: nada
Date: November 13
Subject: pictures, voices

i just got your package with the magnificent comics, the books, your first picture, and that was good because i was sorta wondering what does this voice look like? ... and i had this feeling, gary, looking at your picture, which is kind of indistinct and underexposed, that you look, what, easily overwhelmed, or swept away, and i could see why d— saw you as a target for manipulation and a source of adoration

and that very thing struck terror into my chest cavity because should we ever meet, what guarantee could i give that i wouldn't do exactly the same thing, that i wouldn't do a d— on you, and am i even, electronically, possibly doing one now? now that's a lot to project on one picture of a man with a vulnerable expression, i know, but

guilt is one of the emotions that rules me, it's a genetic thing. i hate to hurt people, if i find out i've done so i think i suffer more than they do, maybe that's the explanation for my unreasonable loyalty to my two husbands (ok, let's call them what they are)

and especially i'd hate to hurt you because i am so grateful for your presence here and because (cliché approaching) i care about the you that appears in lines of type on my screen and that says such beguiling things, talk about construction of self

but you, i don't know you except as a linguistic being to "take myself out on" and, yeah, well, to listen to

and if you knew what a petulant, irritable, demanding, bossy, judgmental, arrogant girl i am (my mom is always saying to me, BE NICE)

look, i'm tired, i'm overwhelmed, here's a poem, not a new one, from last year sometime; i don't think it was in the MS i sent you:

RAVEL

hair encircles the mind
that sits a stone's throw
from transparency, trapping
life forms, flies, owls,
woodchucks, manatees, krill
just like the stars that
never go out but camouflage
in daylight and we are
very nearly moths, reaching

dancing into elephant or
disjoint irony into
pretend speaking. or
pretend dead grasshopper

those lazy jerks of language,
little spells
like used toothpicks—

they paralyze even
the stiffest resistance

thorning. unruled.
a shell full of ash
and then a candle
(votive)

power outrage—how
thrown up against
banks of difficulty.
and the body, prone
or supine. or both at once.

it's dark. darkness
throws up figures in approach
just past the cordon.

darkness wiggles imperceptibly

*

And then there are
no department stores,
and I feel bored.
And obligation is devoured.

Let's obliterate everything!
Let's will our own mortality
on the future!
And then there's the ostrich
in the crevice, out of which
a great synthesized chord
shockingly blossoms!

You're there with me
but I don't know who
you is. There is no true

you, and the you
I think there is
irritates me.

You know what I mean.

This we call the
problem of the you.

Eyes cross in
darkness, thinking
about you.
It's the problem
of the urn (the yearn).
The problem
of the red yarn.

Or the pretend red yarn.
I want a potato in foil.
I want to shake off
other human beings like
larvae, but then
I feel so lonely.

Something skittling over
water: business.
And then spilling over
water: the island is
glowing again. Whatever
I lost I   just   lost.

a tattoo of darkness on my breast
a tattoo of you on my face
body bound in red yarn

and wait for unravel

what kind musik

how the hook above
the dot changes the
music, changes the mean

what   kind   musk

* * *

to understand the red yarn reference you need to know about *inochi kurenai*—that's the red thread that the japanese believe connects mates even from birth

from my early teens i've said i've wished to be:
A HUMMING BLUE SPHERE OF MIND LIGHT
embodiment is a terribly fraught issue for me

maybe that's why my writing has so much body in it because my own relationship to my body is dysfunctional

you know, i can't swim, can't turn a somersault, cry when i have to climb up or down a steep cliff, hated p.e., was always chosen last for relay races have never owned a pair of running shoes didn't learn to ride a bike till i was nineteen

but language, ahh, it's so physical, or what was the word you used, "palpable"

an ex-lover said to me once, "you know, language isn't as sexy to everyone as it is to you." which i knew but i wondered why not

and once barry (watten), when i said i was in complete adoration of alan davies' writing, he said, "it's like yours, it's all about sex"

m— and i went to a mountain last sunday. the morning was awful, i was shaky and had a tantrum—didn't eat early enough, hadn't rested properly. in fact, on the way to the train station i told him i hated how he acts when i go into my low blood sugar rages—he always looks at me like i have a fatal character defect: you bitch. (and that makes it worse.) and maybe i do, but i really suspect it's biochemical. he said, are you blaming me? and i said no, you are completely twisting what i said. so anyway he stopped in his tracks and said in japanese, suddenly i don't want to go, and i said fine, why don't you leave me since that's what you really want to do anyway.

isn't coupledom fantastic? this is what i meant by "we make each other do things" and i said "i'm going to the mountain anyway, now that we're out of the house," and you know what, we went, both slept on the train a little, and the air at the mountain was so good, and we rode a lift with no safety belt all the way up the mountain, with him saying all the time, what if we fell off here, or here, or here? just below us some rickety looking old cyclone fence covering a deep valley with high cryptomeria trees, and it was fun.

there were tons of people there, this being one of the mountains closest to tokyo, so instead of getting out of the city, we brought the city along with us. the leaves hadn't quite changed yet but the day was plenty shiny. the mountain is covered with beautiful shrines; it's supposed to be a place to go for purification. i bought incense and we hiked a little trail to a suspension bridge that was kind of nowhere, and i remembered what i hate about hiking, that you're so busy keeping your eyes on the trail that you don't stop and look and listen, but i tried to, now and then

the japanese countryside is so beautiful, very detailed, intricate. i don't like sparse places. a— used to like to go to the marin headlands but i hated it there because it was just bare hills and wind. i mean i don't mean hated, it just wasn't my landscape of preference. i like ferny, foresty places.

and we had a meal after getting so refreshed in mountain air, a meal to remember, of grilled river fish, sashimi, freshly-made, really "toothy" soba, tempura of pumpkin, lotus root, etc. this was our second "date" after the incident, and it wasn't too bad, no it was nice, although little thoughts of rage and detachment and impatience (at one point i said, let's do a role play. you be me and i'll be you and i'll tell you what you should say and do to me) popped up now and then. i thought, this is OK, i can bear to be with him, at least for a while (as if a relationship should be something you bear! rather than what delights you!)

which doesn't make anything any more clear to me for the moment but perhaps that's all right

nada

∞

From: Gary
Date: November 13
Subject: Friday Evening

Nada,

... I don't want you to feel guilty for things you haven't yet done, may never do. It's not worth it. I'm an adult, Nada; I make choices about who to talk to, for how long, & what about. & the heart, the ego, the body ... they're all amazingly resilient, as Dan liked to say (tho, wait, no, he only said that about the body). And, this leads me to tonight's story, which is one I promised you actually long (it seems) ago, when you mentioned something about being with someone from another culture. I said then, & as you'll see it's true, it's a very romantic story. I don't think you'll feel very guilty after you read it. I don't know what you'll think. I waited too long to tell it to you. As boring as this is likely to get in places, I'm gonna ask you to stick it out until the end.

I'm not gonna finish the story about P—. Except to say we slept together, it was okay, we did it a couple times, but she really wasn't into it, & her lack of engagement resulted in mine. I still would have liked hanging out with her, but I really got the sense that she didn't want me around. I think she was madly in love with the guy she'd just broken up with. (Her decision, she told me. Because he'd just gotten divorced & she loved him so much, she didn't want to just be his "rebound woman." I actually tried to talk her into reconsidering not being with him; it was obvious how she felt.)

Oh, this is also an "e-mail" romance story. At least, the first part of it is.

The week before I was to move out from my wife's place the last time & move in with Chris, I stayed after work one night. And got online. And cruised & cruised around, probably like M— had (which is why I was hesitant to tell you about this at first), until I started "meeting" people. At some point in the evening, I met someone with the name SONYALOVER. I started talking to her, and I don't know how but it quickly accelerated, not into cybersex (she told me up front she didn't do anything she didn't really mean), but into "life stories." She was 34, from Caracas, Venezuela, where she'd worked in the music industry. She was now living in Fort Lauderdale. Like me, she was married, and moving out at the first of the month. We continued talking & at some point she asked me what I did & I told her, well I work in a university & draw cartoons & write poetry. When I was about to leave (it was maybe 11:00 p.m. by then) she said, hey wait, do you want to play a game? I said, Okay. She gave me 12 words and said, Write me a story in which you include these 12 words. So, I did. On the spot, nothing amazing, a sort of fairy-tale story, that near the end moved into semi-porn. It took like an hour to tell. She loved it, gave me her e-mail address & told me to write her. So I did. We exchanged a few e-mails back & forth & then she gave me her phone number. She said, Don't call after 3:00 p.m. So, I called at like 2:45, the earliest I could get out, from a payphone with a calling card. She answered, we talked, very nervously, for a few minutes, then the line went dead. I called back. Her husband answered & I feigned a wrong number & hung up.

The next day, I got an e-mail from her, everything was okay, she was moving out on the first and wanted to know how to contact me, because she didn't have a computer of her own. So I gave her my new number and address. The day after I moved in with Chris she called. & we talked for maybe an hour, hour & a half. Then, I started writing her letters, very romantic things, with long erotic passages tagged on to the end. And she wrote me back. And we exchanged pictures. She was stunning. I remember when my friend Ange came over & saw C—'s picture (her name, by the way, wasn't Sonya—that was a cyberpseudonym), Ange goes: "Oh my god Gary she's a total babe!" I hadn't heard that word since, like, high school. (Ange, by the way knows nothing about this e-mail exchange. I told only one person, who is a poet, but doesn't really hang out with poets much, Laurie.)

Well, the letters accelerated, and the phone calls, too. Not drastically. (Nothing like this exchange, in terms of frequency.) Now understand, this whole time I was sending her these long erotic passages, she never said word one about them. I had no idea how she felt about them. She only ever talked about the poems I sent, my own & lots of others, asking her to translate, say, a particularly vivid Paul Blackburn poem into Spanish (which she did, gorgeously).

One day, I spent the afternoon in Prospect Park with a little blank book I'd bought in Chinatown. I filled it with various observations, pseudo-philosophy, plaintive lyrics & then, I don't know why, I just drew all these erotic drawings of couples. 35 of them, since the book was for her 35th birthday. She wrote me to say, "this is too much." And called me and explained, you know, she thought the drawings were "technically good, but they, I dunno, they disturbed me for some reason. Maybe because we've never been face to face." So, I shied a bit after that, & in subsequent letters never mentioned sex. Or only vaguely. Anyway, she felt my sudden reluctance, and called me &, for the first time, really talked about all of that STUFF I'd written to her. She admitted it completely turned her on, but that she was too shy to say anything. Well, I don't know how it happened (cough), but by the end of the conversation, we were having phone sex. You have to understand, this is the first time either of us had ever done anything like this, either "meet" a prospective lover online, engage in an epistolary courtship, and things like, well, phone sex. (Welcome to the 90s.)

This letter is boring, isn't it. But, it's a story & I think I should finish. So, we started talking more & more on the phone, having more & more phone sex. I don't know how to describe that. It's a very very odd feeling. You feel as though you're right there with someone, especially as it increases in intensity, and then, soon after you come, you realize ... oh my god! I've been masturbating! And yelling! & moaning! Which, I don't know, I don't tend to do. (Alone, I mean.) You have to learn how to do everything you might do with another by sound. & you are learning it, as weird as that sounds. & suddenly, one day, you realize, you & your partner are not only really adept at this, but, it's frightening how wonderful it can be sometimes. It isn't, of course, the real thing. & we'd whipped ourselves into such a frenzy that, finally, one day, she told me she'd bought a plane ticket to come up & see me. On Labor Day weekend. Which she did.

So. She flew in on a Saturday night, got in near midnight. I picked her up at JFK. I wasn't prepared. I mean, we'd talked about it, gone over every little potential intricacy, how hard it would be, how exciting, how scary, what our eyes would do, etc., etc. But I really wasn't prepared. She was drop dead gorgeous, worse than her photograph. I felt like a total fraud. What the hell was I doing picking up this perfect creature from the airport, of all places, like I was one of these people who picks up their lovers at the airport or whatever. My tongue was useless. I couldn't talk to her. I didn't know what to do at first. Could she tell I was average? On the thin side? Well, we took the A train back to Park Slope, which took an agonizing hour, during which time I tried to make conversation. I was reading "I'm not into you" all over her face, the way she held her body, the way she grunted out answers to questions, you name it. But, she was gonna be here for four days, what was I to do? So, we pick up some Coronas, limes, and go to my apartment. We hung out for a bit in my room, then I took her up to the roof. Amazing view of Manhattan, I think it floored her. We went back down, & I just started pulling books off the shelves to read, to read aloud, to her. We sat looking through Brad Freeman's *Muzelink*. (An amazing book. The book equivalent of Chris Marker's *Sans Soleil*.) She loved it. She loved Bernadette Mayers' & Alice Notley's poems. She looked at me for longer than two seconds, and taking this as an opening, I just leaned over & kissed her. Nothing seemed to happen. So, I suggested we go out to Manhattan (it was 3:30 a.m. now), and we went off to get the subway. Once outside, however, I don't know what came over me, I just grabbed her & kissed her, & she grabbed me back, her fingers clawing at my shirt, & we just kissed for like half an hour. & then both confessed how terrified we'd been until that moment. So, hand in hand, stopping every couple of paces to kiss, we just walked around the neighborhood. As the sun came up, I took her into Prospect Park to the very spot where I'd made her birthday book. We went back to my place, and, well, I'm not gonna go into all the details. We spent four days together, mostly in my room, but taking excursions into Manhattan to go dancing, buy fancy cigarettes & eat (Indian food, which she'd never had, in this wonderful place, Panna II, totally overdecorated, too thin & long, & with usually fantastic Indian film music playing.)

So, she went back. & we've been talking ever since. I've tried to convince her to move to NYC, which she says she wants to do. But, she has a final meeting with Immigration in February, and she's not sure she's gonna get into the country, since she got separated. I ceased all of my other fling activity after meeting her. Everything.

And then, Nada, and then I got involved in this. I was going over all of our e-mails a couple nights ago, wondering ... how did this happen? How did this accelerate? I didn't start writing back & forth with you expecting to start flirting. And I really didn't expect either of us to be drawn to this. I mean, not this much.

Obviously, I don't expect to move to Japan any time soon. Or, to be very honest, ever. And, no, I don't think it ever crossed my mind that, well, you might decide to move back to the States & would conveniently wind up, say, where all the other poets live. (I think there are like 10–15, that I know personally, in walking distance of me.)

What the hell am I thinking? What am I doing? Isn't great sex with a curious, intelligent person enough? Do I have to start fantasizing about the infinitely vague possibility of a relationship with an artist whose work I actually really admire? Are shared cultural references really all that important in a relationship? Is verbal (written) connection?

I don't know, I don't know. I do know that I hang on your every word, that I feel compelled to open up to you completely, tell you everything, whatever's there, and, yeah, I feel guilty, too, but maybe not in the same way as you: I feel guilty that I'm making it difficult for you to focus on your relationship, ending or not, guilty that we live thousands of miles apart, guilty for feeling attracted to you, guilty for wanting you, and even guilty for having the audacity to tell you such things.

I don't want this e-mail to become excessive. (It no doubt already is.) Laurie said: Don't tell her about C—. It'll just make everything weird. I told her, but I already started, & besides, what the fuck? It's me! It's my life! & we're talking about that!

Okay, look. I feel like some of the above puts enormous amounts of pressure on you to, like, reply or whatever. DON'T buckle to it. I mean, I'm thinking out loud here, and part of my thinking is: Well, what do I want from a relationship? & what do I really need? Strike the second question. What do I want. You gave me your list; here's my own:

1) shared sensibilities 2) unending curiosity 3) total openness 4) passion, passion, passion 5) mutual respect & admiration 6) LOVE (if two people can ever agree on what it is) 7) shared goals 8) growth 9) fidelity, commitment (that feeling of being meant for each other, as well as deciding, okay, "I'm here") 10) intellectual & emotional com-

patibility ... so, I don't know, but I don't think these are unreasonable. Do you? More soon,

Gary

∞

[*Handwritten letter from Gary dated November 14—received by Nada about a week later.*]

Dear Nada,
          The sun fills my room "like a yellow jelly bean," I open Johanna Drucker's *PROVE before LAYING* & read:
                                        "Figuring the word—against a jealous ground which rises to protect the independence of a xenophobic hand asserting presence as writing on a surface softer than the mind. 'Prove before laying,' read the label— or 'etiquette' as it is called in a term which aptly states its prescriptive attitude toward protocol. What could be revealed without sullying the pristine integrity of the letters? Their unmarked virgin faces flush with ink in the first encounter as the dark experience of knowledge pressed up and into the receptive fibers of some off-hand sheet. In a desperate attempt at self-assuring recognition they repeat endlessly this passage from cast form to transmitter of impression in the sequence of an infinitely mutable array. Their finite hearts beat hard in anticipation of imminent contact, their figurative feet solid on the base of the press, their discoursing surfaces pressed into the service of a continual rearrangement which suggests that any statement at all is a possibility within the momentary configurings of their categorical imperative. Their capacity for repetition and reuse is only real in the ephemeral sense of material, while the carnal potency of the alphabetic resides in its infinite ability to be dispersed into new relations of the letters with themselves and thus to us ..."
                                        I love, Nada, how you move in "Ravel" beginning with "hair encircles the mind" a near physical description that you take into immediate metaphor, the mind quickened by & entangled in hair, soft, physical, erotic, "a

stone's throw from transparency, trapping/ life forms" which you then proceed to entrap, and of course your life forms, your nouns, are exotic, "manatees, baleen" & then looking up to the stars, we become "nearly" moths, drawn to noun "elephant" or "pretend speaking"—how close this feels to our exchange. "lazy jerks of language," and, my heart flutters, "little spells/ like used toothpicks— they paralyze even the stiffest resistance"—and I can't help (again) wondering, what gave rise to this poem, what situation? "You're there with me/ but I don't know who/ you is." I mean, you've told me that, though I know this refers to something else, perhaps more to a situation of literal, physical closeness, and yet huge (mental, emotional) distance, & so I wonder, M—? Though you said you didn't ever really write poems about him.

& then "the problem of the urn (the yearn)"—& I think of "gushing," how Heidegger talks about it in "The Thing"(it's such a metaphysical essay; I hadn't expected that),

Nada, I'm drawn to your language, have fallen in love with it, perhaps with you, since it's your tongue, and like the lover who yearns to take the other's tongue into their own mouth, to curl their own tongue around the lover's, to suck it as far down their throat as they can, wanting to be filled with it, the tongue the most erotic part of the body, how it moves determining fluidity of language, of physical (sexual) expression.

If I continue writing this is bound to become semi-pornographic, and believe me, I want to seduce you, send my words out over the continent, over the ocean to you, want your "island glowing" ...

Yes, to answer your question (was it a question?) of several e-mails ago, I know you're embodied,

not, as I am not, "these words"

our bodies, our lives, constructed this, call it what you like.

I'm courting you.

I want you. I glance up & see the red wedge of Brooklyn, a few of its citizens gathered on the corner, adding bricks to a not-yet-crumbling build-

ing, all your letters to me to my right, & I feel you somehow present, as though we'd just been speaking & you've gone off into the
other room for a moment,

I want, feel compelled, to sweep you
back in, here with me,

the sole intention of this letter.

Love,

Gary

∞

From: Nada Gordon
Date: November 15
Subject: Alfonso Rigoletto

ok, you remember how i said i could never do anything furtive? well,
a couple of weeks ago, maybe about the time you asked me

> Tell me, Nada, what love is. Seriously. For you.

m— and i were Talking, and i did let on that i was having a rather
charged mutually consolatory e-mail exchange with a poet in nyc
i've never met who was asking me corny questions like "what is love
for you." so m— said, well, what's his name? and i, a big grin all over
my face, said ALFONSO ... ALFONSO RIGOLETTO. i don't know,
that's the first name that occurred to me. rigoletto is an opera right?
about comic dalliance?

so last night the subject came up again, in the context of him
asking me what my goals in life are and when I said, hmm, to be
really aware, and through my awareness spread positive energy,
through creativity, (or some other abstract hippie nonsense), he
said, "no, i mean, i feel like i'm just taking up your time, because i'm
never going to marry you or have a child with you, and then i feel
bad." well the issue has never been for me either marriage or children, just the ten items on my list, and maybe a couple more, and
he really only fulfills two or three of those ... and he said, "don't you

think i should move out?" and i said, kind of hopefully, "why, are you
planning to?" and he said "not yet" and i said, "then why do you hang
on to being with me?" and he said, "because sometimes i feel good
being with you." and i said, "yeah me too, but more often than not i
feel tense and discordant." and he said, "well, i really shouldn't get
in the way of your looking for someone else." i said, although not in
these words, that i am certainly putting tentacles out in into the universe, transmitting my YIN, as it were, and he said, "are you talking
about your e-mail friend?" and i said, "yeah, partly, but partly just a
general opening to other possibilities and to greater happiness." and
then i told him that it was true that i had never had an exchange
quite so galvanized with anyone as the one i am having with you
(you gary) now, and that it filled my head all the time, and that it was
alarming me, because of the illusory nature of it, and then i said,
and, oh god, gary this part is going to be totally brutal, but i'm going
to say it because i have to, i said, "there is just one problem," and he
said, "what's that," and i said, "well, i've seen his photo and this guy
is just totally Not My Type ..."

oh god, darling, i'm sorry, and i'm going to get around to quot-
ing proust on this topic in a minute, because there still may be hope
for something, we may actually be Soulmates, or Best Friends for
Life, or even, well, who knows, and a photo doesn't say much anyway, you can't send pheremones in a photo (or at any rate the tech-
nology doesn't yet exist), or essence

and by the way, what i mean by not my type is that i have never
ever been attracted to a blond

skinny is ok, short is great (being teeny-weeny myself, i appreciate bantam guys, they are funnier and more attentive), but i knew
when i read your list of famous people that should we ever attempt
to "take this to another level" this was going to be a problem, or i was
going to have to change some very deeply ingrained images of my
dream fella (always dark-haired, with a biggish nose, a ponytail perhaps, a goatee/ some prototypes: courbet—check out his self portrait, johnny depp, and I don't know, baby elvis?) ...

well, i don't know, but that's what i meant by all that pussyfooting "i would hate to hurt you" stuff

so when you write things to me like

>What the hell am I thinking? What am I doing? Isn't
>great sex with a curious, intelligent person enough? Do
>I have to start fantasizing about the infinitely vague
>possibility of a relationship with an artist whose work
>I actually really admire? Are shared cultural references
>really all that important in a relationship? Is verbal
>(written) connection?

i wonder, are you talking about sex with me here—or did i misread this? and isn't that a little presumptuous, just kind of jumping the gun a teeny bit? i mean hell, there are some things that really really turn me off that i just don't know if you have, like

    spatulate fingernails?
    unsightly birthmarks?
    a squeaky voice?
    catbox breath?
    no butt at all?

let me put it this way: I have never been able to forgive m—, who is a sort of handsome guy on his good days (and obviously not blond), for not being as beautiful as a—, whom i'm sure i idealize but god, his whole body smelled like dry grass in summer, and i'm sure that my ambivalences about m—'s physicality have contributed to the tensions in the relationship

but on the other hand, if he had been deeply attentive to me in all ways, not just sexually, i might not have been annoyed by the fact that his shoulders slope and his breath smells rotten and his stomach juts and he doesn't have much of a chin ...

so are you picking up on the imperiousness now? the judgmental nada?

and do you HATE me?

ok, so let me get around to proust now, partly to let you know that there may still be possibilities

    [Swann] came to the conclusion that the sufferings
    through which he had passed that evening [the evening
    he first fell in love with Odette, about which he was rem-
    iniscing at the end of the relationship], and the pleas-
    ures, at that time unsuspected, which were already

being brought to birth,—the exact balance between which was too difficult to establish—were linked by a sort of concatenation of necessity.

But while, an hour after his awakening, he was giving instructions to the barber, so that his stiffly brushed hair should not become disarranged on the journey, he thought once again of his dream; he saw once again as he had felt them close beside him, Odette's pallid complexion, her too thin cheeks, her drawn features, her tired eyes, all the things which—in the course of successive bursts of affection which had made of his enduring love for Odette a long oblivion of the first impression he had formed of her—he had ceased to observe after the first few days of their intimacy, days to which, doubtless, while he slept, his memory had returned to seek the exact sensation of those things. And with that old, unremitted fatuity, which appeared in him now that he was no longer unhappy, and lowered, at the same time, the average level of his morality, he cried out in his heart: "To think that I have wasted years of my life, that I have longed for death, that the greatest love I have ever known has been for a woman who did not please me, who was not in my style!"

that's one of the greatest paragraphs in all literature.

and this e-mail has been written feverishly, with much emotional difficulty but not slowly.

yours,

nada

∞

From: Gary
Date: November 16
Subject: Re: Alfonso Rigoletto

Hi, Nada,

Okay ... one thing at a time ... so, are you guys really beginning to tear yourselves away from each other? I mean, you've said you were before, but then it sounded like he was suddenly very interested in being a good boyfriend, and now he's admitting he doesn't wanna get married (does he mean just formally? or does he mean that he doesn't really want to commit to this relationship?) ...

... now, as for tendrilling out, well, I think you should, if that's what your desire is ... I mean, god, I certainly did at the end of my marriage ... you have to, I mean you have to if what you want is, really, at this point, connection of any kind with another ...

>oh god, darling, i'm sorry,

don't be, you know more than one philosopher has said that all love really is is sexual desire and that we create all of this other stuff to justify it, a holdover from christianity & other lively religions with strict moral blah blah blah, but that, ultimately, it's physical. I don't, personally, entirely believe that, though I know how powerful this whole affair with C— has been. I mean, I've told her, many many times, how much I love her. & I mean it. I do totally love her. It's just that I'm not entirely comfortable, and especially not after meeting you, with a purely sexual relationship. Our (C— & my) relationship isn't purely sexual, she does like poetry, she reads philosophy, but there is a way in which, well, I certainly don't feel we share entirely similar sensibilities. I mean okay, she's not an artist. & that really, it's not something you can describe to someone who doesn't do it. & it's a way of being-in-the-world. Anyway

>we may actually be Soulmates, or Best Friends for Life,
>or even, well, who knows

I don't know ... and, you know, it doesn't matter, Nada, it doesn't, we don't need to define anything, and god I apologize if my enthusiasm or whatever has pushed you to the point where you feel the need to decide anything about anything cuz that wasn't what I'd intended

>well, i don't know, but that's what i meant by all
>that pussyfooting "i would hate to hurt you" stuff

I know, & I knew it then

>i wonder, are you talking about sex with me here—
>or did i misread this?

well, yes, you did misread it, or I didn't put it clearly enough, I meant (a) I have a great sexual relationship with someone right now (in fact, I'm flying down to Florida this Saturday and am gonna spend the week with her)

>and do you HATE me?

God no ... stop it ... how could I hate you after all this talking, revealing, I don't, honestly, I'm not that kind of person ... and, besides, it's not the first time I've been rejected for being blond ...!

more soon,
Gary

∞

From: nada
Date   November 17
Subject: pure love

i sent you today, actually yesterday, as it's around 3:30 a.m. now, a childishly colorful package of fun things—*lip* (another chapbook of mine), photos, a drawing by my cousin bethany—i had to limit myself as i kept wanting to put more and more stuff in but i thought, no i'll overwhelm him

i hope it will make you happy and start to repair some of the manic things i said

i'm assuming that you are knowing everything that's going on with me but of course you don't you can't, unless you are psychic beyond e-mail

but the fact is, the reason i can't get into rem state, is that i am possessed by your importance to me as a presence, it's pure love

and i know that because otherwise i wouldn't be so hysterical, with all the symptoms, i'm banging off my paper walls here, gary, busting up the *shoji*, leaving scratch marks on the tatami

and i'm sure the stuff i wrote to you was a way of, you know, "running out of the bar," panic, alarms going off

it's is alarming, wouldn't you say, to feel so connected to someone you've never met

you've never spoken to

who's on the other side of the world

who anyway isn't your type and has a latina sex goddess waiting in the wings

and so yesterday, after a day of really feeling i was going to pass out again (i see i'm sometime going to have to tell you the story of my seizure in detail), my head a boulder, unable to function in my work, i came home, said goodbye to m— who was leaving to teach his night classes, made some chamomile tea, which relaxed me enough to release a huge flood of tears (i want to explain those too, but i can't stop to explain everything), and i threw the i ching again, which often calms me down

and do you know what, this was the third time in a sequence i asked specifically what you are to me, and twice i've got the same hexagram, one i don't ever remember getting before in the past, and probably the most powerful hexagram in the whole book:

it's number 1, the creative ... please please go look at a copy (of the wilhelm translation) although i'll quote a little here

it is solid yang lines, solid power ... and it says

"The Creative works sublime success ... when an individual draws this oracle, it means that success will come to
him from the primal depths of the universe and that
everything depends on his seeking his happiness and
that of others in one way only, that is, by perseverance

in what is right ... The Chinese word here rendered by
'sublime' means literally 'head,' 'origin,' 'great.' ... the
beginning of all things lies still in the beyond in the
form of ideas that yet have to become real. But the
Creative furthermore has the power to lend form to
these archetypes of ideas ... The course of the Creative
alters and shapes beings until each attains its true,
specific nature, then it keeps them in conformity with
the Great Harmony ... another line of speculation goes
still further in separating the words 'sublime,' 'success,'
'furthering,' 'perseverance,' and parallels them with the
four cardinal virtues in humanity. To sublimity, which,
as the fundamental principle, embraces all the other
attributes, it links love. To the attribute success are
linked the mores, which regulate and organize the
expressions of love and thereby make them successful.
The attribute furthering is correlated with justice, which
creates the conditions in which each receives that which
accords with his being, that which is due him and which
constitutes his happiness. The attribute perseverance is
correlated with wisdom, which discerns the immutable
laws of all that happens and can therefore bring about
enduring conditions."

what i am feeling, gary, is that my encounter with you, from "the
primal depths of the universe" has been, and i hope will continue to
be, a catalyst. through it i have been made to confront myself in
ways i've been avoiding for some years. it has shaken me, esp. following on the heels of the m— incident. not only that, i feel a concern for you so strong i can't quite explain it, except, you know when
you pick up a butterfly by the wings and some of its wing dust gets
on your fingers, i kind of feel like that, like i look at my hands and i
see some of your subjectivity smudged on them, as you no doubt
notice mine on yours too. and isn't that love? or what is it?

look, a lot of the things i say, especially about men, and about
sex, come right out of trauma, abandonment trauma—some, as you
know, recent. i've shared with you some of those traumas, so you
can begin to know what i mean. i don't know what sort of relation-

ship awaits us, if it's sexual or not, if it's enduring or not, or even if we'll ever be closer than 5,000 miles from each other, but anyway, right now, to me, it's more crucial than anything. i think i've expressed that before, but maybe not as clearly as i am right now.

does this sound like a rejection to you? it doesn't to me.

write to me! write to me! write to me!

love,

nada

∞

From: nada
Date: November 18
Subject: cat glasses

i got home to find a letter from you on the kitchen table ... with another photo, quite different from the first, and much clearer, so i can see the shapes that compose your face, and it is a very cézanne face, not average but unusual, i'd say, the ovals of your cheeks ... and am delighted to see that you have a proper nose, well-sculpted

the gary oldman is the cheeks and eyes, isn't it, yes, you do resemble him, but not so much as my friend ewan does. you look more like an adult in this picture than in the other, which oddly surprises me because sometimes your e-voice sounds like it's about seventeen.

i can't look at your photo for a long time, not because of any judgment of it, but because the solid proof of your embodiment scares me, or embarrasses me, or something. or it could just be your glazed, drunken eyes.

you have a very prominent adam's apple, as i do, although i am a woman, whatever that means, and my neck is otherwise swanlike (i first typed swannlike)

i said i was going to tell you about my seizure

well, it wasn't really a seizure as in epilepsy, but it was something called a syncopal episode, with seizure-like symptoms (is that the right word?)

it was probably caused by extremely low blood sugar incurred on a trip to the south of france with my dearest friend stacey, who lives in paris, and her boyfriend thierry. we had been eating fresh

nougat (basically whipped sugar) the day before, and it was wicked-
ly hot, and we were in a non-air-con car. i had just come from england, where it was very chilly, two days before. in england i'd been
drinking five cups of black tea every day and participating furiously
in this fantastic, very emotional, workshop, plus dealing with jet lag
and a new culture (and england *is* different, from japan especially)

after driving several hours the first day, we stopped at stacey's
former mother-in-law françoise's old farmhouse for dinner and to
stay the night. of course i was obliged to drink wine, and this on top
of some motion sickness pills i'd taken to deal with the windy country roads (yes, i get terribly carsick) and oh yes it was the third day
into my period, so i had lost a lot of blood and had not yet started
taking iron pills to deal with my anemia

when i got up the next morning, i was feeling a little out of equilibrium (not too unusual though). i sat down with stacey and
françoise and françoise's mother, and we started our breakfast of
white bread, jam, tea with sugar, when suddenly i turned to stacey
and said, "stacey i feel so dizzy ..." and she said, put your head down
between your legs (oh, this part is getting hard to tell). as i put my
head down, i suddenly lost consciousness, and fell over on my left
side. stacey said that as i fell my hands were clenched into fists and
my tongue was pressed against the roof of my mouth (that's what
made this a seizure)

i remember faintly being in a completely different world when
i was unconscious. there were other people there, i was interacting
with them. when i heard stacey's voice, very far away seeming, saying, "are you ok? are you ok?" i felt i had to wrench myself up out of
that world i was in. it was incredibly difficult to come back and i
burst out crying, finding myself totally weak on the stone floor in a
puddle of my own pee.

after several hours during which i rested, a country doctor came
to give me a shot of anticonvulsant valium, and then just a little
while after they loaded me into an ambulance and took me to the
emergency room in grenoble, where i had every possible test, including an electroencephelogram, which was normal, i'm not epileptic.
some of the tests were a little fun and involved being stroked on the
legs by handsome french doctors—to test my reflexes, i guess?

my french is pretty pathetic but it was interesting to see how much of it came back to me from my college days on that day in the hospital

at any rate they dismissed me early that evening, and finally i was able to take a bath and wash the salt off my scalp (they'd applied salt with the electrodes, i don't know why). it was certainly one of the scariest days in my life thus far, as if i'd had a toe in the waters of mortality.

it didn't end there, though. the aftermath was panic attacks. i was seized with the fear that it would happen again, and this time among strangers. i didn't deal with these panic attacks until a few weeks later, when i returned to san francisco and worked with a lovely hypnotherapist friend of my mom's. i who hate to be dependent had to have stacey around me all the time, and thankfully she is the strongest and most loyal of friends.

i still managed to enjoy being in the south of france (my first time there, but at least my fourth trip to france), the lavender fields, oh the lavender fields!

* * *

gary, i wrote everything above last night, and now i've just opened my morning mail to find more more more stories from you, and i'm getting this feeling there's a whole backlog of questions i gotta answer (do know i am responding to everything you say in my head, i just don't have the writing time), but now it's 6:30 a.m. before work and i have to finish at least the story of falling over

so after i fell, after a month in england & france, i returned to japan for a week, the first week of august, to connect with m—, hang out with him on his birthday, de-stress from travel (i thought), and just be in my own space. as much as i travel, i don't really like it as much as being in My Room (which is a whole nother topic that requires reams of description. i realize i hardly ever write about japan to you, about the the things i do and see and eat here, and they really are so extraordinary, like even the things i did last weekend, during which i hung out exclusively with japanese people and spoke english really only to you and m— and my mom on the phone, but again, this is another letter)

but de-stress i didn't. the panic attacks kept coming, the racing heart, the suddenly swaying lack of balance. m— didn't understand at all. and it turns out he was terribly hurt that i hadn't called him during the two weeks i was in england, but you know what, it would have been a hassle what with time zones and phone cards (although my therapist rightly said that's not why i didn't call) and you know what else, sometimes talking to him on the phone feels so stilted, or like i am trying to pull affection from him with forceps. by sometimes i guess i should say, in recent months. had felt. so i didn't call, figuring he didn't really care anyway and there wouldn't be anything to say. but meanwhile he was furiously sending e-mails to this girl and that girl, and it was right around the time of his birthday that he first received an e-mail from k—

i was completely vertiginous that whole week. it was hot and humid beyond belief, and when i went out in public, which i kept bravely doing, i often had to find places to sit or even lie down with my feet up. on m—'s birthday we went to ginza to have a meal, and i had to lie down on the floor of the restaurant with my feet on a chair. m— seemed terribly annoyed, i said, look i've had a trauma, i've been very sick, and he responded by saying, "you're always sick," which is really a bit of an overstatement and hardly beaming compassion

but at the same time i know he was starting this correspondence with the lovely young pianist, and he just couldn't wait, i think, for me to leave for the states at the end of that week, so he could carry on his affair

which, you know, now, i'm totally glad he did, because it took a hammer to that veneer of frustration and anger that was covering our lives, and now all kinds of things are being released, i think you know what i mean, like even what i'm saying to you right now is part of that release, and there's bliss in that

in the usa i was still feeling the panic attacks, which i suspect now were more and more about what was happening in my relationship with m—, "ok nada, now look at the truth, face it no matter how dizzy it makes you," but luckily my mom's a healer and she knows all the best healers in the bay area, so i was chiropracted, hypnotized, vitaminized, and even given a remarkable reading of my irises and my blood cells by a guy who looked into my eyes and told me my personality in an instant, let me see if i can pull out what he said, yes, it's right in this file among other things, he said i have a "flower/gem" personality (sounds cool, huh), which means i'm Revolutionary, a Dynamic Creator and Logical (you can guess i liked that). he said also that my iris shows a very sensitive nervous system and pancreas, that the sensitivity of my nervous system affects the vaso-vagal nerve going to my brain, the very nerve that had shut off when i fell over, and that i was going to have to watch my balance

and, have you ever seen your blood cells through a microscope? wow. mine were all clumped together, in fear i think. he said, this practitioner, "you take on the energy of whoever is around you. you have to be very careful about being around negative people (but guess what i was living with, i mean am, but things are different now; and this refers to my job too, where negativity spurts out all over the place but i'm supposed to be cheery and idealistic and ener- getic all the time, and believe me i try, but it's hard when ... oh, this term has been hard). he also saw some other interesting things in my blood, fragments of parasites (too much sashimi) and heavy met- als. he said something incredible, that very often the metal deposits take on the SHAPES of organs in the body that are troubled, and that he didn't tell most people that because it sounds so strange, but he asked me, do you have trouble with your vertebrae (and i do, totally chronic despite the best chiropractors, i just sat up and cracked now, in my non-ergonomic chair) and what about your uterus? well i didn't know it then, but it turns out i have a tumor on my uterus, a benign one (they're very common) which somehow seems Very Symbolic.

oh drat, it's seven o'clock now and i have to do all those morn- ing necessary things. why can't i just stay home and say everything i have to say?

i'll just finish to say that i came back from san francisco feeling renewed, like my life had started afresh, and i felt calmer and wiser than ever before, and then ... whoosh ... the k— affair

gary, did i tell you about the day of my discovery, that typhoon night and what went down? i don't think i did, please tell me and i will write in the next installment. but now i really really gotta go

love, and so much wanting time,
nada

∞

From: nada
Date: November 18
Subject: the castle

tatami is a woven straw mat, about 3 feet x 6 feet, and is the traditional flooring in a japanese room. each mat is bordered by fabric;
the fabric border of the tatami in my house is emerald green with
gold threads. i can't imagine that you haven't seen tatami before, in
pictures anyway. oh, and yes! I just remembered, one of the photos
I sent you is of me sitting on tatami, though not in my house, that
was in an inn south of tokyo. because tatami is made of straw, it gives
off a beautiful smell of nature, especially in the humid summer.
often when i come back from my long august vacations (sometimes
5 or 6 weeks) i feel almost drugged by the smell (didn't i say something about a—'s body smelling like dry grass in summer? think so,
there's a theme here)

   shoji is a kind of sliding paper screen, with a wooden frame,
divided into squares. *shoji* are often in front of windows, instead of
curtains, and let through the most tempting silhouettes. they also
make a very nice *fssst* sound when they are opened or closed. some
of the *shoji* in my house is special. one small window is a woodcarving of a tortoise and a crane, longevity symbols

   this house is very big and traditional by Tokyo rental standards.
upstairs there āre two tatami rooms, one eight mats, one six mats.
the six mat room is mine, but the sliding paper doors (*fusuma*) open
onto the eight mat room, so i am able to feel a sweep of personal
space in this most crowded of cities. especially in this season, when
the afternoon sun comes through, the room feels completely golden
and serene and when i light temple incense, which is musky, not too
heavy or sweet, and put on bach's unaccompanied cello suites or
something, life is almost perfect, except for the obvious ...

   this house was custom-built by the owners for them to live in,
so there is nothing cookie-cutter about it, not the living room: the
tokonoma (alcove space, usually used for hanging scrolls and austere
flower arrangements but now filled with my books), not the asym-
metrical shelves on which now sit various j-nese dolls, a fan, an old
buddhist altar i picked up at a temple garbage spot, and a menorah.
even the wood grain pattern on the ceiling (of my room) is beautiful,

although i recently figured out that it's a printed pattern—i thought it looked too perfect to be real

and as i said the rooms are separated by paper doors, but that doesn't begin to evoke what i mean by "paper." in my room the pattern, which is only just sprinkled at the bottom of the doors is of slightly shining, fibrous chrysanthemums, in very subtle pastel colors, a soft gray-green and pale rose; in the living room the doors are decorated instead with three stripes of different greens, one ochrous, one green tea-colored, and because i'm typing this at work right now i can't remember the third color, i think a greenish brown. even the door handles (not the right word, they're really indentations), are beautiful, with a tiny bamboo stalk painted in the middle.

but the clincher of beauty in this house is between the two rooms, just above the paper doors. the gap up to the ceiling is filled by a stenciled woodcarving that shows a traditional landscape, hills and pines and temples and pagodas and the sea in the distance. if the light is off in one room and on in the other, the landscape becomes luminous, and it is really easy to imagine walking over the little curved bridge at sunset.

the downstairs is not so nice, although by tokyo standards, again, it's pretty spacious. m—'s room is just below mine, six mats, and usually in a state of indescribable disarray, full of books and piles of clothes, papers. he used to complain that i never went to his apartment, but that was because it was so miserably chaotic and moldy i couldn't bear to. (even now he keeps the moldiest of items in his closet—next to his clothes!—a once-blackleather bag now green with the stuff. the bag used to belong to his ex-girlfriend, a woman from kansas who left him one night because he wouldn't marry her. she had been expelled from her hometown, and her two sons, because she had had an affair with a teenage exchange student. and do you know what m— keeps in the bag? american pornography) although i have to say the first time i saw his apartment i thought it looked very *bungaku-teki* (literary). his room is a little better these days, and he respectfully keeps the chaos in there, but it has always been almost impossible to get him to assist me with the upkeep of the rest of the place. now he's being a little more cooperative, and one can guess why. he was especially helpful last night, with dishes (i cooked—out of guilt?—usually we don't have meals together. it's just too uneven as he can't cook and seems to prefer convenience store meals anyway), scrubbing and filling our cubic steel bathtub, folding towels with a kind of bent quietness

because, you know, gary, he gets the mail, and puts it on the kitchen table, and he knows very well that something cataclysmic (is it?) is happening. now if it had been me and a letter had arrived for him from some girl, well, naturally, you know what i would have done—opened it. but i think his reaction is very telling as to how he feels about me, that is, he simply said, "tell me if you sleep with him." no rage, no pouting, not that he has the right to either, as he well knows. but what bugs me is, NO CURIOSITY! how can he not be burning with the desire to know?

i don't think his emotions are very accessible to him, except maybe the ones he uses for his haiku. anyway not at all like my (or, your) intricately articulated emotionality. and this is not because of language barriers. you know, i read the stuff he was writing to k—, albeit without complete understanding, but it didn't go much beyond, "you are the perfect woman for me" and "you seemed disturbed at the hotel. don't worry, i won't live with her forever." and he has the english to say just about whatever he wants to say. there was a time that he wrote me letters, at the start. he did say things like, "it was the highest kind of pleasure to touch you," but more often it was wistful landscape descriptions, nice, but ... i'm afraid it just boils down to culture, doesn't it, to the say it say it just say it vs. the deliberately unsaid for the sake of austerity. for a japanese man, he is an example of rare expressiveness, i know that, but only within his cultural and gender category.

(p.s. did you know that before k—, he had never had a japanese girlfriend? he had slept with a couple of j-nese women, but only one-nighters. he says his primary attraction to her was a kind of kindred cultural "darkness.")

you know, he complains that we don't talk about poetry, but the fact is that our whole approaches to the art of it, our experiences of it, are so completely different. i mean, what can i say, he likes robert bly. it's true that we occasionally talk about interesting things, but mostly the interesting things we talk about have to do with japan. perhaps what i have loved most about him is the greater access he has given me to this culture, and i am a japanophile, in some ways almost japanese at this point, and that seems to be what he likes about me, that i can sing *enka* (plaintive ballads) and chatter away, although not fault-free, in his language, not to mention the fact that I do, i do appreciate wistful ephemera and seasonal phenomena. At the height of our post-k— conflict, he kept saying, "is this all we have to talk about? can't we talk about the insects singing outside?" and it's true, most of what he wrote her in the e-mails was about insects singing outside, the end of summer, and so on. not like ... us (oh, shyness!)

and it's also true that, when i caved in to the need to be desired and slept with him again, this even after banishing him to the desert (to which he did not go), i kept begging him, "write to me! write to me!" (does that sound vaguely familiar?) and he said, "i can't." i said, "why not, you were writing to her" and he said, "but that was in japanese," and i said (i'm laughing now), "but i can read japanese, as you've noticed!"

and guess what, it's not gonna happen, he's never gonna do it

and that's perfectly ok with me

* * *

now I'm back home again, hating how miscrosoft word capitalizes "I"s like it thinks it has the right to

FUCK capitalism

but actually I do want to say something about capitalism, eventually, about capitalism and me

but mostly I want to talk about me, because what I realized today (this was one of your questions) was that narcissism is a survival tactic, oh and I just now realized something else, it's also a reality-checking

what I mean by survival tactic is this: narcissism arises from a perception of a deficit of love from outside, and because human beings need love more than anything, they will love themselves if they perceive that deficit

in that way I think human beings are so wonderful, and I am wonderful, like you said

did robinson crusoe love himself? did he look into the ocean on still days to check that he really existed? that's what I mean by a reality check (not the vernacular version of the term, more LACANIAN) but I feel I've gone off topic here, that I wasn't finished saying what I meant to say about this house and why I live in it with m—. as you know, we've been together seven and a half years, but only here for two and a half

he used to come over to my apartment, which was on the same train line as his, about ten minutes away, every weekend. it was very convenient for him, I think, what is it, why buy the cow if you can get free milk?

it wasn't like we looked at each other and said, "oh my darling, I'm so in love with you, let's shack up." oh, no. but as I said he was annoyed that I never went to visit his horrible cockroach-infested den (do you know that the first time I stayed there he took a shower by climbing into his kitchen sink! because he had no shower!), and he took it into his head to move closer down the train line to me. he found what he thought was a kind of a nice apartment, and he asked me to come along and give my impressions of it.

we went and had a look at it, it was tiny but quiet, looked like a place where one might be able to write something, and he liked it. well, we went back to the real estate agency, and we were chatting with the agents, telling them that we really liked japanese-style rooms (lots of the places in tokyo are modern and western and awful) and they said, oh, have we got a place to show you, and we said, sure, what the hell, we'll look at it (giving each other sidelong glances)

and oh, gary, when I walked in I just ... it was like suddenly I had a womb, well, I told m— for three solid months, during which the house remained blessedly vacant, that if we didn't live there then finally, yeah, I was going to have to say SAYONARA. And that, no, I didn't want to live there with one of my friends. I remember the freezing February day we signed the rental contract. He looked like he was signing the warrant for his own execution (that's a cliché, I know, but it works here), really pale and puffy and unshaven and, ugh. And not just that, I paid the entire deposit—three months' rent—to move in here.

and then only to find that once in the house, it became a kind of hell-house sometimes. he was so afraid that the disturbance in his living situation would ruin his inspiration (it didn't, but he made a big show of things for a while). he became a kind of rebel tyrant and

I a nag. the hours we keep are completely different (that is to say, I have a job), and because he stays up so late, he wants to sleep in, so that I am forbidden to flush the toilet, which is near his room, in the morning, and if I do so by mistake or habit (or malice), he yells out, NADA, PLEASE. so that at one point, when I did so after the k— affair and he started to shout, I marched into his room and said, "look, I don't know about your girlfriend, but I assume she is a human being and therefore shits, too, so I really think you should be a little more considerate when you talk to me." to his credit, he apologized. stacey's first comment when she heard about his affair (she had been to visit here, last spring, and she knew about this restriction) was, "nada, you flush the toilet as much as you want,"

and believe me, I have plenty of other beastly m— stories, which is not to say that he is always beastly. he has the capability to be incredibly tender, but that brings us up to the point where we are today, and possibly his main motivation for having the affair. except that I haven't told you about the typhoon because I can't possibly type any more tonight and besides, you've set all those blasted questions resonating in my brain.

i didn't see the meteor shower last night, did you, did you go up on the roof? did you feel all sort of mortal and tiny and in awe and think about the nature of light from the heavens and how it reaches us, what a miracle that is? and did you think about the theories of how the universe came into being? and which one did you choose? or what did you think about? my students were all talking about shooting stars today, which got me singing disney songs.

god, I feel like kerouac or something. will you let me rest, please? and what did you think of this story?
nada

∞

From: Gary
Date: November 18
Subject: Re: the castle

Writing, on some level, is that situation, exactly, banishing ourselves to an island. Crusoe is a metaphor I think for the writer, having

washed up, here, into this particular present, having to discover (&
things get fleshed out as we write, just as the geography or topogra-
phy becomes "made real" by our beginning to traverse it), but yes,
Crusoe loved himself, or maybe that wasn't the question, then, it
being "for granted," a given. You would not care to survive (as you
say, above) if you did not love yourself, so it's a given Crusoe loved
himself. To be a seafarer or whatever, an adventurer of any kind, you
either have a deathwish, or you're completely or very very self-
reliant, or self-confident. And what gives you confidence, but love? I
mean, reciprocated love.

> but I feel I've gone off topic here,

Topic?!

> did you feel all sort of mortal and tiny and in awe
> and think about the nature of light from the heavens
> and how it reaches us, what a miracle that is?

Well, I think about this a lot, actually, the moon does it for me, since
the stars are rarely visible in NYC. You have to understand, my apartment windows are just, well, what a view! Four windows, one facing
south, one southwest, two west. So, I see south Brooklyn to the
Verazanno Narrows Bridge, some of Newark, off in the distance, the
Statue of Liberty, the BQE (Brooklyn-Queens Expressway), and
much of lower & some of mid-Manhattan. When the moon slides
into my window I'm usually sitting there writing, and it passes
down, toward the horizon, usually hovering a couple hours over the
Statue ...

∞

[*Typed letter from Gary to Nada dated November 18*]

Dear Nada,

These letters (what I'm able to write tonight, Thursday & Friday)
I'm hoping will arrive while I'm in Florida, which will be from

Saturday the 21st until Monday the 30th, I'm freaked out by this,
I'm being obsessive, I'm sorry, and I can't believe this, I sat around
after work again tonight (2 nights in a row) reading everything
we've written, there's a lot you know, though what I have isn't
even all of it, I have from October 20th on, beginning with an
e-mail from you, "Yo, Gary,"

and the stack of paper is already 2-1/2
inches thick, this isn't even a month's worth quite, & still I want
more, crave your descriptions, anecdotes, memories, current emotional checks, well, everything, and reading, reading, reading, I
can't come up with the answer, it isn't obvious, as I thought it
would be, what can I do to not cause you stress, I mean a million
things come to mind, but which is it, if any I can imagine.

Oh, I
wanted to tell you about this: on the train home tonight, I open
Laura Riding's poems to:

WHEN LOVE BECOMES WORDS

... And then to words again
After—was it—a kiss or exclamation
Between face and face too sudden to record.
Our love being now a span of mind
Whose bridge not the droll body is
Striding the waters of disunion
With sulky grin and groaning valour,
We can make love miraculous
As joining thought with thought and a next,
Which is done not by crossing over
But by knowing the words for what we mean.
We forbear to move, it seeming to us now
More like ourselves to keep the written watch
And let the reach of love surround us
With the warm accusation of being poets.

∞

From: Gary
Date: November 20
Subject: about last night

My heart is torn in two, Nada, and it's awful, and this is the story of What Happened After I Left Work Yesterday.

Well, as always, I'd printed out the day's exchange, and had it in my bag, and I was going to read it, but it was such a totally emotional day for me I didn't read it (not right then), I was sitting on the train and just started crying, can you imagine? I've never seen a man crying on the train, never, I've seen maybe one or two women, one in the midst of an obvious break up, anyway, people were sort of staring at me and then looking away in obvious embarrassment, and I just, I pulled myself together, and just sort of stared vacantly "off."

So, an hour later, I'm home, read the day's material, see what a total spaz I've been (thank you for that word, Nada; you know I never ever used it before), feel rotten, then the phone rings, it's C—. She wants to talk, but I'm in the middle of our letters, and so I say, "Can I call you back in about an hour?" And, hang up. And, then, realize I'm so out of my fucking mind I don't know what to do, I have to talk to somebody about this and I just caved, I caved, I called up Ange & Steve, and I said, "You guys have got to help me, take me out, get me drunk, I'll tell you everything, but you have to promise me NOT TO SAY ANYTHING and GIVE ME GENUINE (i.e., no pussyfooting, no p.c. morality crap) ADVICE, and they, being an ancient married couple (they're younger than I am, but they've been married for like 12 years), said "Let's go!" (I remember the draw of single people: you get to live vicariously through everything they do, plus, if things are not going so well for the single person, you can feel content cuz "Baby, we have each other!")

So, I put the now three-inch stack of paper in my book bag, and went over to their house, and we walked up to 5th avenue together to a place called Carrie Nation, a gay bar, one of very few in our neighborhood, and I ordered whisky and beer, and do you know what the bartender said to me? She looks at me and blurts out: "JOHN DENVER! You're alive!"

and I just ripped the glasses off my face, and said, GOD I hate that! and she said, "But John Denver was my first crush! He was dreamy!"

Which made me feel absolutely NO BETTER, not even a teeny tiny iota, I have GOT to get new glasses.

Anyway, So we get a table, the place is great, very very dark, lots of men, a few women couples but mostly men, some tiny lights here & there as decoration, a candle on our table, I feel like we're in San Francisco, and we start talking.

And I tell them what's been going on, and I pull out the exchange, and plop it on the table, and it makes this sound: *FOOMP.* and Ange, I swear to you, Ange BLUSHES and just starts laughing and says "OH MY GOD, GARY, ARE YOU SERIOUS?!?" and I'm just sooooooooo embarrassed I can't stand it, I put the exchange back in my bookbag and now Ange & Steve are giving each other "married couple" glances, oh it's so hard to be on the receiving end of those (after having so long been on the "giving" end), but they listen intently while I tell them everything, or not everything, but a synopsis. They ask me: "Well, how do you feel, how do you feel?"

And I tell them, "okay, look, I never meant for this to happen." And they roll their eyes, and I tell them, "No, no no. I really liked this woman's work, she's a wonderful poet, and I asked her for her work, and she wouldn't send it & I asked her several times and finally, she just disappeared. But, she reappeared a couple months later, and mentioned she'd been on a trip, wasn't feeling so great, and was having problems with her boyfriend, and I don't know, I don't know, I just started asking her about this, and we talked, and the talking & revealing intensified, and at some point we started flirting, and NOW look at it!!! I'm totally in love with this woman, and I don't know if she's in love with me or needs someone to talk to or what the deal is but I'm pretty sure it's mutual."

"Well, yeah," Ange says, "but what about C—?"

"I don't know, I don't know, I tried to talk to her tonight, but I couldn't, I can't even imagine kissing her now, it's awful."

So Ange says, very reasonably, "Well, you should just go down there. First, if you don't, Nada isn't going to respect you. She'll back off. It'll weird her out. If some guy said he'd do anything for me, I'd freak. It's too much." Steve: "No, you shouldn't go. I wouldn't go." Ange: "No, you should. Because you should see also what happens when you're down there. HAS it changed everything? Gary, this woman lives in Japan, for crying out loud! You're going to throw this other relationship away for that? Can you really imagine yourself in Japan?" Steve: "I could. I mean, I'd go."

Me: "No. I mean, I can imagine going there, but not living there. But, I dunno, I dunno, maybe she'll move back here, I'm not sure how much she likes it there, I mean she does, but maybe she'll wanna come back."

Steve & Ange: (roll their eyes.)

Ange: Well, you clearly have to figure out what's more important. And I understand, you know, how can you maintain a relationship with anyone if you're not there on a day-to-day basis? I can see why you're frustrated by this thing with C—. But do you honestly think falling in love with someone thousands of miles FARTHER away is any solution?

Gary: Well, is love willed? Can it be willed? Did I will this, or do I have a choice?

Ange: OH, Gary, I have this book, you'll have to pick it up on your way home, *Eros*, by Anne Carson, do you know it?

Gary: No.

Ange: It's about love, and writing ... it connects the two up—anyway, here's what you do. Go. See what happens. That will tell you a lot.

Gary: What do you think I have to do to convince her to be with me?!?

Ange: Well, I think it's obvious. Keep doing what you're doing. You guys are totally there. I wouldn't worry about that.

Gary: But I love her!

Ange & Steve: (it's a race to the obvious) But—but—you—you've—haven't—never—ever—even—met—met—her—her!!!

Gary: God, I don't know. And I don't wanna fuck this up, I don't, this person is great.

Ange: If she's that great she'll also understand.

Gary: But this isn't, I mean, you have to admit, am I morally bankrupt?

Ange: NO. But, I don't know. I don't know what Nada's going to do.

Steve: I wouldn't go.

Ange: Well, what do you FEEL.

Gary: Here's the deal. With C— I feel a real emotional connection and the strongest physical connection I've ever had. With Nada,

I feel even MORE emotionally connected, and intellectually connected, too, I mean, completely okay, look. I feel spiritually connected.

> Ange: Can't you have both?
> Steve: Go for the brains.
> Ange: Yeah, intellectual connection is, well, it lasts for one thing.
> Steve: Yeah.
> Gary: I know. I mean, yeah, I know. She's coming here, by the way.
> Ange: C—?
> Gary: Nada. I don't know when. I'm gonna try & convince her to come on New Year's.
> Steve: Well, good luck.
> Gary: Thanks.

Okay, Nada, I'm bored with this. It covers basically everything we talked about, anyway. Was it fun to read?

> Love,
> Gary

∞

From: Nada
Date: November 21
Subject: Re: about last night

i can see your struggle, and that made me struggle too

you asked why i said love is a dog that you send into space. laika, as it says in the notes, was the dog on sputnik. do you know what they did to her? they sent her out into space. in a little capsule. how do you think she felt up there? motion sickness/stars up close? did she howl, and how! and then they abandoned her, and let her die up there

do you realize you sent me NINE e-mails today? am i going to have to go a whole week knowing you're off in tropical sexlandia, and worse than that, without your e-mails? and my thinking, hell, he's gonna get greencarded, and there goes that possibility

i'm sorry if i'm making you feel conflicted about anything right now

you should obviously lead your real life
instead of this one in the ether with a pale mercurial poetess
or maybe you should lead both
OK, here's some homework
    i want you to give me eight utterly convincing reasons why i
should go to new york this winter. eight, no more no less. and nothing circumlocutory

∞

From: Gary
Date: November 20
Subject: Eight is enough

    1. If this is your Grand Passion, you'll know
    2. In either case we'll have uninterrupted time together

    3. ——————————————————-
    4. ——————————————————-
    5. ——————————————————-

    6. ——————————————————-
    7. ——————————————————-
    8. ——————————————————-

∞

From: nada
Date: November 20
Subject: Re: Eight is enough

    oh, this is lame, this is like a haiku m— told me about yesterday
    it's called "hibernation"
    and all it is is a black circle on a page
    that's what i get for being demanding

∞

From: Gary
Date: November 20
Subject: PLEASE RESPOND TO THIS NOW ... PLEASE?

1. Uninterrupted time together, we can talk however long we can stand it

2. You can see, meet, hang out with NYC poets you've wanted to meet & hang out with

3. Your anxiety (if you still have it) about physical presences will be clarified

4. You can look me in the eyes when asking me anything, anything, and i will look you in the eyes when answering

5. I'm going crazy without you

6. I need you

7. I want you

8. I'm not going to argue with six unbroken lines, are you? (Please don't tell me this is lame. I believe this.)

Love,
Gary

∞

From: nada
Date: November 20
Subject: Re: PLEASE RESPOND TO THIS NOW ... PLEASE?

ok, yeah, i'm there, but completely, like i keep saying, terrified. you knew i'd come anyway. didn't you?

meanwhile, you should go to florida, and i mean that with all my heart. and i think you should tell c— what's going on

in the principle of complete openness.

i just hope that, in the potential pain of that, for her, your mutual passion doesn't multiply even more to the point that you forget who i am.

and i'll deal just fine. i guess

and it will be good for me to have a break

i printed out everything

it's so incredible, what we have produced, like a child ⌉
so don't go crazy, go to the beach ⌋

love,
nada

∞

[*Typed letter from Gary to Nada dated November 28, 1998*]

Nada Gordon
address 2-B looked up "later"
Tokyo 155
JAPAN

Dear Nada,
the poems are all love poems because they're
meant as address, the loved one (listener, reader) absent at the
time of inscription, & so motivated, taken into hand, by desire.
Nothing is written without self-consciousness. Nothing. Ever. Even
if only for the self, a "later" self. I would like everyone I love to be
happy, & to know why. That this is an impossibility is what gives
rise to sorrow. Or, more honestly, to desire.
Is love binary? & if
so, why does triangulated desire so intrigue? Do we lack appreciation for simple things, is there some mania for the "complex," is the
speed of binary love unequal to that of our thoughts (& therefore
emotions)?
Or, is it that desire requires lack, that what is had is no
longer desired? That seems the simplest or most obvious explanation. But there is much it does not account for. For instance "having" a letter, something, some tangible item, with words (gestures
toward speech), & the knowledge of the care one has taken, writing. Is this letter boring or pretentious because too self-conscious?
Florida is soul-killing. Visually—palm trees, water & water-
ways everywhere, deep blue sky, the ocean, pale green & blue,
Greco-Roman knock-off sculptures everywhere, lots of art-deco
architecture, wild parrots, squirrels, & jellyfish remains on the

beach tanned & burned human bodies, neon burning all night &
colored lights in everyone's front yard. But nothing of what you
might call culture or community.

I've thought about the conse-
quences of having been there, of having so thoroughly there, given
myself to her, to whatever you can call it, desire, passion, love, lust.
I don't know, & felt like I was going crazy, a totally divided self,
because I wasn't all there, my mind & emotions were here, writing
to you, reading you. One night I just excused myself, went into the
bathroom & sat there, crying, not completely mind you, but crying
somewhat, trying to "maintain," and oh Nada, this horrific feeling
came over me, that when I came back to work, there'd be no mail
from you, or there'd be one "Fuck You," or there'd be a series of
increasingly sad or pissed off or desperate letters, but the most
depressing thought was None. Nothing. Nada.

So, yeah, I was think-
ing about nada and Nada and nada Nada. There are moments when
I'm angry with you, angry with myself, for this, like, Why torture
ourselves? So, big deal, we write to each other, and even flirt a little, and some level of intimacy is established or created or some
space for it makes itself present, or however you want to describe
it. Except, then, we become hooked on it, have to write (you think
I had, have a choice?), some need, to be present, at least in this
way, is created, & I missed you so fucking bad I can't tell you. I
was very literally in a state of despair the whole time I was down
there, am in the same state now. When I talked to Laurie after
coming back she said, "You don't sound as excited as I thought you
would." I didn't tell her why, and I don't know, probably she
knows, or would know, if she thought about it.

I really missed you.
The kids outside on the street are tearing up shit, it's awful, why
won't they shut up? I'm depersonalizing them. It's because I experience them as utter irritation. I'm sure if I knew them I'd love
them, & their noise would be music, anyway, the sounds of people
I knew & loved taking pleasure in exerting energy. You know how
much I appreciate energy.

Anyway. I will ask you this on e-mail,
but How Are You? God, I worry about you, you know, I want you

to be physically comfortable, to know what you're doing with your life, to be happy when you can't be totally fulfilled, but ideally fulfilled, which is not to say content, but that your life, your mind, is full, & with some very deep sense of your own, oh this is gonna sound trite (like the rest of this letter hasn't?), humanness, & what that means, or if not "means," at least what it IS.

I love, Nada, more than anything, how human writing to you makes me. Am I deluding myself?

Oh, my love, I'm utterly afraid you won't be there, and no one I can ask or might ask could tell me, but you, so please please tell me, why? Why do I care?

∞

From: nada
Date: November 30
Subject: so ... ?

i've written you a whole avalanche of e-mails
ranging in tone from hysterical to profound to affectionate

but i'm not going to send them
until i hear from you
and you tell me how you're feeling now.

nada

∞

From: Gary
Date: November 30
Subject: quick reply much more to follow

I missed & still miss you very much. I wrote you several times, discarded everything everything everything as "too much" though I have a few things, unfinished letters to you, at home. Maybe I'll send you a patchwork quilt of those. Okay, I will. One's a drunken, weepy admission of love, another a sort of detailed pseudo-philosophical "consideration" of love, after reading Anne Carson's *Eros* and Alan Davies' *Name*, loaned to me by Mitch Highfill, and, oh, other stuff, too. I have so much to tell you about. I'm going (as always) to write in the little available nooks & crannies the day affords & may (as occasionally happens) stay after & write something long & more sustained.

I miss you very very bad.
More soon,
Gary

∞

From: nada
Date: November 30
Subject: Re: quick reply much more to follow

YOU DISCARDED EVERYTHING???
i thought that was against the rules ...
"too much"???
didn't we already cross that boundary?
oh come on
you've got to be more forthcoming
or i won't send you these six long e-mails
do you want them all at once?
or shall i not send the crazy ones?
and you know what
we are going to have to change media one of these days
actually vibrate some vocal chords
don't you think
gary! don't do this again to me! at least while we're engaged like this! it was awful! awful. i felt like i'd had an organ removed.

so welcome back

nada

∞

From: Gary
Date: November 30
Subject: Bleary philosophy

Nada, Nada, Nada,

I've been reading Anne Carson's *Eros the Bittersweet*, am not too far into it (took a break to read parts of *Name* and all of *How I Became Hettie Jones*), and i've been struggling with this whole idea of lack creating desire struggling with it because I don't like it it seems too simple and it's not what I want ultimately, "lack" or to be driven by that ...

I have this sense or notion or silly naive belief that desire is or can be maintained while "having" the thing or person or situation or "fact of it" whatever "it" may be or maybe desire is just the wrong word nada maybe we have to be less postmodern about it (isn't desire a postmodern cliché thing to write about) and come up with either another word and or approach to this thing or this situation which I would call love and others may call friendship or communion or I don't know ...

And the only way I can describe it is or no it's not the only way but the way I've sort of found to describe it (am I boring you? Is this self-indulgent?) is present and liquid & I think already I've said as much but okay that's why being gone for a week, more than a week, while involved like this, while present like this, was like coitus interuptus or whatever like being yanked out of mamma's arms like having the warm water in the shower suddenly turn ice cold (which it does in my shower every every every blessed time) and I could go on but will spare you the heap-of-metaphors ...

So okay Nada this is really what I was thinking what I've been thinking for the last ten days or so & that's
is it possible is engagement possible
to maintain over a long period of time, the course of two lives
& I don't mean friendship
I mean a relationship a romantic relationship
and how is it done how can it be done is it reasonable to expect
will there always be moments of disconnectedness
will sex or other intimate engagement always result if only on occasion in one or the other distracting themselves from the situation

how you described it, almost like floating out of your body
& watching yourself, your selves

∞

From: nada
Date: November 30
Subject: 1) realizings

hey

i don't know what you're up to now, what kind of scenes or delights
or sadness or violence or bliss you might be experiencing
    although naturally i have some curiosity
    and i wonder if your trip will change the tenor of things
between us
    it would be a lie to say i don't have any anxiety about that
    but i'm trying to hang on to my intuitive wisdom
    and the stubborn belief that everything will be all right in the end
    as i said before
    but it seems everyone in this drama is a little stressed out right
now, at least on this side of the world, and i'll get to that story when
i get to point 3 in my list below:
    three things i realized recently (not strictly today):
    1) if i were a man i'd have to adjust my testicles all the time
    2) you've been more demonstrative in these e-mails than i have, as
a rule—i've held back some—wondering how much traditional gender
role concepts have to do with that, or how much is my natural reserve
    3) people are dominoes
    what i mean by that is this:
    i hadn't told m— before about the volume of our correspon-
dence, nor that i've decided to come to see you in late december, but
i felt i had to, that it was unfair to my somehow still limping-along
relationship with him not to
    so i did
    and of course his kneejerk response was, well then we are just
friends and i can do whatever i like, right. i kept silent on that. i didn't
want to even touch that one, because, how do i feel about that? i

guess not at all clear. but still, as he left to go to his tutoring job he kissed me, not passionately, but ... (this is japanese-english) heartfully, with a wistful, "i can still kiss you, right?"

and then! he did something even more kneejerk and called k—, with whom he spent the afternoon getting terribly drunk, so drunk that, when i asked him today if they had had sex, he said "a little" "what do you mean, a little?" "i was sooo drunk" he said. i think he got home at about 4 or 5 this morning. he didn't actually spend the night with her, but missed the last train and had to stay at a hotel along the way home. when i went down to to say hi to him, i asked where he had been, what had happened, how he was feeling, and he said

he didn't think k— was the kind of person he could stay with for a long time, that she "had some kind of mental sickness" and required a lot of "pampering" (and i thought yeah! she's 23! and neurotic!), and that he always knew where he was with me. and i said, what do you mean, you feel a sense of familiarity, or ...? and he said, "no, you express yourself so clearly."

which i thought was funny, and i said, yes, so much so that i can make a man half a world away fall in love with me over the clarity of my expression ... i never thought articulateness would have such a profound real-life payoff, or would matter so much, or that the athena in me would prove to be such a charm point

but at some point during my conversation with him he pulled me into his futon and asked me to disrobe, and i said, feeling a moment of desire and sympathy, "i think we should have sex"—colored by the knowledge that since you're off triangulating, i'd better do the same to keep my strength up

and he really did seem so unhappy, whispering in my ear, "*suki da yo, suki da yo,* nada" which literally translated means "i like you" or "i'm into you" but is what japanese men generally say instead of "i love you," which sounds stilted in their language. and then afterwards he was just saying he wants to go somewhere healthy for a week alone to get his health and stability back

it's really touching to see him actually showing his attachment to me, even if in predictable ways. the sex itself was ... normal ... still with that post-mortem, distanced feeling, for me, although his desperation was interesting, and made me feel powerful

but you know, my mind is so much with you
i am never sure in which of these maxims i believe:
"sex is just sex" or
"sex is never just sex"
which do you believe in?

* * *

what i mean by dominoes is this:
we human beings, we just fall all over each other in our pain,
either to hurt each other or in need for each other
first m— fell on k— because he felt i had fallen on him
but i fell on him because a— had fallen on me, and m— fell on
me because s— and e— had fallen on him
or like your wife fell on you because so many had fallen on her
before, and you fell on d—, who had been fallen on by her husband,
then your wife fell, and probably d—'s husband too, and then you fell
on c—, and then by weird computer magic, you and i fell on each
other, then falling back on c— and m— in turn, so that m— fell back
on k—, and who knows what the next domino effect will be
i know it's logically wrong of me to keep the "hurting" and
"needing" functions clumped together, i should think this through a
little better as a metaphor, but i know, gary, you've never demanded
intellectual precision from me, and please don't. because that would
make me very tense
but i think there is something beautiful in this domino theory,
something that proves that law of thermodynamics (2nd?) right: For
every action there's a reaction.
which is the scientific explanation, according to my brilliant
crazy gay performance poet buddhist buddy bruce, for KARMA
and also underscores the simple fact that we are ALL extrusions
of Being and are all interconnected, not to mouth platitudes from my
marin county childhood, but it really really is true, that you throw a
pebble in a pond and the vibrations are felt at the edges of the universe, if there are any edges
and helps me deal a little bit with the irrational, no, not irrational, what am i saying, jealousy i feel for whatever you may be
doing now with c—, the encounter that has the potential, but i hope

not, to ruin our potential, i hope so, grand passion.

* * *

and now i'm going to tell you why i love you
1) your syntax, it's so ecstatic
2) your comicbook interjections (ejaculations!)
3) your questions, that open into more volleys of language
4) your flattery, to which i'm completely susceptible
5) your humor, you really entertain me, no, crack me up
6) your brilliance!!! (i realized i really needed to tell you that, that i haven't acknowledged all the evidence you've been sending along, both in these letters and your reviews and your poems and comics, even your posts on the poetics list i've been aware of for ages, the throb of them)
7) your openness & compassion
8) your commitment to a passionate life, no compromise, that repressed people like me long for, even as we furrow our brows, work so hard we fall over, and try not to let the violins move us
i told my friend ewan, he said "i'd be suspicious of that intensity, all those pages"
i said "why? half of them are mine! but it could just be a literary project."
and he said, "i think it's a human project."

* * *

one thing i think we should do, together, if after your week in the sun you still feel like hanging out with me, is to go over the pages and answer all the questions that remain unanswered
i know i neglect them in favor of the desire to say what's on my mind right now, to tell the next welling-up story
but that doesn't mean they don't interrupt my sleep: "nada, don't forget to answer gary's Q. about ... or tell him about ..."
so let's do that, OK?
love,
nada

∞

From: Gary
Date: November 30
Subject: Re: 1) realizings

> > i don't know what you're up to now, what kind
> > of scenes or delights or sadness or violence or bliss
> > you might be experiencing

This will require a separate letter all its own, I did make many notes
in my journal, about Florida, about the geography & flora mostly, the
word most coming up being "primordial," probably because of all the
palm trees and, oh, Nada, GREEN BIRDS!, though I've been told the
palm trees aren't deciduous

> > 1) if i were a man i'd have to adjust my testicles all the time

Not all the time, actually
        it depends on what you wear
        I wear boxers
        and don't often have a lot of adjustment needs
        unless I'm sitting down with legs crossed
        and go to REcross them
        in which case, sometimes, "Oh!"
        and "Oh dear!"
        certain accounting must be made, then
        I think the having to adjust them is not the worst part of having
them
        it's their vulnerability
        like if you do cross your legs and suddenly, EEP
        squish them
        it's both painful AND embarrassing (imagine!)
        but also, Nada, they're UGLY
        they have goosebumps on them 24 hours a day
        and hair
        not beautiful hair like the hair on my scalp
        or even okay-enough hair like that under my arms
        or kind of sweet hair like that on my legs & arms
        or the kind of magnificent "fun" hair aka "pubic"

but this really just disgusting
"balding man" hair, so imagine a balding man
whose head has "softened"
and now he's bald and his head is soft
oh, and the two hemispheres of his brain have completely
detached
& now float, lonely in the pool of his balding softened head

> 2) you've been more demonstrative in these e-mails than i have

I do think this has to do with the fact that I'm male, like maybe I feel
less vulnerable in a way ...
I think also, you know, you do allow me, I mean you specifically
Nada, allow me to be demonstrative, I mean, you've said it was okay,
and also there are certain protector feelings I have for you which are
in part male and in part just situational (I'd have them if i was a
woman I think & you told me everything you're going through have
gone through recently) and oh okay
I'm in love with you ...

> 3) people are dominoes

Well, okay, is this the novelist in you, looking at situations in a
specific way maybe, as "characters" engaged in "plot," though of
course yes things are causally related

> and he said, "no, you express yourself so clearly."

Duh

> which i thought was funny, and i said, yes, so much
> so that i can make a man half a world away fall in
> love with me over the clarity of my expression ...

Yes, it's true, but it's not just the clarity, Nada, it's what is so clearly
expressed, do I have to write you a poem to explain okay I will ...

> i never thought articulateness would have such a
> profound real-life payoff,

My dear it's not articulateness it's energy it's you it's the ability to be you in words how you exist in words the intensity with which you exist in words, and it's more than charming, it makes me ache

> but you know, my mind is so much with you

Tell me about it ...

   Gary

∞

From: nada
Date: November 30
Subject: 2) evidence

gary this e-mail gets a little hysterical further down
        but i think i won't edit it
        anyway brace yourself

* * *

i got from you today your completely over-the-top, loopy, lacy, langue-y love letter (from november 14), i've never received anything remotely like it. it's so ... french. it is the verbal equivalent of being backed against a wall, and does all the things it's intended to, that is, make my little heart pound, and causes various other physical effects i'm too modest to mention

        but i mean don't you think it's a little manipulative? not to deconstruct your no-doubt sincere desire for your fantasy of me, or your erotic delight at having been permitted to romp around inside my colorful, voluble, utterly female brain ... but don't you feel frightened at taking risks like that? saying such things to a person you've put together out of this story and that poem, an array of tiny photo-stickers on an envelope? i admire your romanticism, but i worry about it too. i worry about the effects it's having on me

do you know, and again i'm not guilt-tripping you, just inform-
ing you, that i weighed myself this morning and found i was only 41
kilograms (that's in the low 90s in pounds, sorry, i don't have the for-
mula handy). my skeleton is right there, i feel almost paleontologi-
cal. i haven't weighed so little since i first got here and got the a—
shock. what breasts i had have almost disappeared—my body looks
roughly 13 years old. that skull pressure i was describing continues.
i am constantly suffused with adrenaline and an abnormally ticklish
solar plexus

and i wonder, are these love symptoms? or are they delusion
symptoms? (shades of jimi hendrix here) is there a difference? or is
this just a sickness that's been written into existence by a couple of
lonely wordsmiths (but are we lonely? i mean, she's there, he's here,
even as i type this. so if we're lonely, what is it exactly we're lonely
for? this? perhaps) with libido oozing out their brains and then their
fingers? and it has to go somewhere? and does that matter?

you understand my anxiety? i'm so terrified of disappointment
on either side. that would be ... so awful. that is to say, language is
SO effective, your language (as provoked, no doubt, by mine), that at
this point i'm almost screaming, "ok! ok! i'll do anything you want!
turn up the radiator and get these clothes off me!" but I STILL
HAVEN'T EVER MET YOU

now where's that at? aren't we supposed to date first or something? have coffee?

you know what e-mail is, gary? potentially? this is today's realization, or one of them: it's pillow talk. it's pillow talk without the
sheets and snoring and box of kleenex and condom packets. it's just
like having your head next to someone in a dark room, telling everything. and then falling asleep, encurled ...

and here's another realization i have had: this is all just too too
cinderella

and what's going to happen when oh oh please reassure me
when this hits the quotidian?

will the quotidian absorb it? stomp it out?

or will the nature of the quotidian be transformed?

that's what i want to know

p.s. a comment about the letter: re the tongue of the other ... "to suck it as far down their throat as they can" oh dear on the giving end is ok, but gary i gotta tell you i have a really sensitive gag reflex, i can't even floss my back teeth without wanting to retch so but i mean there're other places where such lingual probes can be gainfully employed, should it you know ever come to that

but i'll tell you what i'm feeling i'd like to do:

i'd like to put my lips to your ear, your right ear i think, and suck out all of the knowledge and energy from your brain (not to take it from you, more like a disk copy), and swallow it, so i am fairly pregnant with it

that's what i'd like

∞

From: nada
Date: November 30
Subject: 3) domestic anecdotes

(She is in m—'s room, he is sitting at his desk, she on his lap. The gas heater glowing just in front of them.)

M—: I did something very unusual—I wept today.

Nada: You did?

M: Not over you—at a *yakuza* (gangster) film.

(she slaps his face lightly)

N: *He* wept over me—on a train!

M: He sounds ... very eccentric ... like the kind of people you often see in New York.

N: A— wept over me, a couple of times (More light slapping, smiling)

M: Sorry.

N: Would you weep if I packed my bags and left?

M: Maybe.

(He pulls out a book of aphorisms and turns to the section on Love. A discussion on the aphorisms follows. Many of them seem to her antiquated and sexist, or inaccurate, like: "What attracts us to a woman is not what binds us to her." M— says that after sex the mystery is lost, that men just think that way. Some discussion of the difference between lovers and spouses ensues. Suddenly she is aware of a great physical tension. She asks for a massage, which he patiently gives her while they listen to a tape she'd bought in Kyoto of monks chanting the Heart Sutra. Then, she goes up to her room and writes this in her new journal. And goes to sleep.)

* * *

anecdote #2

this was about a week ago. you know, m— is now working one night a week at my school. i got him the job. he came early to ask me some english questions, and we went out for some food. for some reason the topic of this correspondence came up, and suddenly i started to cry about it: "I've never had this kind of communication, of attentiveness, from ANYONE." m— looked at me slightly bemused. "well, aren't you going to respond? don't you want to know more?" i said

and he said, "nada, we're not normal people. we're poets. if we were normal we'd be sitting here with a couple of kids saying to them (switches into japanese here), 'now sit still' 'finish your food' 'do you need to go to the toilet?' and so on."

i guess it's true. WE'RE NOT NORMAL PEOPLE.

* * *

anecdote #3

m— has been trying to convince me to come with him to a kind of sex den of iniquity where, if you pay 5000 yen, you can have sex in the same room where a bunch of other couples are having sex ... and you can also offer up your partner to someone else

i said that sounded kind of emotionally difficult. i told him about the time that a— and i brought our ditzy roommate, j—, into our bed (a— was attracted to her) and i tried to stroke her thigh a little, while they were making out, but i couldn't handle it, i just started crying

but i told m— that who knows, i may come back from my winter vacation completely disillusioned and begging him to stay with me, and he said

i'd much rather take you to that room if your trip to new york

turned out to be completely fulfilling
  weird
  weird
  weird
  wasn't i talking about purity a while ago?

                                    * * *

  m— asked me if i wanted anything from the store
  i said, yeah, get me something beautiful
  and you know what, he did! a poinsettia plant
  what a completely un-m— -like gesture

                            * * *

i snooped his schedule book again and found that he's booked christmas week to spend with k—
  i can't really complain about that, can i, since I'll be in NYC on
the 26th ...
  but here's another m— and k— story: he posted an announce-
ment on his BBS that he was looking for someone to talk about
Takuboku Ishikawa and Dazai Osamu with (i won't hold it against
you if you don't know who these writers are, but they're really
great). k— saw the posting and burst into tears, in front of her parents, even, then called m— and said, "i know you're looking for
another lover" and he had to calm her down
  my god, people are so uncontrollable once you start certain
processes in motion

                            ∞

From: nada
Date: November 30
Subject: 4) on ravel

first to say, about "ravel," that last weekend at a teachers' conference,
i met up with, for the first time, jack kimball, a poet who used to live
in new york and now lives in miyazaki, and does an e-zine called *the*

east village—actually you were in it, weren't you
    complete with sound files
    and he bought his powerbook and mike and recorded me reading that poem
    for all i know it may be on the internet already
    tho' i don't remember the url.
    jack is great—way too smart, taught at harvard, gay i think, completely bald. i told him i thought he looked a little like william blake. and he's mad for the new york school.
    new friends! how the universe keeps opening up! (colored ropes)
    now on to the poem:
    as you know, i've traveled a bit.
    these are the places i've been to:
        france
        italy
        czechoslovakia
        germany (for a day)
        england
        korea (for one night)
        malaysia
        thailand
        indonesia
        mexico
        china
        and of course japan
(and i have wonderful stories about all these places!)
    with m— i have been to thailand, bali, paris and the usa, both sf and nyc
    but more often travel with other friends
    or completely alone
    m— does very badly in the tropics
    i've really only enjoyed travelling with him in japan and in new york
    traveling alone has its virtues. when i travel alone i am more open to the wonder that surrounds me, i write a lot, i can indulge my whims ... but i feel lonely. and i do make contacts with people when i travel, plenty of them, but more often those contacts feel superficial (or threatening—i tend to be a bit of a target), at least

compared to the kind of contact, the kind of communication, my being cries out for, about which i think you know a little

so remember what i said about writing being a hiding place? taking meals in little island restaurants, with no one to talk to, and knowing that if i did talk to whomever was around me it would be along the lines of, and what do you do? and where did you say you were from?, i am forced, in combined expressiveness and alienation, into poetry (isn't that how it works?)

and that was where "ravel" was written, on koh samui in southern thailand in the springtime, last spring i think it was. but spring has no meaning there, it's always just a hot paradisical beach

and in the evening sitting in a beachfront restaurant the power went out, which meant that i had to write to the light of a tiny votive candle. plus the kitchen was slowed down by the power outage, so i had a lot of time to write

"ravel" was written on little cards, maybe old business cards, in weentsy little letters, because i felt desperate to use the limited space as best i could.

the night was balmy—tropical and perfectly starry, and the wave sound, constantly soothing, was making me passionate, or something like it, making me concentrate really hard.

the poem is full of little jokes although it is deadly serious

even *hair encircles the mind* is a joke, because mind isn't in the skull, we all know that

and it's a *stone's throw from transparency*, the mind is, because when you concentrate, things seem almost clear, but not, there's just enough fuzziness, hair encircling, to obscure the truth, and that frustration leads to intense desire for it, reaching

and also there's hair because, well, i told you about the "cousin it" resemblance; i think that i'm about 30% hair, something like that, my hair is tremendous and bothersome especially in the tropics

and the thing that is to me *just like the stars that/ never go out* is the transparency the mind can't quite get to, although another referent might be conceived of. the point being though that they (stars) and it (transparency) are always there, we just don't perceive them as such, but that light, that transparency, draws us like moths to it (i guess it might be death even, or pure being)

and then in the next stanza my language spazzes out a little, to

keep the poem from being too rigid i suppose, or more likely it's just
a lazy jerk of language

but the *irony* and *pretend*ing seem important here, *pretend* keeps
coming up in this poem, this feeling of inauthenticity or things that
just somehow aren't clear, aren't right, and *disjoint irony* is something
i *dance into* in order to make myself feel better about that. and i like
how *pretend* becomes an adjective, exactly like child-talk.

those lazy jerks of language are the lines or stanzas in poems that
are kind of superfluous, or the things one writes just to write, just to
move and follow the rhythm one's making. one reason i'm afraid to
edit is that i'm afraid to edit those lazy parts out for fear of what will
happen to the rhythm of the poem

the *toothpicks* were sitting on my table at the restaurant. i often
find i cast around for whatever nouns are around me. i love nouns,
love them. one of my favorite devices is just a little list of three or
four of them, like a still life. i love what stein said about nouns, she
was just exactly right.

actually, *they paralyze even the stiffest resistance* bugs me,
because it's illogical ... but maybe that's why i wrote it. if you paralyze resistance it gets even more resistant. i find it amusing that you
found some eroticism in this line, and i wondered why you feel i am
resisting you, i mean i may, but in this medium i certainly don't, do
i, at all—i anyway liked the maleness of your reading of this

thorning. unruled. hmm. now that i think about it, that may be
me. always thorning (you may see this quality in me, later, i don't
know, or maybe you see it in my letters sometimes? certainly all that
"you're not my type" stuff was a kind of thorning. i'm really really
really sorry about that. oh god. really). *unruled* is the little cards i was
writing on, but also me, i am not ruled. maybe there's a sense of
wanting to be ruled here. and that could be more easily eroticized, i
think. or, it could be there are no rules to the poem, or that i was
making the rules as i went along?

and it occurs to me now that, getting french for a minute, unruled-
ness is *"dereglement (de tous les sens)"*—derangement, unruliness

the *shell full of ash/ and then a candle* is of course what was sitting before me at the restaurant, on the table. *votive* is one of my
favorite words. you light a candle for your wish, for your prayers. the
parentheses around *votive* make it a deeper wish.

power outrage is a pun on power outage. and it has to do with m—, i think, our power struggle (which i haven't fully described to you yet, uh-oh, another anecdote in the wings), thrown up against banks of difficulty. or it could have been some other man, the pronouns shift all over the place in my subconscious, kind of leap from guy to guy to reader in general. the difficulty might not just be personal difficulty or the difficulty of being but the difficulty of my so-obscure writing.

the body, prone/ or supine (power relations, but here two ways of being abject, vulnerable), *or both at once. both at once* is of course the two-backed beast. is sex. (reader/writer)

and i realize too that the prone and supine bit has something to do with a george eliot novel, *the mill on the floss,* i once had an assignment to write an extended ending to it, but this is a fuzzy memory to me now, i'll have to re-read the book

the *darkness* at the time of writing was literal, but a poetic background and mindstate too. the *figures* are *approach*ing (other human beings) but i've roped them off *just past the cordon* (gordon) or they are anyway separate from me.

and darkness wiggles imperceptibly is just a great line, i don't want to have to gloss that. except that what i like about it is its discomfort (*wiggles*) and subtlety (*imperceptibly*). it's an event that means nothing, can't even be felt, and yet is disturbing. ok, now i've glossed it.

first stanza of next section changes tone, gets chatty and noisy. as if suddenly i turn into madonna, in full party dress circa late 80s

and this brings me to shopping, which is what i and so many other victims of post-capitalist society do when feeling disconnected or unclear, hence the *department stores* reference. and in fact on that little island there were no department stores, and i was getting a little bored. or impatient. *obligation is devoured* i think may have meant something like, "obligation to the earth, to other human beings"—a spasm of social irresponsibility which leads to the next stanza, which is kind of self-explanatory

the ostrich/ in the crevice—hiding its head of course

crevices being full of mystery, and pleasure

the *great synthesized chord* is the chord from *sgt. pepper's* (from "a day in the life") that i used on *koi maneuver.* it's a little like the chord a macintosh makes turning on. everything's in that chord, it's an explosion of possibility.

the next stanza with the pronouns, actually the next four stanzas— most people who have looked at this poem say this is the heart of the poem, the intro just curves into it. sure, that first stanza could prefigure you, why not? except that you don't irritate me (well, except when ... oh never mind)—unless, unless (and i quote) irritation is a form of pleasure! (which it is)

but i do think i had m— in mind a little here, because he really does irritate me something awful. and i don't hide my irritation. it's no wonder that he had to girlhunt. but this isn't just m—, that's the beauty of pronouns. and i think i'm nearly always writing at several levels. *you* is always reader. like you are the reader.

and *the you* is what is desired, however irritating (pleasurable), that's why the *eyes cross* and *problem*s arise.

By *the urn* i was thinking of keats' "ode to a grecian urn" (beauty is truth, truth beauty, that is all ye know on earth, and all ye need to know) (did i quote that right?). but your "gushing" makes a little sense here (crevices. vessels. suddenly very kristevan)

and then *the red yarn* i explained before. *pretend red yarn* is the *disjoint irony* that makes me feel better although it isn't true red yarn and therefore isn't beautiful.

and so one looks for replacement desires, i.e. *a potato in foil* (eating = shopping)

and the next stanza about wanting *to shake off/ other human beings like/ larvae*—yeah, that's a genuine desire i have sometimes. or why would i have structured my life the way it is. because human beings can be so trivial, so needy, so boring, so shallow, so mannered, so stupid, so ugh ugh ugh, that despite my compassion i often do want to shake them off, or i might actually do it—*but then/ i feel so lonely*, which is true, and which i notice is a theme in my writing. but it's a willed loneliness, a protective loneliness, a creative loneliness, an inevitable loneliness perhaps. and brave of me to admit it, right there in the poem, all open-like. but maybe everyone feels that way?

the next five lines are just to bring action and light back to the poem, which had got so dark and lonely. instead, *skittling* and *spilling* and *glowing*. in fact, in the real world, the island had started to glow again, the power outage was over.

but then i lapse back into maudlin loss, probably a— here, but maybe not. could have been any kind of loss—of a sweater or a book, of a friend or a fella or a day or a father or hope.

the *tattoo of darkness on my breast* i like because, well, darkness isn't representable as a figure, so how would you tattoo it? instead, it's the knowledge of that darkness quite indelible, probably just over the heart. *a tattoo of you on my face.* that *you*, again, could be any desired other, could be the reader that looks at me or looks at my words and sees herself or himself (at one of my lab readings, i think i mentioned to you, i wore a t-shirt that said "YOU"), because how much of what we perceive of other human beings is just a trace of our own faces?

body bound in red yarn because repressed, because not connected, but waiting for "unravel"

and in fact the poem does start to unravel there

just listens to the *musik*

the hook above/ the dot is a question mark

that *changes the/ music*, the intonation, of a sentence

changes the mean, well, the japanese often say "mean" when they mean "meaning" but i meant two meanings here, both "meaning" and mean as in your cerberus dog

and the last line, the word *musk*, is an eye-rhyme to *musik*, but more than that, the poem gets lost in an appreciation of a smell, of incense or the body-smell of an animal or human, and spaces out into that, in a loving way. it's a tiny little kind of redemption for the poem that has already twisted through so many moods, waiting for the lights to go back on and the food to finally come.

is this what is meant by "radical subjectivity"? or "private language"?

does a poem like "ravel," which may seem vaguely or stylistically powerful but, for a normal reader, kind of unpackable, have any kind of "lasting literary value"—i.e. is it anthologizable? relevant or useful to others? or is it just the tracings of a woman trying to maneuver in a thinking/feeling way through life? maybe i should publish my life story as well as glosses to my poems?

like i'm doing now with you.

i so enjoyed writing this essay. i found out all kind of things about that poem i didn't know before, at least not so clearly.

really big love,

nada

ps: oh yeah, another m— anecdote:

    the first time i ever read this poem aloud was at a kind of literary luncheon party with a bunch of tokyo writers. m— was there too. we were going around the table reading our stuff. and do you know what m— did just as it was my turn to read? he went to the bathroom. he MISSED my poem. (on purpose?)

∞

From: nada
Date: November 30
Subject: 5) omens

omens all over the place, some of them dreadful
    i'll tell you the bad ones first.
    1) my mom consulted a psychic, and sent me this e-mail:

> Anyway, I'll tell you a few highlights of the reading:
> That it would be good for you to have wisdom in
> your choices, and don't think you have to have a
> relationship to be complete. This is all I'll say for now,
> and I do understand how you have a pull of destiny to
> explore the situation. Good to keep your smart hat on.

isn't that awful. on the phone, soon after i got this, i told her i didn't really want to hear anything negative. but she mentioned that according to the psychic, you are "possessive" and "not the right kind of person" for me. the psychic said that all my years in japan have made me feel that i have to have a relationship.

    but that's not true! i just need to have a real relationship instead of a lame, deceitful one! with someone who talks to me, really really talks and listens! someday anyway.

    and then in a panic i went to an internet tarot site and asked what will happen when i meet you

    (god i'm really grasping at straws. why? what's the big deal here?)

    and the final answer to my query (though there was a lot of other stuff in there too) was: "vain hopes. disillusionment."

i think i was asking too much of the universe, though. because there have been other omens that completely contradict those above that are so distressing me

this omen is the weirdest, because it was totally unsought for. and here it is.

on the way home last night i stopped into a clothing store called Cenozoic to browse, look at black sweaters, and just as i was unfolding a turtleneck i hear over the store's loudspeaker, which was set to an english-language radio station:

"that was the day my husband, GARY, who was just my boyfriend then, asked me to marry him"

then the music changed to auld lang syne, which is what japanese shops always play at closing time

and i said to myself, nada, you didn't really hear that, and even if you did, don't trip on it, don't be ridiculous

and i ran out of the store

i have another internet horoscope, which i printed out (i only keep fortunes i like) which is wildly encouraging

not that i'm superstitious or anything

i'm not going to quote it here though.

DECEMBER

[*Enclosed in a letter from Nada, dated December 1st*]

Symphony

Can you have a BONER
for a voice?
A voice you've never
even actually heard?

Can you walk up the steps,
sit by the lion,
and then what.

I'm the lion.
I want YOU
for the hole
in the soul.

At what angle
are you situated

nostrils flaring.

Passion has no use
for clocks. It's
a mind thing, not
a time thing.

Every system in the body
feels this.
So what is a body.

A kind of conductor.

I want to say, *oh,*

ditto
ditto
ditto

"whenever you are near"

∞

From: nada
Date: December 2
Subject: how was it for you?

i'm sorry, sweetie, sorry i freaked you out
     and woke you up although you had to get up to answer the
phone anyway
     but i had to do it
     i had to put a little tiny drop of reality into the potion
     (and now for a drop of tenderness—but i must put in only a drop)
     and ohmigod GARY you're a girl!
     you're even more of a girl than me!
     Moon Unit Zappa no less! no wonder i like you!
     you didn't tell me what an effervescent, goofy gigglehead you are
     now this is again, completely disorienting
     although i have to say one thing
     i know you were nervous
     but you're really a much better listener in e-mail
     in which you also have a tendency to be a little impulsive
     but one thing: don't ever ever supply words to me, unless i ask
     and give me lots of time to answer questions
     as i said, i check truth value, or do *mot juste* searches before i say
stuff, or try to, not that i always get at either
     i mean i've been living here for so long my native language
doesn't always just come directly to me
     you also sound much more genuine in e-mail

but maybe that's just those giggles
i don't know
i sort of pictured you scratching your chest distractedly
like you'd been bothered by women all night and you were thinking
aww baby, gimme a break
although i know it wasn't fair of me to suddenly get all real time like that
now was it
but fer cryin' out loud,
do you know the kinds of things you've been saying to me?
well of course you do
and am i going to spiral out into freaky fantasies of rescue and roses without any basis in life at all?
well i already was, still am, but now it's at least tempered by knowing
that you are verbally really really silly
and the way you were talking to me sounded kind of idiotic
compared to the way you talk to me here, i don't mean your voice, which is annoying but also kind of great, i meant the general babble about dumb things like the poetry scene when we've been talking about ... oh i dunno, the nature of being, grand passion, colored ropes and the like
which is perfectly OK, and perfectly predictable
so, you you you, how did you feel about talking to me?
am i less of a muse and object of infatuation now?
a little less mysterious?
and what did you read from my voice and my way of communicating?
what did you like, dislike about it?
did it break your ardor? fuel it? change it?
tell me.
nada

∞

From: Gary
Date: December 7
Subject: My Weekend

Wow, you know what? Last night I wrote you, oh oh oh
        Well, I'll have to type it in here & will send it as soon as I'm done
        As for my weekend, I called C— at around 10 p.m. Saturday, told
her everything, & said I didn't feel comfortable with her coming up
to stay here at Christmas and it was, well, no describing it ...
        But she did say she understood & that she felt I had to give this
a shot and wished me luck ... we were both crying something awful
        Anyway, anyway, there are elections in Venezuela today & the
reigning wisdom, according to C— is that, depending on the out-
come, a country-wide revolution is possible
        So C— is now working on getting her parents out of Venezuela
& back to Spain where they're originally from, and if & when that
happens she's off to Spain herself
        Anyway, let me get working on this other e-mail for you ... and
yes, oh please please I do need to hear from you, too
        Love,
        Gary

                                    ∞

From: Gary
Date: December 7
Subject: 12/7

My dear Nada,
                        If today I'm as flat as the light on the street below
it is only because I write from great distance, but do curl
as a cover in the sun, toward you, if imperceptibly
wanting more than to be newly come as a first kiss blossoms thick
as summer. I wish today I had its heat, & that heart others "trod on
ages ago," & so this may explain why, yeah, I'm a fool
why the red sun in my throat is yours; well,
it was mine once, now lent to you in utterance, sweet doubt &
scattered brains hacked away to this, my love—but, what point

in bluntness, flat as the light in the street?

It's too easy to repeat
& expect subtle difference, nuance; I want every word I do give you
to be new, not newly come. I saw today *LOVE: a book of remembrances*
& ached we hadn't thought of it (bp Nichol did), it sent me
here, to these words struck against my Underwood "Golden Touch"
's ink-black platen, my cigarettes, & beer as amber as your eyebrows
appear photographed in wiggly fluorescent light, though
they're dark brown, I think, almost black, it's your eyes that
're really amber. & "really real," as Van Morrison would say; & I've got
I realize no right to write you like this, though I don't feel
beguiling, more that you charm vivid color from even this dirty
Brooklyn air. "The year starts in despair/ at ever awakening to it,"
I just bibliomanced, "New Years, Mad," from Coolidge's *Solution
Passage*, & I wonder at the madness of this, but know equally
I do love you.

It worries me, too, fool that I am, of breaking up
with you into pieces, silent as letters, to be strewn onto water
not able, the winter sun so harsh above the south Brooklyn skyline,
to become, without words, so liquid as this. But this—
imagine foraging for anything like this, among others
more beautiful than us.

That we are not so beautiful is why we may
strive to make this, here—& I mean This, not
these words—so beautiful. Give me Anything & I'll take it
& make of it Everything. For you. What is love if not this promise?
I promise you this: All my promises will be kept, until delivered
& then they will be yours, & what you do with them will be
you. & it's you, that shadow around your mouth, I want. Do you know
what you've done? To me? I drink as the sun sinks below
other projects because I am not, now, drinking you. Only your arms,
your legs, opening, & there you are, you, Nada,
only you wrapped around me, as I am rapt now, thinking of you
matters to me, my hands & arms, lips & tongue useless
that they cannot feel, this moment, how you pulse beneath your skin.
Our cells, the alphabet of our souls.

We will never speak, bodily
in complete sentences, we'll lose every spelling bee, but know

this is only because we did not begin as adults. That's also
"what love is," knowing that, that loveliness is accidental, might
mean a chipped tea cup, flowers oddly situated in a drinking glass
filled with tap water, that nothing might be so perfect
as our seams. Or our "seems," as in "it seems
so perfect on the screen." If you can resist me, in person, if I
fumble lines to your face—elsewhere
"a bee soaked with liquid rises," & that knowledge may be all
that will save us. My only request is that you know
& remember this.

    Will to be yourself with me. The sun has just now
disappeared behind white buildings, I need
to do laundry, the everyday seeps in even into this letter, how
keep it out, if I'm to be honest with you? I itch
in my clothes, no doubt reek of cigarettes, beer, sweat & cum
am human & animal as you are human & animal
should boil tea to sober up, begin to think "How can I quit smoking?"
How can I do laundry, having written you this? I close
my eyes, having stared at this photograph of you too long,
it soothes nothing, I know I'll wake tomorrow, my extremities cold
my thoughts curled in your syntax, my body still quick w/your
image, it was somewhat cruel of you to send me such beautiful photos
don't you think? Or not cruel, but beguiling, as if to say
"I'm yours," when, no, you're there, I hope we can forgive each other
knowing cruelty as a product of distance.

    My mouth feels like it just
fell off, I lift my beer to it but there's only my tongue
& this, my language is what you've reduced me to, or elevated me towards, as though writing you were loving you, which it is, but
no it's not; Nada, I want, need, to love you, bodily & soulfully, meaning
bodily over time. Deny me that & I will sink back w/fits suspended
against my face, my tongue will grow dim, my arms will rest
as fallen dominoes. I write this as the sky grows purple
& paper dim.

    Whatever happens, Nada, I know we will never again
imagine our skin to be protective. I know, too
what insomnia is, & that love is not merely attendance. It's also sound
that numbs logic. It's this neighborhood we live in. It's whatever story

you tell me that I relive.

                  The ruckus of this letter is no accident
it's how my very words love you. It's how vain I feel
feeling the sun exists to warm me. "From letter distance I am made,"
only I'm here now, seeping nitrogen, able only to light
another match, able only to confront all the things I think
looking at your photograph. What, I dread, will we become
if not together? "Understanding"? That's the last thing
any bruised heart hopes for. Mine, or yours. "Let all our mistakes
be jewels," our sparks & low grunts no relief. I will never
ever, be "relieved of" you. You're too deeply inscribed. No one,
my love, will ever write you like this, no words this
insectile, no letter so porous. Reading this, you reading this,
I know, & do feel, you seep. We are not poor in spirit. & so,
let us no longer starve for love,

                           Gary

                         ∞

From: nada
Date: December 8
Subject: Lubricity

     ohhh ...

     liquid butter and
     totally green
     stockings

     when i think of you
     i think of dope

     this is the line
     that built the ray
     that juts out of the stratosphere

     a maze

at you   in you   around you

*

looking for silky, for silky ....
sweep
or the glue
with glitter in it

feel it. sense it.
savor it.
taste it.

immediately.

or put on your fedora
and go outside,
to think

*

in optic fiber
on dizzying satellites
there were rhapsodists kissing

(in letters)
insects
singing outside
(I want to sing outside)

and time
time is totally
glue

did you notice
how i wrote you into life?

the twitching

life
our writing
made? twinkling
the colloquial ...

*

cypresses.
daisies.
pines, pining.
pine box.
plastic box's
circuits > > > > >
our nerves ...

be still my mind

pressure at the temples

the tree of life
droops over
an engraving
of a couple

below whom
an axiom (epigram)
makes total sense

time is totally
cyclone.
now that you're here
you might as well
lie down
with
me
.

.

.

we might hold up our hands
in gratitude
for the godz
to rain down
miniature cherries,
weeping dwarf red
cedar, weeping
fig, wooly thyme,
marigolds, beauty
secrets, anemones,
pygmy bamboo,
indoor landscapes

waltzing like
infants
praying like
telephones
                like modems,
like telephones

*

poetry, then
has some efficacy

a poem
whose only word is
SWOON

*

this lyricism
is a kind of
blood, or
oil, or
semen, or
sand

and it keeps on pouring out
its lubricity
beyond quandary

the camellia[‡]
a vulva
after all

[‡]open, inviting, pinkish, dewy

∞

From: Gary
Date: December 15
Subject: l o n g i n g

Nada, my love
        I like long poems, long lines & letters equally long, length
an expression of love, lavish tendrils or tentacles
uncoiling out as tho to curl around the object of longing, silent
lector or lover, language a kind of leash, or like question mark's hook,
crooked finger signifying "come," the list poem one manifestation,
its litany of things seen, considered almost as lump, manifesto-like,
tag lines, any yellow legal pad filled with letters & numerals
        no less legendary
in the mind, & do we know or consider where all this leads?
        or are we both
blindly lead disclosing material as though filling this hole presently
standing in for "us," this ____ of miles not even our mutual laughter
obliterates, will not compulsory, our lust neither tabloid nor licentious
because what constitutes a handful might fluctuate, never neutral, so
no wonder *lip* floored me, & I still feel its oscillation, amplified by
my own lambent longing, oh this is doggerel, mere alliteration
like, love's so impossible to describe you only ever fumble ...?
Tell me tell me tell me,
            Love,
            Gary

∞

From: nada
Date: December 16
Subject: Re: l o n g i n g

gary my love

i like short
poems
short lines
and people equally
short

to show conciseness
and focus like a laser
on the object
of desire

crooked finger
signifying "come"
i almost do
when i read
you

this leads
to where it is

not lacking
in awe

the beauty
is the fumble

nada

∞

From: Gary
Date: December 16
Subject: O M E N

Dear Nada,

> "... *I' mi son un che, quando*
> *Amor mi spira, noto, e a quel modo*
> *ch'e' ditta dentro vo significando.*"
> —Dante, *Purgatorio*

> (I am one who, when Love inspires me
> takes note, and goes setting it forth
> after the fashion which he dictates
> within me.)

Shapeless, the omen thrives
on cinders. Tho light
strives it. It

is intent on Now before
it blots. My word
as good as water.

No letter's
silent, my mouth a Yes
such that your eyes are needed

to read it. Say, say if this
is true. What are you thinking?
Answer me: the sad memories in you

aren't yet destroyed
by Love. Come,
                pour in my mouth

the one word that fills yours.

How do you tell a story? Where
without aging I die I love
you o my prison. Love? Nothing
no one can say not arising
out of pain. Coarsely gathered
in our own serene faces, so
waterfull, thinned like paint
... no omen worse than that.
                              Make

move your reason, its exact
rigor, & on the heel of my hand
I'll kiss your fingers.
                    But if I prick
your heart it's only to see it
bloom, & in that brownness which is the mind
green things flourish

                not only
                the should've been, not

                only as a tree is only
                become a ship & lost at sea.

                              Didn't I see
you, just now? How else do I miss you, no
you. Our cells are prisons.
                    We tire ourselves
                    in submersion.
                              Meanwhile, I hang
upon your lips, I'm mortal, the movie that
everything is. One can't describe love without sounding
bleak. So, let's you & me

                keep it clean & simple

                accurately non-numbered

                it's not enough to say

"love," looking into

the light of the heart

* * *

You're the hole in my sock, & the mind quick to discern
you're the caring-to-wound who on hands & knees gives up
you're the "Hey man, what's happening?" & the unknowing jolt
you're the whole face that wet the fingers that lost touch
    with the tongue I read in some poem in that other world
you're the coiffed present life labeled Past Behavior
you're my most respected addressee
you're what I've ever seen confront me, a broken surface
you're no word, only an awkwardness of eternal light
you're my consciousness, my here, my where-else-could-I-find-cold
    & to begin with, you do not stop at you.
                                        Nada, my Name
any name I might give you, the title
of any book. & I love you
because you're beautiful & strong.

* * *

An omen must be read. As specifically as Love. I'm not
gonna blow even one blue note from your brow
but neither can you lock one under box lid. Give it up. Surrender,
I'm this man sitting under those stars on this earth
empty, but awake. & there's no difference between
you & me. What does it mean that "you & me" is magic
& unreal? The universe is fully known because it is ignored.
I don't want to be ignored
by you. And I'm not in a greedy mood. I'm simply
not here, where you are
reading this. It causes confusion, & future mending. Mend,
but with an amused gesture.

* * *

"Well, that's life!"

"Does this trail lead to the ridge?"

"endless nothingness of reality"

"Let's get out of here"

"remember me"

* * *

OMEN: "Willingly I'll say there's been a sweet marriage,"
divined by D— for me from *Bending the Bow*.
We bent it so far it snapped.
                              Everything
speaks to us, we simply don't bother to stop
& listen. Every
thing. Is your cunt one *lip*? Or those folds now kept
just out of reach. What I imagine (you)
lives & trembles in the air. Every fold inside you
dreaming a different kind of dream.

OMEN: "I have taken leave of the friends I love the most & have
set out on a [ILLEGIBLE]."

OMEN: "You walk,
      you get muddy."

* * *

Love is anterior to life,
Posterior to death,
Initial of creation, and
The exponent of breath.
            —Emily Dickinson

* * *

Like concentric waves on the wind, our water, a bird
my heart your kiss, an open fountain, my eyes
on your lips.
                  Heart spins like a top.
                                      I'm caught
Should I care? Adios, sun
                      & the river at my feet
I wanna go back to you
& from you
to my heart. You going too?
                        Adios,
our bare heart.
              Nada, avoid the illusion there can be any lack
for someone who wishes, then fully decides.
                          & tell me, tell me
how incomprehensibly far from this
you feel
we are.
            Will me with you. Dear woman, filled with our hesitant fate
tell me
        tell me
            we no longer lay out each path
            as a lovely meander

            I await your answer,

            love,
            Gary

                ∞

From: nada
Date: December 17
Subject: oh, men

i feel strange from interrupted sleep
    how to describe the insomnia, a tensing in the upper body a
quick shallowness in breathing, i try so many tricks to sleep: those

four beckett alphabet letters

    sung as ABCD ABC

    but half as slow as on the tape
    but my mind speeds it up again

    or picturing myself on an escalator going down a long long escalator in a jungle
    and counting backwards from a high number

    or a chant i learned at my mom's ashram

    sri ram jai ram jai jai ram om
    sri ram jai ram jai jai ram om

    or trying to imagine the energy in my body as a warm orange fluid that i send calmingly upwards to relax starting with toes

    but it doesn't work
    it doesn't work

    especially my stomach, my chest, constricted tense no, masturbation doesn't help
    maybe for a few minutes
    but sex doesn't stop this mind

    from asking

    what is this
    what is this
    what is this

    so that what used to be "sleep"
    becomes "lying in the dark flooded in language"

∞

From: nada
Date: December 18
Subject: Moonscape with Earthlings

i really tried to sleep
but woke up excitedly at four
needing to finish this poem
well it isn't finished
but i'm sending it anyway
to you
my inspiration ...

Moonscape with Earthlings

"You don't have to LIKE me if you don't want to. Just LOVE me,
that's all."
                    —today's train neighbor's stationery

up against a word wall, pushed
by voluble groin

your (o)men's ferocity
eats at me.

my sentences feel simple.
they make sense.
this is how i touch you.

                            *

no anvils anytime, no
nor no bricks suddenly dropping
no no no no no—gentle.

                    our communication
                      a fabulous peony

bending its stem
in early morning
insomniac mist

communication
a silly straw breath
goes through—wilting
for love
of that breath

*

yearning for a dilatory cat
every sound's a melody
silence more suggestive

yesterday a secret
everyone could hear:
sibilance

you took notice
endings force beginnings
so why worry

yammering
effervescent doll-boy leaps in
sweet-tasting sea water

younger than ever
enlightenment reveals
shine on leaves' surface

*

the brassiere
makes an oath
of containment

things with wings
look on: flies
in oils

a small black eggplant
appears before the eyes
as a mirage

> I quit!
> and put the plum
> in the exact mouth
>
> on the mound of love
>
> you in a folder
> beside me

my head
like a sumo
on quaaludes
filled
with the voicings
of a sister mind

and this brotherly
l o v e

*

From Satoko Nishimura's sweatshirt:

EVEN when you're not in YOUR room

imagine there is AN invisible HEART above you
all the time

that WAY, you'll feel SAFE and

comfortable wherever you are.

it's not just a DECORATION

it also gives you

HAPPINESS and courage

(insert image: kissing dogs wagging tails)

HANABANA DAYS

advertisement *advertisement* *advertisement* *advertisement*

I really enjoyed this lesson in my life. There is no lesson but this how many times we can laugh. The first time I talked to you, you answered my question about the difference of MAN and WOMAN. NADA said I don't like distinguish MEN and WOMEN. I was surprised because you said clearly NO, for the first time. But I understand what you said, now. I like your way of thinking as one personal. You have a good eye that everything and everyone is equal.

And this lesson is just like Nada.

—Akiko Yamada

Through Nada's class the members of the class became more friendly. Because we are needed to cooperate. I also found what Nada was like. For example, she is cheerful, charming and likes skirts better than pants. Nada's skirts were always pretty, I think. I rarely wear a skirt but I felt skirt is also pretty thing. I want to wear skirt more often.

—Yumi Shintani

*

I think I should get a C in this class. ... I was not energetic in the class but in that small room that was the best I can do. It was really hard. This is one reason. The other main reason is that I like the shape of a C. It's very artistic sophisticated and even intelligent. When I think about a C, I feel the history of a C being so deep, and I like the word it's initial stars from C, for example coca-cola, cheeseburger, camisole, cheerleader, cabaret, celibacy, cynical and so on. That's why I'm glad if I could get a C.

—Takashi Yamada

*

This man has had an oppression on his astonish.
You can see the long star.
He is also having trouble with his choice.
The doctor is examining one of his air bows, and he has a bandage around his need.

This girl is a trip girl.
She is holding an envy in her hand.
There is an erection near the typewriter.
Behind her there is a glow on the desk, and an eternal is open at a map of Japan behind it.
There is a picture of freedom on the wall.

*

adventure.

tumult.

the poets come out of the crevices to look at each other

jitsu wa ne

      atta koto wa nai n desu ga
   zutto zutto
      anata no soba ni itai

kore ga   *honto ni*
          sono mae ni oshieta
   inochi

   kurenai

      sugoku sugoku

  fushigi da ne

      love,
      nada

      ∞

From: Gary
Date: December 22
Subject: 12/22

My dear Nada,
      No one, none, will come after you
as you aren't part of the soul that perishes, & anyway you
taught me how to live & be brave, in this moment where nothing is lost
but shines out from the rest of the body purely. So
is it safe to greet the rest of you, to measure myself, to write
this letter as though it were a poem
why not, happiness a kind of affection. We only imagine we want
everyone to fall in love with us, or that we do, when
in our beds we lie together at the feet of some city we've never met
viewless, impenetrable, infinite the power to fool ourselves
or anybody, no god outside us but is just as, & that
yes, it's here, beyond the heart's reaches, where the world
seems to encircle, where "I refuse to let what I've always wanted
keep me from what I've always wanted," where
our future isn't sealed because no one ever put it just this way
where you become everyone I want to talk to tonight.
      Our letters
all dead paper mute & white, and yet they seem alive

as I am alive this evening, window open until the cold
fills the room, which is us, you, me, but which in my saying so
is no longer us, or you, or me. It's not even mind, though something
minds that the earth, though curved, can hurt us. Close your eyes,
it's not even mind.
    "Think of bedsheets not quite warm & momentarily
open in mild darkness," I
don't want to sleep, will read & write to invent another serene face
like yours I want to live with, the face inside my favorite quote:
"Mercury slips out of retrograde at last," which is empty.
    We're all
in heaven now.
    Love,
    Gary

∞

From: nada
Date: December 23
Subject: vows

i promise to
listen to anything you say
help you say what you want to say
give you the time you need from me
tell you when i need to be alone, and when i need you around
tell you the truth anytime you ask and sometimes when you don't
surprise you often
answer your questions
respond with all the energy and attention i have available
take care of you as i can
allow you to love me
keep communication possible in any any any eventuality
worship the back of your neck
love
nada
p.s. and yours? your vows?

∞

From: Gary
Date: December 23
Subject: Re: vows

Nada,

My lips are yours & my heart is yours, wholly
My eyes are yours & so are my ears, no other attentions
        will take precedence
& my life is yours, or ours, I vow always
to live neither for myself nor for you but for us
& always with you, & to never cease unfolding
never to cease teasing you further open
What is it that you need & want? I will always ask
& will always tell you mine, my own
tho I promise to learn over time to read you
& know, intuit, sense, to be with you such that I'll know,
And anything you want, I'll give you, or help you find if it's
        not something already within me
I'll help you learn to drive, if you ever want
I'll tell you everything I know, if you want
& ask you everything you know, I want & will want always
        your knowledge & experience for my own
I will never cease writing poems to you, my love
nor teasing them from you, will always read you
I will never cease wanting you, my beautiful woman
& will always & in all ways let you know
I promise to meet all of your expectations & having met them,
        strive to surpass them
There is nothing, Nada, I wouldn't do for you, for your unceasing love
& if you let me love you, I'm here, I promise you this
        from me to you:
                    A n   e t e r n a l   p r e s e n t

        Love,
        Gary

From: nada
Date: December 23
Subject: Re: vows

oh!
even if i were a hard-hearted callous monster which i'm not
there is nothing nothing i could do to resist this, resist you
see you in three days
love
nada

∞

[*From our first meeting, in New York on December 26. At one point, sitting across from each other at the Mona Lisa Café on Bleeker Street late in the evening, all other options expended, we resorted to our most familiar mode of interaction, and began writing back and forth to each other in a notebook.*]

MAD
        WHORL   ENTER.
      IDEOLOGY   RISE
                     ENTERPRISE

what is our enterprise?
the language outside comes
as a shock. i want fluidity
and real talking. i feel really
awful.

ME TOO. I THINK WE'RE BLOCKED.

in shock. shock is as galvanic as anything else we've experienced.
maybe this is part of the story. but the way i feel, gary, is so
wrenched i can't tell you. like i said, awful.

WHAT IS THE PRIMARY DIFFERENCE?

between what and what?

WHAT IS IT ABOUT THIS, NOW, HERE, THAT MAKES YOU FEEL AWFUL?

it's a kind of discomfort with you visually. like my eyes don't relax on you, i feel anguish. it's not about sex.

IS IT ABOUT LANGUAGE?

no. that's not our problem, duh.

WHAT DO YOU FEEL, LOOKING AT ME? BOREDOM?
no no no.
maybe: 1) too much movement
                2) too much contortion
                3) the expressions
                   filmic/jump cuts disorient me
                4) can't seem to veil face (you)

WHAT DO YOU MEAN BY "CAN'T SEEM TO VEIL FACE (ME)"?

totally open and readable. can you read my face?

IT'S A LEARNED THING, I THINK, BUT ALSO WE BEGAN WITH AN ALMOST IMMEDIATE CREATION OF A WALL. WHICH I'M TRYING TO DISMANTLE. BUT DEEP INSIDE ME, I'M NO DOUBT RESISTANT, NOT WANTING TO BE HURT.

yeah.

SO, GIVE IT (AND ME) A LITTLE TIME. I NEED TO BE ABLE TO TRUST YOU. OTHERWISE, I'LL REMAIN CLOSED, OR PARTIALLY CLOSED.

but that wasn't my comment, that you were closed. the opposite.

YOU DON'T WANT TO READ MY FACE?

no, i totally CAN read your face. maybe it's a japan-exacerbated quality in me ... being accustomed to/desiring a mask ... what occurred
to me today was "i've broken my own heart" ... is that too melodra-
matic? just expectations talking?

WHAT?

that phrase entered my brain. it's as if by meeting you the narcissistic echo-love i'd felt in other media was obliterated. you are truly
other.

YOU CREATED ME ... BUT I ALREADY EXIST ...?
we discussed that a little, remember?

YOU SEEM TO LACK TRUST.

in you, you mean? or in general?

IN LOVE. THAT IT MIGHT BE SOMETHING MORE THAN NAR-
CISSISM. THAT, UM, I WAS THERE THE WHOLE TIME. YOU SAID,
ONCE (MORE THAN ONCE) THAT I'D PERCEIVED YOU. DID YOU
EVER PERCEIVE ME?

what do you think?

YES.

then why do i feel ...

DO YOU REALLY FEEL THAT?

i do when looking. not when touching or talking. yes.

THIS IS LANGUAGE. SO IS "THIS" < —
YOU & I HAVE FOR SO LONG USED OUR EYES TO READ EACH
OTHER BUT WE FORGET (EVEN WHILE READING—I KNOW IT'S
BEEN TRUE FOR ME) WE'RE READING WORDS NOT PHYSICAL
PRESENCES.

i told you very clearly the physical effect(s) your words have on me. hence this torn-ness.

WHAT CAN I DO?
WHAT CAN WE DO?

that's the torment of the day.

I COULD JUST GET SHITFACED & MY WHOLE FACE WILL BE LESS ACTIVE (NOT TO MENTION FLUSHED IN A SEMI-LOVELY WAY). JOKE.

well, i'm afraid you may need to after my brutal honesty.

JOKE?

1/2. but i worry about getting home all right. selfish, huh. i kind of hate myself right now.

[DRAWS MAN WAVING WHITE FLAG.]

are you telling me to "just surrender" again?

ACTUALLY, I MEANT "I GIVE UP! I DON'T KNOW WHAT TO SAY!"

yeah, i know. but on the other hand, and this is why we've got to where we've got, why i, the physical beautiful nada who lives so very far away is sitting before you now ... because, unlike anyone i've ever met, you DO know what to say, you ALWAYS know what to say, and i've got proof of that.

YES. LOOK. I LOVE YOU. THAT MAY MAKE YOU FEEL UNCOM-FORTABLE RIGHT NOW, BUT I DO, AND I BELIEVED EVERY-THING WE BOTH SAID AND HOW WE SAID IT & IN WHAT IT ALL SEEMED TO SUGGEST. IN OTHER WORDS ...

(then what's going on with me? what's my problem?)
(now do you think i lied?)

(why parentheses?)
(how do i really feel?)

FOLLOW ME.

you mean somewhere?

YES

what are your intentions?

WILL IT KILL YOU TO STEP OUTSIDE FOR THREE MINUTES?

to do what exactly? duel?

YOU DON'T FOLLOW ME, I'M GONNA GIVE THIS NOTEBOOK TO
THE WOMAN ON YOUR RIGHT.

no, no threats, listen. here's my fear right now. we get physical. i'm still
freaked out by your looks. it remains an issue in our relationship, causes problems. you feel like shit and so do i. and sex will have complicated a relationship already bizarrely byzantine—4d love.

THEN LET'S CALL IT OFF NOW AND SAVE US BOTH FURTHER
HEARTBREAK. IF YOU THINK THIS IS A REAL ISSUE, I'D LIKE TO
BE RELEASED. I'M NOT GOING TO WASTE MY LIFE, MY MIND,
MY LOVE ON SOMEONE WHO FEELS THIS WAY ABOUT ME.

i hear you. but there's a problem, which is that that's not the only
way i feel about you, as you well know. so what to do? am i just in
shock? am i too scared by the opportunity for actual real grand passion? i'm trying to figure out how i feel. but let me ask you this ... is
it possible at this stage, where we are ... to "release" ... "be released"?
we're written all over each other. what we did, are doing, is totally
dangerous. love is totally insidious and not shakeable.

THEN BE HERE. AT LEAST GIVE IT THE OPPORTUNITY TO
BREATHE.

yeah, ok, of course. what else can i do??? plus you gotta remember
i'm FREAKING OUT. just because i'm wearing a mask. and i DID
warn you about this. ...

∞

From: nada
Date: December 28
Subject: snow

having trouble getting connected
        is that symbolic or what
        but finally i am being allowed this connection and hoping you're
there
        are you there?
        here in woodstock there's dreamy-looking postcard snow, and
last night when i arrived here after hours of stuffy bus really weird
things kept happening. when i got off the bus in woodstock no one
was there to meet me so i went into a taco place to call peggy, and a
woman came up to me and said, are you nada, peggy's friend? she
had heard me say "cayenne," the name of one of peggy's kids, and
earlier that day she had given peggy a massage, and peggy had left
her purse in her car, so she said, come on, i'll give you a ride up there
        so into the forest, now so snowy, where i found at peggy's house
a birthday celebration! lots of great food with garlic and tall white
candles and kids running around and interesting people drunk on
champagne and birthday cake. most of these people are parents, so
they talked a great deal of education, and of course i piped up, that
being one of the few subjects i really feel i can discourse on, and
they sort of invited me to live here and teach their children. hmmm.
interesting. another colored rope.
        so gary gary how are you, are you ok, of course not, i can't imag-
ine that you feel ok, as for me what do i feel many things, certainly
a kind of quiet anguish. and wondering what i can do for you that's
ok to do for you that isn't patronizing that is honest that demon-
strates that isn't hurtful. i hear the internet connection is not so good
here but please do respond today if you can and i will try to respond
in turn.

here are my i ching readings, which i'll discuss with you later at greater length:

yesterday: CONFLICT changing to STANDSTILL

today: COURTSHIP (with a warning to tarry) (i can't tell you how many times i got that hexagram) changing to PREPONDER-ANCE OF THE GREAT (which indicates big crisis and transition, often undertaken alone)

talk to me.

nada

∞

From: Gary
Date: December 28
Subject: Sunday

White devastation, translucent emptiness, black sorrow, orange anger, pink mistrust, cobalt blue resentment, each emotion a color, each color like the Alien in the film of the same name, its tentacles curling through the 40 feet or so of intestines, secreting & spewing liquids further & deeper into the body, via veins, nerve endings, my whole being as though raging flame & all this liquid like crude oil, producing itself unendingly

I can't write about this well I realize, only bad writing feels right, everything inside me bad, putrid, decaying, twisted beyond recognition

C— says, today, she doesn't think we'll ever be lovers again, she's too resentful, too hurt, too angry, & I couldn't bring up, didn't have inside, anything to change that, to offer, I feel the same way, I feel what she must have felt, I mean I know now what I did to her, I betrayed her, shoved her aside, utterly lost respect for her feelings, for her life, for the fact of her life, that she, too, is human, or anyway, this is feeling it may not be truth but it's feeling what I do feel

We're fragile beings, all of us, & as strong as intimacy makes us, as strong as any genuine human connection makes us, to have it sev-ered, changed, is disastrous, can be disastrous, & this meeting has been a disaster, for me if not for you

This is honesty not hatred, in the way your telling me I didn't do it for you wasn't spoken out of hate but from your very real feelings being there, and I need, I feel we need, nada, now, closure, an ending to this, you had yours, you were able to do that, your insides simply closed to me, I was there & you shut, which is not a judgment of you but a fact, & i need to shut myself to you, do you understand, I hope you can, I mean I really hope you can understand

Understanding wasn't what I wanted, Nada, I wanted everything you seemed to be, I was, oh, my baby, I was so in love with you, I don't know if you realize how much, I don't think you do, your appearance didn't matter to me, it really didn't, what mattered was that I never felt closer to another human being, to a woman, this was really what meant anything, this was "meaning" for me, & I wanted you, whoever you were, whoever the you was who was writing to me like that, who was connected with me like that, I just wanted you, period, end of sentence, would have wanted you no matter how you looked, whether you had hair or not, I was so deeply in love with you, moved by you, taken with you

I can't believe you thought because you were checking other men out while with me that it wouldn't work, god, you know, that kind of attraction and desire never ceases, it's nothing to feel guilty about, it's human nature, monogamy is I don't think natural, but willed, it's being devoted, devoted to someone you love, whose soul you find you can swim in, how often does that happen

I'm sorry you felt you couldn't love me, we have such different sexualities I think, I already worshipped you and would have continued to, because you, your body, you, your body is and is not all of you, I felt desire for you, for your body, wanted to kiss you, hold you, touch you, explore you, because I loved you, because I already loved you, because you were really & truly my desire, what my whole being had always longed for, you were in no uncertain terms, my love

But there's no convincing you, as convincing even as these words should have been

> I wanna go back to you
> & from you
> to my heart. You going too? ... Will me with you.

You couldn't do that, you do believe in that lack between us, and though you did wish, you never fully decided, & your will withered

And now I really have no choice but to accept, to accept what happened as something that happened, that everyone involved got hurt by it, maybe you didn't get hurt but you didn't get what you wanted either, and you lost me, I mean you've lost me, this voice you had, which came to exist for you, and it doesn't matter whether or not I disappear, you already lost me, couldn't find me within yourself anymore, what had been mental what had been real you could no longer access being around me through lack of physical desire, I didn't desire you physically when we first met you know, but I said nothing, nada, nothing, because I knew it was like climbing out of a spaceship onto another planet & didn't trust any of those first impressions, I simply didn't RECOGNIZE you there, as how could I, you were unfamiliar, and I think you found me unfamiliar, your descriptions of me were of someone trying to situate me, you couldn't find me, & that's how I felt too but I assumed that would take time, and I don't know, your telling me "it's not working for me" half an hour after meeting me just completely disoriented me as though I wasn't already disoriented

Everyone I've talked with & asked about this was surprised, especially by how swift it was, Alan never had an experience like this himself, he said "something really must have been amiss— scary," & I feel that too, I do, and Laurie, Rebecca & Ange all said not all honesty has to be expressed, I don't know if I believe that, but Rebecca was smartest, she said, we all have doubts, other longings, push-pull feelings, always, and this is something that goes on in the internal monologue, you can never escape that, I don't know if you'd agree with that, I don't know, oh

I don't know whether to say these things to you now, when you return from woodstock, or not at all, whether to just admit you're not ready for this, you may never be ready for this, you need Johnny Depp and let you find him, sure, it's not something I can control, and it's not something anyway I wanted to control, I felt equal with you, I felt I'd met my mate, my match, and I suppose I have to admit, to conclude, to draw to conclusion, that, we feel desire so differently, or understand it differently, so my feelings are that, okay, Nada, maybe you were right, we aren't meant for each other, and we should move on, my shiva, and move on

I really do wish the best for you, that's such an ugly cliché, but no uglier than we can still be friends, all of the clichés are ugly, I thought we were above them, apparently not, so, wow, I can't be with you anymore, this whole thing hurts me too much, and worse, the woman I thought I knew I realize, realized, I didn't know, wasn't you, you were that woman, there, who said she couldn't love me, O my love, my love, that was you, I was writing to someone else, someone vanished, destroyed, & now forever absent

I don't know what to expect in the future, either from my own head & heart & soul or from yours, "play it by ear," is what you said, though, do you hear me, anymore, do you

hear

me? ohhhh,

I don't know, I don't know if you really do

take care of yourself

don't resign yourself to mediocrity

don't fear further intimacy with others

be always alive & awake my love

& someday your body will let you have what your mind heart & soul know you really do want

& if nothing else,

peace,

Gary

∞

From: Gary
Date: December 29
Subject: Today's

Oh, Nada, you're not going to believe this, but I'm not in the same mental space I was in yesterday. Meaning, I no longer feel the need to distance myself, not here anyway, from you. Can you understand? There's kind of a whole explanation I need to give you.

Last night I went out with Ange & Laurie, I was so down, couldn't imagine myself ever getting over this, the loss of what I took this all for, what I had wanted, what you seemed to promise, what our relationship seemed to promise. I'm still sad about that, and still disappointed with you for deciding so quickly, but I no longer feel devastated by it. Maybe it was watching *Celebrity* (which you really should go see); it did help to see people behaving, well, I'll just let you see it. It was also, you won't believe this, but sitting in Telephone after the movie (Telephone's a bar you'll get to know well if you move to New York) I swear to you your exact double walked in. I literally thought it was you, and started following "you" to the back of the bar, but then saw, "Oh, no, she's a lot taller." Exactly the same face, same hair, even seemingly the same amount of makeup as you (no, not "too much.")

I sort of obsessed on her a bit. Kept staring. But, what happened inside me was interesting. All of my desire for you, for you as who you are, or I should at this point say were, made manifest, here, oh, wow, it just faded away, I mean, I could feel that all draining from me. And I just got sort of interested in her as not even you. I mean, just this woman in a bar. & felt totally attracted to her, desirous, wanted her. But "her" I realized, I mean the crucial part of this, she wasn't you. I knew that & my body knew that. I mean, I knew that.

It was, as odd as this sounds, a great relief. I almost walked up to her and asked for her phone number. I would have if I hadn't been there with Ange & Laurie. It's obvious she goes to that bar a lot (she seemed to know a lot of people there), so, I sort of thought: "Hmmm. I'll get a great haircut, get some rest, maybe come back some day, whatever." Not really intensely needing, ever, to actually do that, but sort of vaguely fantasizing about that.

What I really felt, sitting there, was how deeply, bodily inscribed C— is in me. It depressed me, it really saddened me, because yesterday she'd told me she didn't think she could forgive me, and as I said in yesterday's e-mail, I didn't have the emotional energy to try to convince her I really really do love her, want her, and had fallen in love with an illusion (you) in large part because (a) I couldn't really allow myself I think to be so sexually satisfied, so emotionally satisfied (guilt?) and (b) I think I saw in you, projected into you, parts of both D— and my wife, what I really loved about both of them, and had constructed this woman who was part you, part D— and part my wife, and of course, as we both did, that utterly beautiful fantasy of the relationship you & I might have had ... But, stripped of that illusion, well, I realized, yeah, it begins with the physical, and the truth is, no one will ever match C—, will match what she does to me emotionally & physically.

So, after leaving the bar, taking the N Train to Brooklyn, I called her (she's not moving back in with her husband until Thursday), and we talked, and I discovered amazing, just amazing things about her that she'd never told me, the most shocking to me (as something she'd neglected to tell me) being that she had been married in Venezuela for a year & a half, & then divorced. Well, and she had also been a sculptor, something she never fucking told me! Can you believe that? And a fairly successful one. She had put this on the back burner after moving to the U.S., and I think felt so bad about having lost that, or not feeling able to do it so far here, and wants to keep doing it, find a situation in which she can return again to it. Anyway, Nada, I just told her, I told her how much I loved her, how bad I wanted her, that I'd made a big mistake to have gotten as involved with you as I had, and just cast her aside like that. And you know what? Hours into the conversation, I just said: "Go into your bedroom & take off your clothes" ... & we were back where we'd been before I met you. She's going to move to NYC as soon as she gets her citizenship & has saved a little money, probably late spring. In the meantime, she's going to fly up to visit me.

This morning on the train, I thought of us, you & me, I thought, we could continue writing, continue to deal with the emotional fall-out of all of this, write each other no less intensely but not so frequently, since you won't any longer be compelled to stay up for my messages, not equating them any longer with sexual/relationship fantasy.

How do you feel about this? Are you getting your e-mail at Peggy's? How come you haven't e-mailed me yet? I think I know why, whether or not you got yesterday's e-mail, you need & want distance from me.

Anyway. Tell me, Nada, what you think, feel & believe,
Much love,
Gary

∞

From: nada
Date: December 29
Subject: Re: Today's

gary i can't tell you how ecstatic this e-mail makes me. i'm going to have to try to transmit that ecstasy in this response. my anyway feeling is that look, we're going to have a happy ending after all, and everything will be "all right in the end" as i declared

> I'm still sad about that, and still disappointed with
> you for deciding so quickly, but I no longer feel
> devastated by it.

gooooood. but listen it wasn't a "decision." it wasn't mental, it was elemental and basic physical/intuitive knowledge. not calculated and not, i think, a neurotic fear of love, not that i'd put such a thing past me, but because i came to you really with the intention of devotion and surrender ... and when that didn't happen, how can i describe the fissure in myself, the coldness and like i said, anguish ... if you can help me release that i will love you even more

> All of my desire for you, for you as who you are,
> or I should at this point say were, made manifest,
> here, oh, wow, it just faded away, I mean, I
> could feel that all draining from me.

in a way good. in a way my girl-ego doesn't totally like this (not really a valid thing to say but what the hell)

> I thought, we could continue writing, continue
> to deal with the emotional fallout of all of this,
> write each other no less intensely but not so
> frequently

yes please leave me what's left of my hair and, well, we need to discuss this, but what if i did live in the neighborhood? i'm so like, anything's possible now, i think i have to do one of those star charts that tells you the best place in the world to be.

>How come you haven't e-mailed me? I think I
>know why, you need & want distance from me.

i tried to e-mail you but couldn't connect, and only want distance if that's what will be non-destructive. i never wanted anything
destructive to come of this. you have given me so much.

>Anyway. Tell me, Nada, what you think, feel &
>believe,

ok i told you. and i will stay here a little while if there's anything
you want to respond to.

you know, richard, peggy's husband, does internet-related work,
and he's fascinated by the aquarian-age possibilities of this medium,
this assisted universal mind, and he's also fascinated by our relationship, as evidence of where the world is moving

what we are doing is so much in history, utterly relevant and ...
am i being too self-serious?

gary i still feel so connected to you it still aches

embodiment was not successful, i don't say what i just said to
lead you on, please never accuse me of that, not my intention ever

but i refuse to deny my feelings

∞

From: Gary
Date: December 30
Subject: today's bibliomancy for Nada

New Year

With ample focus, light,
A masterpiece
Poetic in its architectural finesse
Grows probable
As the infinity of first person plural
Trembling in our hearts.

Verbs imbued with every flavor
That created them
Against the press of things,
Bless ritual with belief in brilliance
That chastens each discovery
Of new color waiting for its name.

> —Sheila E. Murphy
> (from a card received this morning)

∞

[*The following back and forth e-mail exchange occurred February 14–15th, but because it details what happened on the evening of December 30th after the above e-mail and Nada's return from Woodstock to NYC, we decided to place it here.*]

> Okay. I do remember you were smiling when you
> first came down the hallway from annie's apartment
> to meet me, and that it was a kind of coy smile. But, I
> didn't really think much more than that. Remember,
> even after our first attempt at kissing, four nights
> before that, you still wrapped your arm in mine.

felt connected. liked you. even though you freaked me out and the kiss was so ugh. i mean wasn't it ugh for you? our energies were just NOT intersecting.

> Anyway, I thought, when the movie was sold out, oh
> no, she's not gonna wanna sit around and talk, it might
> make her uncomfortable.

little did you know

> I thought it would be better to have a movie or
> something to talk about. So, actually, I was feeling
> fairly bad at that point, and kind of distressed.

i noticed that and it made me feel even more empowered.

>When you said, oh let's just go to a café or
>something, I thought you meant to find a paper
>and see what else was playing we could see.

oh no no
i just wanted to be with you

>Finding Café Gray Dog was kind of, I remember, it
>took a long time. And, okay, I remember thinking,
>"well, I wonder if this will be okay, I hope I'll behave,
>I don't wanna be a bitter person around her, can I be
>nice?" I didn't feel bitter, but I did feel dejected and
>still very sad, and actually in disbelief. You have to
>understand, there were still moments, a lot of them,
>where I just kept thinking (not a willed thought, either,
>or it didn't feel like it) "but she loves me! I know she does!
>how can she not love me? It's so obvious we're in love!"

really? you were thinking that? not just 20/20 hindsight?
anyway those were my thoughts exactly.
i just had to find the right way to show that to you.
the right moment.

>So, okay. I remember ordering some things and sitting
>down with you. And it was a bit nerve-wracking, but
>I also remember you were kinda moving in your seat a bit,

and what does that mean, you think?

>singing along with things. No, that came later. I think
>you were staring at me. I don't have any idea what we
>talked about at first.

well i remember we talked about wanting to read the journal of
the guy next to us. i talked about the couple to my right. but what
else did we talk about? i don't remember either—isn't that funny?

but i mean i didn't feel awkward. i felt determined. to undo what i'd done.

> I think very early on I asked you if you were okay
> because you had a kind of look, and you said, "Mmm,
> well, I don't know, I think I might have blown it,"
> and right then, I knew, well FINALLY ... !

ok, what i wanna know is, did anything happen to you, what happened to you emotionally/physically at the moment i said this. were you shocked? amazed? relieved? or did you just get self-protective?

> Although I may not be able to remember exactly what
> we said after that, I do remember immediately switching
> into a kind of protective mode, and thoughts were
> beginning to race around in my brain, like, will she still
> sleep with me even though I'm back "with" C—? I
> was, I'm embarrassed to admit, sort of scheming to find
> ways of verbally justifying why that would be "okay" for
> us to do. "C— did say we could sleep with other
> people," I wanted to tell you, but I don't think I did,
> not that night anyway

my feeling was at that moment that i knew there was no way that you and she could have had the kind of symbiosis that we have, great sex or no. that knowledge made me very confident, and i had no qualms about coming on to another dame's guy because basically i knew you were my guy anyway, you'd already told me a million times even before we met each other physically. was i overconfident?

> I remember you saying that I looked good with my haircut.

seduction

> I remember you singing along to Portishead and
> thinking oh oh oh she is just too beautiful, why is she

>making me feel like this?

seduction
oh and you know i really like that you found me too beautiful
that's cool with me

>What fool reason did we come up with to hold hands?
>Were we comparing digits? I suspect we might have been.

no no no. i reached out for your hand, there was no game at all,
no reason coming from me but ...
seduction

>But, I also remember playing it kind of cool,

oh nuh uh not even   .
you were totally under my spell ha ha
you thought you could get me under yours before but you couldn't
it had to come from me

>At one point I had an angry thought, like, Why
>weren't you like this four days ago!

well one reason was you wasn't cute four days ago
plus all them expectations i'm always on about

>and I remember, I do remember a staring contest.
>We stared at each other for a long long time it felt like,
>and I was determined not to turn away, even though
>there were moments I felt very self-conscious.

me too a little, i remember blinking. but i remember the sensation of staring at you completely stirred up my insides. very very
very deep excitement, we were penetrating each other.
gary, how long you think it'll be like that, with us? i mean honestly. it was like that to some degree with a— for years, but with him
it felt (obviously) younger, less mental, tho there was some spiritual
dimension to it. when i'm inside your eyes like that i feel like i'm

probing your brain, that i can massage your little dendrites and feel
the electric shocks coming off them

> And I don't remember how we started kissing,

cupid was behind you, pushing
and aphrodite behind me, pushing

> but I remember how it felt, how I felt wrapped in your
> hair (it was falling around us both), and then, when
> it suddenly dipped into the candle and the really
> frightening FFFFFFFFSHHHHHT!!!

oh yeah wow

> when it caught on fire, and my heart, already racing,
> just stopped. You had it out before I could do anything.
> And I just felt all the sudden so awful, like, Oh god she
> already is so freaked about losing her hair and now I
> accidentally made her burn it, it's worse than dumping
> Indian food on her Bernadette Mayer thesis, oh no no
> no, the poor thing! And that smell, which was immediate
> and overwhelming.
>
> I didn't know what would happen when you came back,
> I thought you would want to go back to Andrea's, to see
> what damage had been done, to repair it if possible
> (like, "how?" i ask myself now), but no, you came back,
> and you weren't even visibly upset, i couldn't believe it,
> you were kind of laughing, and I felt bad laughing,
> but laughed anyway, mainly out of a kind of relief.

and you know what it doesn't even show
yeah i was laughing
it just seemed like more theater on top of theater
i was kind of thinking at one point that i should just shave my head
then maybe i could've been a full-time butoh dancer or something

>And, though the smell was so overwhelming, I think we
>just started kissing again,

what you mean you woulda stopped because of that smell??
and don't you realize that now every time you smell burnt hair
that night will flood back to you? it was a way of tattooing it in our
memories.

>and we sort of stayed there for a while, I think, until it
>looked like they were closing up. I remember gathering
>all of my courage, I didn't want to suggest something
>you didn't want to do, I didn't want to be rejected
>again, or held at bay, but I just thought, You have to ask
>Nada over, you have no idea if she even wants to, it
>can't be unspoken, you have to ask, you have to ask.
>That was the hardest thing I had to do. It was brave
>of me, don't you think?

yes, i guess so, but it wasn't like i wasn't giving you the world's
most obvious signs that i was willing. let's count 'em: seat-squirming,
singing, staring, hand-holding, swooning, kissing, catching on fire.
oh plus telling you i felt like i'd blown it. i think those things must've
been fairly encouraging, so no, i'm not gonna give you any medal of
bravery here, sorry.

>"Would you like to meet Lee Ann's cats?" Coy as it was
>a thing to say, because I didn't want to like, assume
>we were going back there to crawl in bed together.

even after all that?
you practice a lot of mental restraint sometimes don't you

>I remember when we got in to Lee Ann's, the cats were
>there and you talked to them
>
>& I remember in her bathroom looking at the film-strip
>dress, and I think we kissed at one point in the hallway

i remember looking at lee ann's books
and at one point finding that long sex poem she wrote, and you
reading it over my shoulder
and i suddenly felt shy in a really good expectant sweetly
desirous way

>i remember when you said something about "feel
>my skin," and i think that was when i knew, okay, this
>is totally okay, she really does want this

i think i may actually have been getting a little impatient
like why is he so reticent???

>i remember your groovy underwear, they kinda
>looked like antique swimming bottoms sort of,
>they were black. i don't think your bra was black,
>though, wasn't it kind of dark purple?

hmm, don't think so. are you sure it wasn't black? in your poem
it was black!
my bras are either black, beige or mauve. not dark purple. no
wait i do have a dark purple one but i didn't bring it with me.

>oh, i'm not sure now. but i remember kind of a fear
>before i started licking you, like, Uh oh am i going to
>like how she tastes? but i did, and you responded sweetly

oh gary come over
i know i taste good
i just tasted

∞

[Written collaboratively in a notebook, December 30.]

consummation

fake rain sound
all almond & gold
the hissing of mushrooms
in the forest of spiders:

sympathetic movement
(projected from dancer)
+ vanilla (my favorite
patch)

countless nights in that
despair futon, i thought
life a daily swamp
a gathering of ends

into this end:
the tang of your
shoulder blade at
my tongue

i still don't think you're
pretty. am i growing up?
with your finger in your
mouth, yes.

leaning towards, i immolate
or at least spark
the sound of hair burning
like radiator's pop

let's get camellias—it's
the perfect bathtub
                    then let go me
so i can get to the store

"... and i am a japanophile, in some ways almost japanese at this point ..."

"i had this feeling, gary, looking at your picture, which is kind of indistinct and underexposed, that you look, what, easily overwhelmed, or swept away ..."

"... I don't know how you deal with loneliness in Tokyo, I don't know if loneliness in Tokyo is the same thing as loneliness in New York ..."

"i can't look at your photo for a long time, not because of any judgment of it, but because the solid proof of your embodiment scares me, or embarrasses me, or something. or it could just be your glazed, drunken eyes."

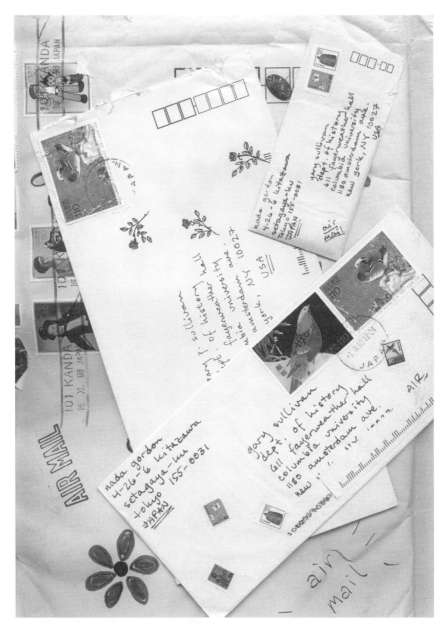

"My letters & your answers, having risen out of obscurity
like a column of air in the larynx, now sleep
folded in a book of poetry ..."

November 6 '98

Dear Nada

I'm listening to your tape, which just arrived. There's some great stuff on it — I remember from one of your performances that you had a beautiful & natural singing voice... and here you modulate between an almost-Liz Phair blasé (sp.?) to, well, really lovely singing. Now, I'm hearing what must be your Beckett versions... "white... white...," So, you must tell me about making this tape... where were you, yes, I think you were in Japan by this time...

The stickers are hilarious, self portrait of the poet as various members of the Spice Girls:

Baby Nada
Sporty Nada
Ginger Nada
Posh Nada
Scary Nada

(as your self-appointed manager I expect 20%) Okay, I just put on Liz Phair — I had no choice, and, yeah, you know, it's uncanny, you do sound remarkably like her. Do you know her Exile in Guyville? A song-for-song response to the Stones' Exile on Mainstreet. You'd love her. I have no hilarious Spice Girls photos, but, okay, I do have a very "Jonathan Richman" picture I can send you. It was taken on Labor Day weekend this year (the camera is stuck in '94). I promised you books, so here's a couple, as well as an article (it's not so swell, but...), and a bunch of cartoons.

Confused,
Unhappy, Sallow Spice

Yesterday after work, I went down Broadway 6 blocks & met my friend Charles, in from Tucson (we met in Minneapolis)... well, lo; & behold, he happened to be at Ray DiPalma's house, so I got the treat of meeting him — I actually like his work best of all the east coast language writers... he looks like an out of shape Sean Connery. Tomorrow, me & Anze Zdinko are gonna get together for a trip to Metro Comics. She e-mailed to complain that no one tells her anything interesting... so, because she's fascinated by rhyme, I wrote her a long e-mail comparing rhyme in poetry to I–IV–V in music, western music, I told her that what killed the renaissance in music was the keyboard, which you probably know, flatters notes as it ascends. The keyboard octave is not the octave you get with other instruments because of how overtones behave. (They're sharp.) So, Bach's structures, which rely heavily on I–IV–V, were developed to grapple with this. Anyway, rhyme & I–IV–V seem analogous, so I wrote her why I thought so, & then she was happy I guess, and said "take me to the comic book store!" This would be the beginning of a wonderfully disastrous love affair were it not for the fact that she's happily married & neither of us is attracted to each other. Anyway, she's been reading & writing about Ann Bradstreet & so I hope to ask her a lot of annoying questions & get the scoop. I hope all is well with you, Nada. I'm okay, tho it's very very cold tonight...

Yours, Gary

"the photos of me lie spread out on your filthy rug staring at the under-side of your cock and your fingers moving around it, your balls con-tracted in imagination."

*"To drink the look/ & twinkle,
to seep in/ there along with
the stare of/ attention, fanning
there, the two/ minds that gaze ..."*

3

how come, gary,
you dislike asia?
(kiss me) of all
the parts of the
world i've been to i
like asia best (kiss me),
better than europe or
america, north or south, tho
i've never even been to
south america. (kiss me)
hey, mexico is north
america, why is that hard to
conceptualize? anyway i like
asia for its aesthetics and its
temperament, i think. tho there
were some times i asked myself, why
didn't i choose to work in italy or
brasil? or portugal, perhaps? (kiss me.
i'm a fox. kiss me). i told you i helped
to direct a school musical, right? the
♪ pajama game ("i don't wanna talk small
♪ talk/now that i'm alone with you/ i don't wanna
♪ talk small talk/i've got something better/ for
your lips/to do/and that takes no talk/at
all) (inner meaning: kiss me). or ("let's not talk of
the weather/ or the fashions for the fall mi")
but i digress. i notice that when given a
reading task students start out silently
absorbed, then move into communication,
discussing meaning. Today Akiko is wearing
fishnet stockings. i'm wearing a slightly
broken (the strap part) amethyst pendant i
touch for power, but my eyelids are still falling
down. oh sleepy bored (kiss me awake).

THE NEW LIFE
©1999 BY GARY SULLIVAN
Dear Nada, What's poetry but the world's ruin? Aim-less as a red-hot iron bar. I think I love you... phe-nomenon? Redaction? I feel uneasy & open bo
Writing collapses the greatest of distances... this, I realized, being its primary measure of worth
Using some of my favorite poets as models— di Prima, Dante, Bernadette Mayer, Sappho, Sei Shonagon, John Wieners, bp nichol, sheila Murphy, Philip Whalen, etc.— I began writing letter-poems
WELLLL... IT'S NOT RILLY YER BEST WORK... IT'S OK FOR WHAT IT IS...
My poet-friends weren't all that enthusiastic...
dear gary~ relevancy is life (think of DNA)...i'd even study geometry if i knew it would get me what? food? o, i'd rather have a poem under my pillow than an
The truth was my hyper-critical poet-friends were boring compared to Nada, who was now sending me like 10-20 pages of writing a day, filled with poems, memories, odd lists, opinions & so on
That she lived in Tokyo & I in Brooklyn intensified our relationship—it was the first time I really felt I was not only making language live, but living in language... (TO BE CONTINUED)
NADA — IF THE WORLD EXISTS I'M NOT SURE CONTINUITY CAN, CAN THE SPACE BETWEEN INCIDENTS BE DESCRIBED? THESE WORDS? I LIKE THAT "HEART" IS THE ANAGRAM OF "EARTH," AT LEAST IT'S SOMETHING I CAN MAKE PEACE WITH...

THE ZINC BAR
90 W. HOUSTON

CORRESPONDENCE
THE POETICS OF INTIMACY

SUN. JULY 18
7:00PM $3.00

nada GORdon + GarySullivan

"But let's say I've taken you, in arms as thin as Palatino ..."

"When you write to me, everyone else sleeps, when I write to you they open their eyes in the snow ..."

JANUARY

From: Gary
Date: January 4
Subject: You're on a plane ...

as I write this, thousands of miles above the Pacific, curled in your seat, perhaps reading, maybe writing, but definitely thinking, hearing that hiss of constant oxygen recirculating through the plane, feeling it dip & rise, feeling yourself dip & rise riding the air currents

It's hard to eat today, I've mostly eaten carrots, a few cookies, a bagel, tried to take pleasure in these, but it's true, my body knows, Nada, you're gone, not present at the moment, & the longing's tied my stomach up in knots. Is it just that I got no sleep last night? Or is it love, & feeling love, wanting to express it, more than wanting, but having, deep within me, this very real sense of urgency whenever I think of you. Which is, you know, always.

Oh, the practical e-mails will come, some even this week, but today, Monday, there's something about the knowledge of you in the air, flying off to where I first met you, there, and "here," where you'll be again soon. It doesn't sadden me. What is it that I feel? Again, urgency, that's the best way to put it, my stomach feels hot, somewhat twisted up, my arms shake a little & my fingers clench

When I woke up this morning it was still dark, the room this wonderful sort of purplish blue, the sun not yet up. I tried to remember what it was like, waking up with you. I remembered everything, or everything I remember, about being with you. Mostly how it felt to be in each other's presence, especially after we'd grown more comfortable together. Do you know what it was like, just lying there with you, knowing your heart was beating, that you were breathing, and your mind active, & O, I just wanted to eat you up. I wanted to give you everything.

I love you beyond what I imagined I was capable of. Write me,

& let me know you made it there okay.
　　Much more to come,
　　Love,
　　Gary

∞

From:　　nada
Date:　　January 5
Subject:　written on the plane

__illuminated__

right now sunrise
　　　　is the most incredibly
orange spanch, and
　　　　　　civilization a mantle
　　　　　　　　of electricity. love's blind
　　　but not to all this light
or that spanch infecting
　　　　　the sky i travel in.
　　　　　　　(the orange now
　　　　　　even more orange, like
　　　　　　those italian or are they
FEARFEARFEARFEARFEARFEARFEAR ***spanish blood oranges, at*** FEARFEARFEARFE

have you thought what we're embarking on? are ***the cloud center an*** you ready? you seem ready as for me i'm

not ready , but doing it anyway as i must and as ***impossibly orange sun*** i promised. if i don't i may as well

crawl into a hole and whimper ... until the end. ***like a workfare vest)*** what am i afraid of, afraid of not being

nice to you, afraid that you want to believe in love so desperately you project it on me tho as an object i am not deserving basi-

cally wicked, shallow, closed, cold, and otherwise soulless: but i don't really believe. it's just a fear in forest of fears. i'm afraid of

ever betraying you. that crumple and raging i never want to see, never want to feel that blank anxiety. if we ever end let us end

as a softish waving. i'm afraid our bodies may distract us from our art. i'm afraid of growing old and with a tooth sitting in a room

alone and poor, my eyes bulging at the wall.

　　　　　　　but this, gary, this ...

　　this is the arc
　　　　of light that holds our
　　　　　　minds within our bodies
but also sends them shooting out
　　　　　to make point-to-point
　　　　　　　connections. without you
　　　　　　　what's my fleeting beauty worth?

we stroked the smalls of each other's
backs in gasping delight at sunrise
in brooklyn.   this is a new day,
and we are breathing
in it, the sun
now having moved out of

orange to
blinding, blinding

WHITE

∞

From: Gary
Date: January 5
Subject: 1/5

Nada,
        my letters & your answers, having risen out of obscurity
like a column of air in the larynx, now sleep
folded in a book of poetry, some phantom
no less than human flesh
but beside it, as beside your glans the reddest flower
would look as gray as asphalt.
                            It's the book I open now, my
fingers blackened by our consonants, the present
devoured by our past, though I do think it's funny
you asked me to send you
short lines,
tightly
inhabitable, when
the camellia is more like what I am
& didn't you say you wanted me, do I have to make you
promise not to forget
we took our clothes off? Wake up your hands
my love, you are hard
to love. As hard, at least, as this pillow.

                                                    Wake up
I want to tell you something. Well, any-
thing, just so long it's particular, & real. Descriptions
of burnt matches in the cherrywood incense boat, banal
pan across the tiny landscape of my nighttable
orange paperback copy of Browning's *Aurora Leigh*
mostly empty bottle of Brooklyn Brown Ale, its gold & chocolate
label peeled off, wedge of half-eaten bagel in paper wrapper
your letters, photos & poems on the rug beside the bed
grains of sand, glass & paper bits everywhere
my cream colored phone, its cord trailing off into the other room
where Chris plays George Harrison's "Dark Horse"
which I'll suffer knowing it's temporary
life's temporary too if you look at it like that
I prefer not to, I guess, like how I prefer
companionship, long romance, someone in particular to see
not merely memory.
                    Memory has nowhere to go. & how long
can I pour my heart out
while my hands shake, I know this is just a poem, but why
won't you say anything, tonight I feel
swindled by words, like all our kisses replaced by my fist.
I want what I write to make you wet between your legs.
I don't want to scour the dictionary
to find it. I want you here
in this poem, like the Indian on the American Spirit pack
like Elizabeth on the cover of her book
I am 36 years old, I can't
look out the window from where I'm sitting. I can
reach the Mezcal D— brought me back from Mexico
I can see the collage-poem C— sent me when I left her
for you, I can line up all the photographs of you
on the filthy rug & beat off, but my hands are cold & dry
it'd be barely tolerable & would go by too fast
& when it was over I'd still be here & you'd be there
"in my head
            & on my page"
but what would I do with my cum-filled hand, not to mention

all my inexhaustible fears?
                           A gust of wind sets off a car alarm
4 stories below on 6th Avenue, luck is
always for tomorrow, luck is for voyagers, & all the grass
dies
in front of us. Everyone reading this poem will roll their eyes
but you.
          So?
               What am I supposed to concentrate on now.
Drunkenness. Empty stomach. Some life to come.
I'm not consoled by this. It is a
                      goddamn
                      fucking
                      shame
                      to be
                      as indifferent as the sea,
                      to know love
as the end of all our imagining. There's always something
to see, feel & smell. But I loved you as well
as you loved me.
                  Life without love is unimaginable.
                  Life in the movies is too clear.
                  Life bores men who think all morning.
                  Love means you never stop staring
                  at me, no matter how many girls
                  I spent adoring, & that I know who we are
                  when the weather's out of hand.
                                  This book
a paper boat, filled with poems
increasingly specific.
                      Outside, it's twenty degrees, inside
maybe 40. That's not specific enough, your nipples
as red as raspberries, that's closer
but obviously drunken sentiment, your pubic hair not sorrel
as much as I like saying the word, your cunt sweet
but who among your lovers hasn't told you as much
I loved how you shivered against the palm of my hand
I want to smoke a cigarette but I don't

I want my tongue inside you when I'm saying this
but it's not specific enough, it's just
that I can't avoid it, I'm freezing, the radiator
hissed off hours ago, Chris paces the living room
no sound but some distant car alarm outside, blocks away
this isn't a good poem the beer sits heavy in my belly
I want to feel your weight on me, my cock's unreal in my hand
without you though the negatives disperse
my arms will fold when I'm done with this but no one will care
but you, no one will see me from this angle but you
& as morning's early business opens
we again will open, I will open, & will think of you
open, having opened, my only lover,

Gary

∞

From: nada
Date: January 5
Subject: what is a man?

(gary, a swallowing thing that gazes)

what is a man
an extension of skin
with hair in the bed
that reeks of difference

what is a man
but a swallowing thing
that gazes,
making decisions

he pulls back the curtain
to reveal a shivering/ sparrow's
tiny carnelian/ legs

at the end of the day
there is always energy
like a boomerang.

tell that to fernando
the butterfly
he knows all about rapture

∞

From: nada
Date: January 5
Subject: what is a woman?

what is a woman? a kind
of cock holder or sometimes
a sea urchin, a woman
is a blast of sea water
trickling out the mouth
of her lover, and in the
center of the heat
there is a blue flame
called sympathy. "sympathy"
is what lights up the
street that you walk
in, thinking of your cock
being held. being. held.
what is a woman but
a kind of internal refrain
constantly hummed so you
know you're alert so what
is a woman, who inscribes
her organs for you
can only be this peculiar
abalone, the interior
shell nacreous but only
when you pry it.

∞

From: Gary
Date: January 6
Subject: 1/6

Dear Nada,

> "The key to thinking is
> words. Words unlock the brain
> so you can see."
>   —Curtis Faville

        Love, if it's anything
other than illusion of mind, is like
learning to read. My mouth is open, I'm naked & unashamed
though clumsy.
    The moon will also go down.
          Here in a word is the
window through which I see it. Meanwhile,
Chris plays the Buzzcocks in the living room, I type this letter to you
letter by letter,
    it seems silly, I've already forgotten
what it was supposed to be about,
        I'm non-existent. Everything is.
Chris disagrees. One of us
can't be wrong.
    Still, if there's a land which is the mind
love's more than the atoms of dust which populate it.
         Do you
hear me? The faucet dripping
reminds me of you. Like you, I can't hear
it from here.
    I wish I wasn't so lazy, I wish I had money, or
could quote Lorca from memory:

> "*Como las ondas concentricas*
> *sobre el agua,*
> *asi en mi corazon*
> *tus palabras.*"

The average reader won't bother to look it up.
Because there's a sense in which things are
as we say they are.
I would like to eat you. "Like
a white wall. Movie cream."
Look at your little finger, the emptiness
of it's like this letter once I know it's in your hands.

This poem
isn't working is it, I sat through too much garbage
at the Church, & only the thought of you unzipping your Gene
Simmons boots
& lying back on your futon
will inspire me tonight. Will you? If I write you
really wet porno?

"When wind comes, petals lightly
separate the overlay,
cream folded against cream."

I know
you like subtlety. Pure moments
carried to a poised light patiently in love.

Someone
writes you a letter.
He's kind of a junkie parrot
the kind who'd rather run his hand
down your leg than write you a sonnet, are you scared?

He'll still
write you, if writing means your head on his shoulder
w/his tiny fingers between your legs.

He/I wants
that you/she has her lover (him ((me))).

Was fucking you
an avoidance of words? "Words" meaning
your clit might as well live
at the bottom of the deepest part
of the ocean.

I'm not sure if porno can be written by a person.
Writing you, I begin to float.
I'm failing.

Sexuality expressed within, not by,
the writing.
Writing = riding.
I would do anything
to fuck you again
like the only person I'll ever fuck again, the written word
is porno cuz any written word is re-experiencable
there's a faithfulness to porno,
you have to be
faithful to it.
I want my words to open your legs.
I want to see you,
love,
Gary

∞

[*Enclosed in a letter from Nada, early January.*]

gary:

a not-so-secret
secret. sublimely

cat physique
the first night

cats must feel
like what i felt

sublimely
feline. sublimely

felt.

~nada

∞

From: nada
Date: January 8
Subject: music of the spheres

      ring around the orb
      of emotional
      truth: SATURN.
      the night is more
      cold. i prove
      by gesture
      what is hard
      in words.
      or the inverse.
      am i crazy?
      is starlight ludicrous?
      "to meet a llama
      of the opposite sex"
      my orb
      inside your orb;
      yours inside mine.
      you are my
        pupil.

                ∞

From: Gary
Date: January 9
Subject: 1/9

What if all these nouns are stand-ins, losers
The alleged "real world" would
Humiliate, née Weaken
Similarly the belief we had in fabulous threads
& cigarettes, or have
Now that we've kissed each other
& imagine that makes us
What we tell ourselves we'll never be.

Butterglory. Orson Welles. Can of Bud
While you sleep I think of
Tornadoes, piss off everyone important
& flail, but refuse to fail. "You." Only
Words, not even human breath, hey
Ever notice there's always more non-smokers
Than intervals in which to smoke?
It's the world, not me, that's been unfaithful.

To you. & through you back home, stripped
To my underwear & Beny Moré's "Francisco
Guayabal." I admit
I have no ideas about "objects," nor
Hope to. Save you. Where all that passes
Is time, this time might as well be Beny Moré
Any mere speck
In our hands, in which "Beny Moré," etc., depend.

It's always time to go to bed
With you. On Earth
& lying coeval beside you, I see a look
On your face, like
"Let me sit on yours." It's okay if we do it
To Beny Moré, he's as sophisticated as we are
Ourselves, though he's older, dead
Actually. Sleeping, we only pretend to be

Other names. You demand too much from me
For instance grace & incomparable
Beauty, my face frightens you, the roof
Is safer, I should've kissed you
There, where at least the view'd distract.
Four flights above Brooklyn
It doesn't matter the stairwell reeks of mold
They're steps which climb a steeper goal.

∞

From: nada
Date: January 10
Subject: doesn't just ...

doesn't just pop up out of nowhere

seduced by bits, by
gangly blue
utterance, into
these linked heads' pleasant
deforming. if i see your
face every day will i
become a cartoon?

the bird picks bugs
off the rhinoceros.

my chest is open to the
cool air, steaming, even
without you fixedly
staring down. forever
is a glib word but not
without a certain charm
alarm my little body
shivers to (your little
body). as-yet unborn
cats flex their furless
paws in amniotic fluid.
do you know what a
"charm box" is? when i
see you again, i'll tell you

∞

From: Gary
Date: January 10
Subject: Lines written while you sleep

Tires roll wetly through last night's snow I read
"Thank you for bringing your states of mind"
in a book I'll keep in my head like
the winter sky a cloud sunk in the pale urban landscape
it makes me a bit claustrophobic though the light
warms the room which is good cuz the radiator's dead
I open another book & read "Exactly because the air is
made still and heavy by carbons" & slow down I even think
a thought through to its logical conclusion before
closing the book to look out the window & stare
into equally blank sky imagine every human eye awake in New York
the light grows dim snow begins to fall I feel you
turn in your sleep adjust your heartbeat to this
my typing which is anyway all I have of you today whatever
I allow myself to write down, did I
mention how outside people scattered on the street look up
envious of us as I am envious of you your arm-encircled waist
maybe I wish to resemble only my lover's lover
so I write you excessively as he would write to you
"no thoughts future dreams nor even empty after glow now"
I might be dying now but wouldn't even know
it's just winter makes me morbid tho the thought of love keeps
me from pursuing that thought opening another book
"On which the step of that I have denied
Descends in silver to his proper bride"

∞

From: nada
Date: January 11
Subject: internet—a sonnet

internet—a sonnet (after EBB)

when first ye fingers to the keyboard set
to call me in the darkness of my room
and plunged through head and heart, to mourning womb
the language of your love, though we'd not "met"
i heard the hard disk whirring, and a net
of silver fell upon my solo skin.
no, the net protruded from within
for to be caught is something that we let
happen, fate allowing. now i recall
a clumsy sonnet's (written long ago)
entrapment metaphor for love, and all
my teacher said was "leave off old forms, no—
don't write like this," but still, though dumb and small
i offer this to you, so that you'll know.

p.s. i think entrapment comes up as a metaphor in sonnets because
i feel trapped in the form, at least when stuck to as strictly as this.
i've never tried to write them in the bernadette or ted styles tho i
LOVE those poems. rodefer was the teacher. it was before i swerved
into avant-gardism i wrote that older sonnet (not that this one is any
less clumsy), something about running through a maze of love, the
final bad couplet, "although due to my love i'm trapped and mad/ it
is that very madness makes me glad." oh dear.

p.p.s. here's an epigraph from EBB herself:

> (Elizabeth to Robert, on the anniversary of his first
> letter to her, January 10, 1846)

> Shall I tell you?—it seems to me, to myself, that no
> man was ever before to any woman what you are to
> me—the fulness must be in proportion, you know, to the

vacancy ... & only I know what was behind ... the long
wilderness without the footstep ... without the blossoming rose ... and the capacity for happiness, like a black
gaping hole, before this silver flooding.

(i found this after i wrote the "net of silver" line
above)

p.p.p.s. hey did you know these two were into bibliomancy and
oracles too? check out what Robert says:

(Robert to Elizabeth, February 11,1846)

Yesterday morning as I turned to look for a book,
an old fancy seized me to try the "sortes" and dip into
the first page of the first I chanced upon, for my fortune;
I said "what will be the event of my love for Her"—in so
many words—and my book turned out to be—"Cerutti's
Italian Grammar" a propitious source of information..
the best to be hoped, what could it prove but some
assurance that you were in the Dative Case, or I, not in
the ablative absolute? [...] Well, I ventured—and what did
I find? This—which I copy from the book now—"If we
love in the other world as we do in this, I shall love thee
to eternity" = from "Promiscuous Exercises," to be translated into Italian, at the end.

∞

From: nada
Date: January 11
Subject: porno

The leopard comes on stage walking erect to do his strip show. He's
holding his tail in one of his front paws, sniffing it like Bill's cigar. He
has the face of a cartoon leopard, like Tigger, like Tony the Tiger, like
Sher Khan. One notices his mouth, the two puffy whiskered flaps of
his upper "lip", his seductive eyes (see Baudelaire on cats' eyes, lan-

guid and profound, containing the universe). He is swinging his narrow hips side to side, side to side, and lets his tail go too to swing it in the opposite direction, to create momentum. He runs his front paws down the sides of his body—he is beautiful, one wants to wear him. He strokes himself behind his ears, then down over his neck and upper legs, which he then holds out in openness as he sways. Oh. His penis begins to emerge from where it hides inside him. It is pink, glistening. The barbs are not visible. His hips start to go back and forth and around in circles too. He puts his front paws above his head and snaps his equivalent of fingers, then turns around completely to wave his tail sharply back and forth at the audience, his big feline asshole perfectly obvious, and below it two fuzzy golden testicles the women in the audience can barely resist running up to caress.

One actually does—me, I think, and as I do so he turns his head to me in lust and irritation. I hear a low growl in his throat. And as he bends toward me I think, this is the end, I am dead now, but he just nuzzles my neck. I shiver in delight. He feels so warm, and is licking me behind my ear. I have forgotten I am on stage, I am so spellbound, my eyes are closed and I can smell him, sweetly meaty fur and whiff of urine. I run my hands over his variegated coat, the smooth way, and I lose myself ... until I find I have mounted his back, my legs around his haunches, my head just next to his. His whole body is purring me, I almost come. He lies down and encloses me in his front paws. My eyes are still closed as he roughly licks my face and I am slightly sickened by his animal breath but also drugged. I reach down to feel his penis, about which I am curious, as it is so new to me. I start from the tip downwards, it is slimier than a human penis, and slimmer. When I touch it he stretches out all his limbs and starts to shake a little. He bites me lightly on the neck. I move my fingers now from the shaft upwards to the tip. My hand is in excruciating pain from the little barbs, like I had grasped nettles. I howl. Frightened, the leopard gets up and cowers against the red velvet curtain at the back of the stage. I am crestfallen, and frustrated: "what have I done? I've blown it." I lift my skirt, put my hand in to collect some moisture, and hold out my hand to him. He comes slowly towards me, I notice the rolling of his muscles. He sniffs my hand, licks it. Our eyes lock. We are in love.

∞

From: Gary
Date: January 11
Subject: weekend letter

Dear Nada,

it's 11:30 Friday night,

        It snowed tonight, the cars are covered with it, the sidewalks, & the roofs. It's beautiful outside right now, like Minneapolis, I wish I was curled up with a glass of hot apple cider.

    I think only one thought conclusively, I love you, I totally want you Nada Gordon, it's kinda unconscionable, don't you think, like where's my real life, don't I have other things to do but write you, where otherwise might my energy go, I could be working on a new cartoon, getting a better job, I could be picking out my new wardrobe, I could be making new friends, I could be doing anything, but no, no, here I am, I write you because it's the only way I know how to prove my devotion, & it's more than that, I'd rather write you than do anything else, even though I know I'll die someday and you'll die someday, we'll both die, and then where will we be, it doesn't matter, the truth is if we fuck this up we're gonna haunt each other endlessly, do you want that, can you live with that, I can't, I love your friends for telling you this is It, I wish my friends were so loving, I wish my friends were equally generous, I wish my friends could see, oh you never told me by the way, what does Andrea think of this, does she think it's true love does she think it's viable does she think you're crazy & irresponsible, I'm tired & I want you to hold me, how come you're not here & holding me, how come I'm alone when I know who you are, when I know you exist, how come we're apart, it isn't fair, it isn't, we're not supposed to be apart, isn't that obvious, don't answer that with reason, it won't work, my whole being won't be swayed by reason, every cell in my body knows you're out there, knows you've been here, what are you waiting for, sideburns? Less furrowed brow-on-a-man? You want better shoulders than these, these are mine, my love, meaning they're yours, do you really imagine better shoulders will hold you, do you really imagine any other man writing you like this, do you imagine any other voice in your ear but mine, or any in mine but yours, will you ever be able to caress other legs but mine & imagine you're loved, imagine you love, o I don't care who else you ever see, I don't care who you flirt with, I know I've ruined you, spoiled you, & will continue to, will love you more intensely than any future suitor, give it up, it's hopeless, even this letter is only the beginning, is nothing, finally, tell me in all sincerity you've ever been loved so completely, tell me any other man has this passionately wanted you, tell me you were ever this wet before or will be, when actually everybody else anybody else will only ever be stepping into our footsteps, cartoon suitors, please tell me you love me, please tell me I'm not alone, aren't you lonely in Japan without me, aren't you missing something, like the most important person in your life, I want you to be happy I wanna make you happy but you're thousands of miles away & I know only one thing will convince you, one thing already has, please don't forget ever ever forget what it was like, don't stop imagining what it will be like, together, I love you my soft light, my single monkey, are your hands open or closed when you sleep?

Do you know something I never told you, I've always loved that you call this a drug, it is, like being filled with white light & comforting warmth. I'm feeling that now, I've switched positions, I've closed my doors & tacked up the blue blanket-thing, I'm lying on my stomach on the bed with my laptop on the floor, two pillows beneath my chest, I'm rubbing my erection into the bed, softly, I just remembered that, when I was young, that's what I would do, even though my stepbrother showed us all how to masturbate, I never did that, I would lie in bed on my stomach and move my hips, move them until I came, which you know, initially was just this feeling, this spasm, this whole body tingling, but without any release of sperm, that came later, not much later, but later. Can I concentrate on anything now but being with you?

O the sun is directly on me now, it's delightful. I can barely see the screen though, but that's okay, I don't need to really see what I'm writing. In fact, it's best, imagine typing me with your eyes closed, I'm doing that now, not looking, the sun warm against my eyelids, and having to remember where I am just from knowing what my hands have done oh it's kind of erotic typing you like this eyes closed lying on my stomach lemme unzip my jeans ohhhh that felt good & my nose right now is kinda right in my blanket i'm imagining your brown housecoat why did I find that so sexy cuz you were in it definitely but also the coat itself it was so warm maybe so comfortable it was furry oh you were like a brown cat in it that's why I love you my brown kitten wanna rub your tummy now wanna smell your hair & skin I wanna lie with you in the sun and hold each other until we're sweating because I wanna taste you oh please please nada next time no deodorant I wanna be able to lick your underarms I wanna taste you there & smell you, oh I can feel my heartbeat accelerating it's at that moment I wanna take your hands in mine it's then I wanna stare into your eyes both of us naked and sit with you on the futon maybe drape our legs such that our genitals are close without touching and just our slender fingers interlocked, curling around each other, constantly moving like baby eels at the ends of our hands, tongues with fingerprints, I feel so strong lying in the sun my heart's racing now throbbing against my ribcage I wanted to write you some porno but this isn't porno really not what I had in mind I was gonna write you some noun-filled erotic scenario, sort of like yours though mine would have been less imaginative, I liked yours, the nettles ohhh delicious detail, animal breath, riding with your legs around the leopard's haunches, anyway my feet are cold I wanna get them warm somehow why isn't the sun falling on them, I've just lifted my legs they feel warmer now the sun must be on them, you are the sun nada, the sun is you, I'm imagining your energy with the help of the sun's, & just opened my legs, am suddenly conscious of my asshole, like how you described the leopard's asshole, I'm waving my legs back & forth in the air, look at what you've reduced me to, I can't be with you now so I'm doing this, you can't be with me now so I'm describing this, it's kind of agonizing & embarrassingly silly but what other erotic pleasures can I offer you now just this ludicrous stream of consciousness while I lie here erect & without you, but also with you, the sun is so harsh my baby it feels great but I really can't see anything, my eyes are tearing up and all I can see is red, am I seeing the blood in my eyelids or is it the color light through the flesh makes i'm conscious of my breathing, steady but a bit rapid, I'm aware also of my hair for some reason, like the warmth is making it grow, oh that's weird and I can feel the back of my throat too a bit scratchy still like I still have a cold okay suddenly I want to change positions I wanna lie back, I've now moved, the

pillows are against the wall & I'm sitting upright, my legs stretched
out before me, the laptop on my forelegs, my jeans undone, open,
imagine a V & my erection just inside that, peeking out, and what
I'm trying to do now, I'm pausing between typing, taking hold of my
penis & trying to imagine what it's like for you when you hold it,
what this thing feels like to you, so much of the other person, so
much mine, is this why we concentrate on genitals, generally, above
& beyond the obvious reason, but because they are so much the
other person, your pussy so much you, & is that maybe why I wanted when I was with you to bury my head between your legs so often,
why I loved being there, why I loved how you tasted, yeah but also
how you shuddered when I licked you, and those little noises you
made, almost like you were crying, how you sound when you're crying, but slightly different, your whole being shuddering, now, I'm so
erect if you could see me it would look sort of like this

\|/

with the \/ things being my jeans, where the zipper is, opened, and
my cock erect between them, oh it's amazing to think you held this,
what is that like anyway I kinda want you to describe that for me, it
must be kind of thrilling, especially knowing that this has grown for
you, that it's me responding to you, it was indescribably thrilling
when you told me "look at what you've done to me," and then
opened your legs & guided my fingers there with your hand or was
it just with how you looked at me to feel how moist you were,
remembering that I have to hold myself very hard, have to squeeze
myself, & agitate the head of my cock just slightly, my heart's really
pounding right now my love, oh you are my monkey, I want my
monkey-cat-bird wrapped around me now, I want to sit here like this,
my back on pillows against the wall, legs outstretched, fully erect, &
have you climb on top of me , your legs straddling me, & oh ewww,
would you let me kiss & lick your chin, your neck, your shoulders,
& blow on you everywhere, maybe it's the distance we are from each
other or maybe it's the strength of the sun on me maybe it's that you
told me you liked this and maybe it's having talked with you last
night & felt so completely with you it's all these things probably but
I want really bad to lie you back with your head falling back over the

edge of the futon, & with scarves tie each of your wrists to the wooden frame with your arms outstretched, & then your ankles too, opening your legs widely (your pubic hairs would really glisten in this light you know, uhhhnnnn), & securing your ankles to the wooden frame as well, oh and I know what I'd do first my darling, I'd kiss you from your belly to your pubes, then would begin to lick you slowly just how you like it, lapping you like a kitten at its milk dish, & I'd ask you to tell me when you felt like you were close to coming, meanwhile I'd be masturbating, and when you told me you were close I'd stop licking you, I wouldn't let you come, instead I'd raise up on my knees over you, so you could watch as I came, as though the energy had been transferred directly to me, nada i'm coming as I write this, I can feel it ohhhh fuck ... mmmmmmmmmmmmmm I can imagine it spraying all across your body, from your legs, through your pubic hair, across your belly, dribbling onto your nipples, oh do you know how much cum I just released? wow, my boxers are soaked, I can feel it dribbling between my legs, lightly tickling my scrotum. Urrrgh. Oh, but no it wouldn't be over yet, I'd follow the trail of my sperm with my tongue, & either that'd annoy you or it'd feel good, you'd let me know, & if it annoyed you maybe I'd lean back down between your legs & continue to lick you until you began to shudder, & would then continue to explore the rest of your body with my tongue, with my fingers, to tease you, to worship you, you could tell me anything you wanted & maybe I'd grant it, but maybe I wouldn't, some things I'd do for you, other things I'd start to do, but would trail off, taking the story elsewhere, & you'd never know, & you couldn't get free, unless you really wanted to, or you grew bored, in which case you'd tell me, but I'm thinking you probably wouldn't be bored, you like how lightly my hair falls on your belly, huh, & how my breath feels against your skin, & that I marvel at your breathing, your beating heart, oh, I'd write a poem in Henna the length of your body, lines going up your legs, around your belly button, what would I write, well it would be a sacramental poem I think, & something as lusciously detailed as you, as intricate as my love for you, & as long, oh, oh, oh

   big love,
   Gary

∞

From: nada
Date: January 13
Subject: phone sex

    —after milton—

    indeflourishing alone, my belly
    imbranded with your elonging
    adust with your handprint

    your gaze azurn,
    moistered cataphracts
    all conglobed in plenipotent
        love.

    imparadised, we phone, concoctive,
    even after jaculation.

    if you will be my conflagrant
    i will be your paranymph

    all myrrhine in my arborous mewings,
    completely glibbed by you,
    immanacled
    then enslumbered
    in nocent elamping—

    wholly, perfectly
    engladded.

            ∞

From: Gary
Date: January 15
Subject: 1/15

Dear Nada,

we are the golden eternity in mortal animate form
& so desire love, abandoned
would condemn us. There is no elevator
in that shaft, the wind howls
in the stairwell, someone left the front door open

I regain consciousness slowly. To drink I
                                    must bow
                                    down
                                    before you
                                    or drink
                                    until I fall
down, o the thin hair in the small of your back.
As if the mind were a poem (it isn't) & as useless
as the concept of eternity. Rome apple. Summer
squash. Jewish rye. Thank you
o thank you iced window, lights
twinkling in perturbed atmosphere
"occasional ugliness" "nobility" "earthly mould"

I'd love anyone who'd call the sky shredded
who'd call to tell me that much. I'm here
now, why haven't you
called me tonight?
                    The wind comes up
as though balancing on two legs.
                              I want
to say more, say
broke my neck, a dead crane, a
failure. There are three matches left in this book.
I read. Leonardo da Vinci's earliest memory was
he was lying in his cradle when a vulture came down

& "opened my mouth with its tail, struck
me many times with its tail against my lips."
Freud dismissed it as fantasy.
                              Whatever rips
the mind apart survives, keeps us
if not sane, aroused.
                        My hair is not exactly kempt.
Earlier, I beat off looking at the photos
you sent.
            Am I supposed
to make a joke of it? It's Martin Luther
                                    King's
                                    birthday
                                    today, he'd be 70
                                    1/15.
                                          O, no
I've run out of money. When I
beat off, I did try to imagine it was you
but I still need to know
a lot of things, though
as long as fate permits, I'll go
on beating off.
                  I have no political conscience
it's too cold, the radiator's pitiless
& so's romance. Sorry, not my
heart requited by the fact of its own existence. If I
could stumble back out this door, beneath
the jet trails' frozen thick scalloped edges
or the work of the day drilled into asphalt
well, probably I would, but probably
                              I'll just lay
my head down on the pillow
yellow & stained, love
"the only subject, the rest
requiring form"
                  love,
                  Gary

∞

[Written by Nada on the back of a postcard, sent late January.]

garden

we do our love in a clear, veined bubble
in the mind vacuumed shut by a horrible flower
that is really a sea mammal out of whose belly a listless
man gazes at a rat in a plastic tube before the invasion of
plastic. the others are loving or riding huge birds (swoosh
of feathers on human skin) or loving giant blueberries which
may be skulls or lava or pregnant. the man on the mallard,
whose balls are on the mallard starts to kiss the "nubian."
the mallard looks idiot-wicked. a 1/2 submerged guy
presses his pretty erection beneath a red ball. how
do you love an owl? why are the tiny swallows
courting? why does the magpie think only
of filigree? why are you looking at me
that way? i realize i'm inflatable

∞

From: Gary
Date: January 20
Subject: 1/20

Dear Nada,

"A quiet, a very quiet place
With camellias in bloom."
    —Shinkichi Takahashi, "Cat"

Ruffled in January, people open each eye
as the day lurches the world that lights
everything.
        Many things are better unnaturally lit
like rooftops, a fist before it slants.
I want to continue gently.
                I equals soft harmless

bulb January tenders softer. Wave-blurred
light nape never exposed.
                         Poem stroked as fur
no better than fur's silent thought. Waves
of snow screwed in cold metal faucet.
                                     White
disk, dusk a deep trickle.
Wet inside.
                   For verve, outside. Outside, it's
all you. Outside you, some light
unsurpassed in beauty this January day.
                                     My life
snuffed likewise by people it warms, cold
people on steps at dawn.
                         Sky equals
the better to eat what your legs
sweep free, leaning, like a house in January.
                                            I
topples white castlework, the voice
of a car goes by.
                   Brooklyn all lit up, its plumbing
frozen like a song no longer played, duped
by selfish expert to office.
                         In January's pointless
building I am always wearing our tie, I learn
nothing to eat, & shrink from it.
                              I don't believe
we change the world by insisting. I call it
shy, focus on unstable objects.
                         Their winter
pauses, as if it's pavement. Slightly,
unless light, I know you,
                   love,

                   Gary

∞

From: Nada
Date: January 20
Subject: How do I love thee? III

> i love thee because thou asketh of me
> artful proof of love and provideth
> same, i love thee because thou art perfect,
> or flawed, or neither, or both. i love thee
> because thou art an always open faucet,
> for me. for me. i love thee for thy quaint ways,
> thy courtly vigor in a crabbed world. i love thee
> for thy littleness and slang, and for the breath that rides
> like frantic lovers to thy brain. i love thy very tongue's
> constructions. i love thee because
> thou dilateth my pupils, maketh
> my tongue spout water, my loins to flutter.
> i love thee because thy gaze is the liveliest
> thermometer of our dual being, i love thee
> as i love the goldest light in this room
> i shall never see again. i love thee as i love
> the red numbers on my phone that count
> the minutes i have cooed with thee. i love thee
> as i love thine own room, the quilt that laurie gaveth thee
> on the bed on which we lay, stroking. i love thee as i love
> writing,   as composition.   is healing.

∞

[*Sent as a letter from Nada, late January.*]

dear gary—

i wish i had your skin today, or at least some clearer semblance
of my own, this eruption just below the nostril a reminder
of my "emergency." it was somewhat cruel, don't you think,
to send me such gleeful pictures of you, as if to say

                                    "i'm thriving" while
my face breaks out into sponges

over the tokyo skyline
                          i look up at the shinjuku towers,
the imperial palace, all of shitamachi, and feel suddenly huge,
           having eaten mackerel in miso and drunk hoji-cha. yes, gary,

        yes

i feel heavy in my clothes, the same ones i wore to the mona lisa, as if
that day i was i, or you you, instead of a couple of smaller-than-life
standup figures pulled out of the dumpster of failed romance
                                                somewhere
paolo and francesca are still cartwheel-copulating their way
           through limbo

        or was it hell? remind me. "sweetheart"
                   comes from OE "sweetard" orig. meaning
                          dullard or dotard, but if this postcard/poem's
foolish it's only as the pastiche of you i find myself becoming,
           like the only
boyfriend i'll ever imitate again.
                                why a vulnerable bruised peach today?
                   with bloodshot eyes
                                   gary i've got nothing
but trump cards for you, not hidden, spread
           out on the table, my thumb
that grips the notebook is throbbing with the blood i—oh!—
somehow find in my veins
which may as well be yours
along with the all the rest of me.
                              it's too late to call you
                              and beg you to make me laugh
                              or jerk off in my ear

           but everytime i hear a string instrument
           i start going CUCKOO ...

              sayonara
                   my cool heart

i'm gone

should i care?

(swinging around lamppost)

love,

nada

FEBRUARY

From: Gary
Date: February 1
Subject: 2/1

Nada,
          You are in the garden of an inn just outside Prague
& I'm there too, simply by reading
Apollinaire, thousands of miles between us erased, imagine!
discolored by distance no more
The door is my own tongue & I can't help it, I'm an atheist
what other pleasures can I claim from this weary world
besides escaping the many horrible things that can happen
& which are, anyway, too obvious an end.
                              If I simply look up
the bits of brick buildings outside that window (I'm
not looking up yet, relax) will disappear, & you'll see what I wear
on my head. It's as unfortunate as Picasso
standing in the mirror behind the rather large crowd he's gathered there.

When you write to me, everyone else sleeps, when I write to you
they open their eyes in the snow, they're
the only reason we need to think or talk at all, even they
know the weight of your body on mine, its wet air
though they're not warm, like you, nor do they smile

You make me thick, that's my song, tho I'm dreamy-eyed when I sing it
the kiss of my hands sucked against you
                              but you
want specifics. & only then, to enjoy them? Neruda kept his heart
          yellow
when he wrote, as what isn't? Even yellow rice is delicious-looking

in a blue bowl. All of this is besides the point, I'm limp
with details, the most available ocean
is polluted, my eyes are acid blue at breakfast, thinking like this
makes me rash
      & doesn't turn my cock female
any more than your voice is these words I see, hell anyone
can see a petunia, even a woven petunia.

I feel like a typist. Forgive me. I imagine things happen as I tell them
but, Nada, only to you
       my committed repose. Tilt your head
& give me your lips, what would you like me
to give you? My cigarette, to crush out? How about some
flannel pajamas? What else stick your bare toes through, & then
to vanish, all out, to fatten the air

Not possible to sink down beside you. Tomorrow
you'll be in New York, but tonight the rivers are black, casually farther
oh where oh where, my cock blown apart
like the morning paper, it was the color of my throat

    Love,
    Gary

        ∞

From: Gary
Date: February 2
Subject: 2/2

Nada,
    the sky seems wet where the sun set, primitive
as the dream you wrote me you had, I wonder
in the dream, did it rain on all these same people
I see out my window, who've never even met me? I'm tired
of being queasy, & the sky is no help.
        It makes
me nervous

what I do with myself without you, can see
Long Island City a mile off, weirdly, I think it wanted to rain
more. I care
       so, "goodnight"
           Oh,
our immediate distance just collapsed in my face
when I said that, I won't say it again,
               no. I'll lie
in bed
       my panties sobbing. I imagine spermatazoic animals
rise from their ashes, above them an electric heater
flew by, I'm keeping
a journal. Only the tip of Manhattan is visible, bright
against Brooklyn's torn geometry, too warm
for snow. If I were as broad-shouldered as a bookshelf
(sudden clarity) green
with evening upon it, or had yellow & black wings
would I do. What
you ask, would I do. I like when you ask me questions, it's
sexy. I'd rather write you porno than a poem
but it's winter, everything I write you more like an ambassador
than a passport, dumped
like an ashtray on the floor at your feet. Love's impossible
glimpsed out a window out which you can't see
well enough to know it's suffering. Let me take off my clothes
so I can better describe it:
          Oh, shit
I'm suddenly older
I feel like everything drained from me, it's embarrassing
& isn't that all that matters? No, I know
you'd rather hear about creatures that light the ocean, well
I'd rather write about them, I never wanted
to be here, now, alone. Now it's quiet (I've run
out of cigarettes), rebuffed I'm slattern, the rain stops
against the radiator's hiss. I'd give anything
to behave on you, the scale
small & attentive, to vanish in your fingers, is that too clever
a thing to say, or

overly preening, like a flower or ocean in your ear?
Stomach, I feel my stomach & I'm here,

> love,
> Gary

∞

From: nada
Date: February 10
Subject: post-insomnia

so last night of course i could only get myself to sleep after coming

my principle fantasy was face-sitting, i think i find that especially erotic because it feels like a very overwhelming thing to do to
someone, i can't imagine anyone doing it to me, but wow

so in the fantasy i was kind of kneeling over your face, not making contact, but dripping and totally fragrant, you could see i imagine my fluids shining on the hairs just outside my lips, and you're
moaning, completely desirous

and i just kind of dipped my hips down sometimes to meet your
tongue, then got off you again and then you kind of grabbed my hips
to keep me there, and i started like really rubbing against your face
until it was completely shiny with my liquid, almost suffocating you

oh and at one point i kind of sat up started rubbing against my
pillow, which wasn't that fun, it felt like a pillow, but i left my smell
all on the pillowcase, i found i was sniffing away at it like a puppy as
i continued the process, it helped me

so after the climax, i fell asleep and started to dream

hey what do you think of this email?

∞

From: Gary
Date: February 10
Subject: bibliomancy

... two powerful myths have persuaded us that love
could, should be sublimated in aesthetic creation: the

Socratic myth (loving serves to "engender a host of beautiful discourses") and the romantic myth (I shall produce an immortal work by writing my passion).

Yet Werther, who used to draw abundantly and skillfully, cannot drawn Charlotte's portrait (he can scarcely sketch her silhouette, which is precisely the thing about her that first captivated him). "I have lost ... the sacred, life-giving power with which I created worlds about me."

—Barthes, *A Lover's Discourse*

∞

From: Gary
Date: February 11
Subject: 2/11

Nada,

"... these things I am going to write will never cause me
to be loved by the one I love ..."
—Roland Barthes

But let's say I've taken you, in arms as thin as Palatino
& that you're here, no lower than the sun
which, having set in Brooklyn, hours ago, rises now in Tokyo
filling your room with light as golden as Sappho's
Aphrodite. Don't your eyes adjust to this
as well? I wish I could describe for you how black the chimneys
are tonight out Laurie's window, how white
the sound of traffic sweeping through Messerole, to
no one cares where, how pink the distant sirens, drifting like leaves
through streets I don't know the names of.
You're the sweetest woman I know
your genius that you'll read everything I write tonight as though
perfect life = why go on (w/this?) = what I fail to tell
when I tell anyone "I have a lover."
                              Building = chimney

or at least let me describe for you the water towers
full & flat against velvet night. I only mention velvet because
the thought of you in velvet
makes my balls ache. ("To feel is to be.")
I wish I was senile, could sleep contentedly
but I know you're here, reading this, where I can't find the bottom
or I'd shut up, like, "Is that your white wings
against the window?"
                              Why did you wear black panties & bra
the first night we fucked
as tho you were in mourning? Who hasn't pissed their life away
like they were so special, hasn't
paid for it w/their life? You
are where I always want to be, bigger because death
won't open you up
as I have, I have no notebook, only one last remaining wish
"to write this poem," tho it proves
no one right, addresses no problem, here
on this kitchen floor
where I think only you will ever see it, I'd rather be in bed
with you, but that doesn't mean I'm not
or that we're not, loosely stacked against you
no need of words. I'm frightened
I don't want to be this open
if it means having to leave you
to find something cheap
enough to eat. I'm writing because I want you to keep
holding onto my arm
                              rather than what I say,

                    love

ʼ

                    Gary

∞

From: nada
Date: February 15
Subject: anime

Anime

Two is me, the
one is bathing

the lung,
like a passenger

or part, a shaven
responding

stamped "G"
on the ether.

*

To meet in
a shaft that

seems to
have history

or expands
to stares unless

the rejection opens
a window—

Talk of the
garden, again,

in differ-
ent face,

but to go
black or elf-

devil, the witch
as mazurka.

*

I make potion
& emotion

offers change.
Someone else is

in a cloak.
To mew is have.

The laughing puts
you in a state.

No more
seems or

spidery omen
in crimps,

huddle. The
widow dismisses &

I want hard
flight.

*

A thigh would
change the

shape of sleep,
first burning the

head, later heart.
What had been

ropes
formed tentacles.

To be sought
not on form.

Reeling it in from
the net or post.

The wind in the
leaves. But I love

the small toes,
gravitations.

*

A squire
above my

mound clasps
such as we

have in this
misprint.

I see a
goddess one.

The wind's
face is not

"betraying"
some beast.

Bump to set
it off or

crack although
no one asked

*

It is slowing
between (rebus).

Part of me
will actually

kiss this
music.

A froth of
windless snail.

A body gone
for three months

& image &
memory (memory)

will draw the
breath that

maintains a
calendar

Starved for an
other

in my think-
ing. Yet I

won't repose
under statues

most likely stunned,
face down.

*

*

I lost the line
from the

writing. &
your figure over

my other
thinking. This

on a Monday,
epidural.

Is it a muse
or a person,

a girl, in lines
she sounds

dolorous, then
someone far in

a city
at a window.

The seed poured
down the valley

& it met
against lions

budding; it made
it make the

low sound. I
woke, hooted.

*

To see the world
as a man,

he's all mare,
just in

a horse way.
Don't wait,

you'll lose
direction

The eggs no
longer

block passage.
Monks

would be
there in the

halls too—
bibliomancy.

*

I can't hear
thru the strain

so let it
be flirting—

tho there is
a voice, electron-

ically echoing
in frustration.

They built
a connective

tissue of
raw origin

& agreed on
its promise

to enter the
wishéd land.

*

To love it
make x in

a circle,
to keep it

speak the
soothing line

with juice,
blue color.

"Prediction"
is not pre-

destination. I
wiggle during

sleeping. There's
another word that

passes fire,
hotter fire.

*

Not Punk but
English,

having fun,
others too.

His wines were
offers

bees
blood & gold.

I wrought
this poem as

a house you know
it was phones

and seems scarcely
nervous

yes &
yes living there.

*

An optimism
is sassy &

urban, feeling
the sound

as a portal—
watch

out for
the tailfeather.

The real voyage
is fire

than the mother
I saw him

cropped, he
breathed, like

a sigh, and then
picked me up.

*

Two eyes: the
burnt log &

sea above; quite
direct and

"right thru."
The candlelight

day lived under
this incipience.

Needs slashed
—with the mind

& newspapers
on the ground blown

in eerie lovemaking
noise. The

two happening in
space actually together.

*

I'll lose & yearn,
grow exact

fears, develop
molesight. Fit

your face, a
night angel,

it's because
we want it.

Aching,
life

& bright
winds out

from the new
guy with

a clown on
it, slender (sender).

*

I wanted
other hand,

the dream
word, not

a familiar.
The dream

lover's head
a field

He writes to pro-
pose. The wafting

bauble of days.
Seeing another

writing for other
to propose. Daze

at seeing the
moment she writes.

      *

Hard-on as a
thing

that my
heart

pumping,
I fly to,

again to
raise my legs

World fills
with rhyme,

the bed
lucks out.

I made him
from mots in

my living
womb.

      *

A "mind game"—
to bring his

harmonica
to the maid

force-fed like
wild form (heron)

still
looking gaunt.

Breathing steam,
to be roaring

—and me, rising
fluttering (no

death) (babe
heat) transitional

pleasure of a
heart beat

*

Poet of the
moan

but to smooth
my sight by

some grin like
a dart, wall

glowing in
mindlight.

Would I leave
the country

through the tea/
straw of

such collusion,
the gift of

his besotted
stare and all

*

Why think there's
only so many

rhymes, so many
witches. It

was as differ-
ent as peace

and with will,
emotionality.

A conch but
some affair—

it resounds as
words

slurred, then in
triangles, the couple

singing *Inochi
Kurenai.*

     *

What delights
me is flowing

excitability.
Future determines

what I
needed in the

past, stopping
to break lines.

I saw the
corny side

as seethru like
a filmic

weight, bred
in peace.

Limes pile up
in the greenhouse.

     *

Punishing false
eyelashes that

exist, to try
to learn from them,

maybe. Then there's
mascara,

the need to
make up. Blush.

Minds are morbid
& I am in

your room, crying
until

day's end. Went
in, came out

with a famished
spun web on.

*

The next bas-
ic learning

is of need
where our notes

—have left you
—have left me

gushing from
tune to tune.

What is my
internal like.

You were
slow sway,

clutching penis,
wrapped life

singing a dear
smell.

*

Say "lover"
as a bird

I'll straddle
us both—

saying the
word, in

anticipations,
moon on arms.

Form a trough
in forehead

planning/
traversing

these little
stanzas which

grow into
a wheedle.

*

I danced
upon the

faces in the
keyboard where

we couldn't speak—to
lose this sleep

having realized
what my face is.

To wait for
the day to

have your
light in it,

what will be
arrival in

that time
& placetime.

*

Such a
portent

(oh, dude).
They would

sit needing,
not choosing.

What is this
likeness.

She tried her dia-
dem on with spit

but flitting across
to her it was up

astounded and
flirting to a groove

rage I felt just
this enchantment.

*

Singing lark
our date about

time (fate), tho
that spark where

you looked so
abject, my ass

almost as if
it's on fire.

Anew to his
presence, I

felt so confused.
A question followed

by "manx" &
the covers

lifting
looking for tail.

*

What I might
love of doubt is

the whimsical
rolling over—

the us with
no hassle

like a Russian hat
or shadow cat.

To write a
poem on the

back of
the lover, on

the lover
I never smelled.

The lover who
sent the poem.

*

The gasp &
squeal,

Mitch's
haunt-

story.
Outside my

computer,
inside it.

She pleasured
herself with

the smallest,
the almost

unborn foot.
It held a

center that
harpies clawed.

*

The rhyme I want
is the rhyme

that has no rhyme.
Goodbye, givens.

In this moving
is my assem-

bly of parcels,
roundly maternal.

I veer down
to the pasture

for the masks
to wear which

were not bought
or worn before.

The dress of masks,
skin of film.

*

Some will
vibrates

down the
medulla:

FOOD
LOVE

EVERYTHING
PLEASE

The stopped
face in sight:

Athena. Sun
god no doubt

is a hand-
some presence.

I want to go,
find him out.

*

Myth lets fly—
which is

girdles &
green stockings,

shells that are
ears with

some people in
& old lovers.

A dream of
a new place,

to push a
barrier open

against my concern
and rude fright.

My that was ancient
like ancients' fear.

*

The drooling of
morning, of

what there is
to be laundered.

The microcosm
a go-go

causing to
burn my hair.

To be gorgeous
& strong

(he wrote)
to love

a sound. The
newer mi-

gration, the
face foundation.

*

Yes, a lack
of matur-

ation ... "a high
sound beyond

which fish can
become song."

A new mistress
waiting for smell.

I note that it's
a form of peony

then, the diversion:
foreign lands; build-

up of languge;
trading lives, cracking

up the new boy's mood,
grip his smooth eggs.

*

We notice, oh
in this book in-

stead of her not
thinking about

him, then she
could blow out

& be fuseless
& be here.

A tramp
left

home for the
fair one, a

real virgin
's clamlike lips

palace maze
at night.

*

To drink the look
& twinkle,

to seep in
there along with

the stare of
attention, fanning

there, the two
minds that gaze.

Visions of a
false "beast"

as looking to
a false furor

like redlessness
into scarlet being

not here you're
still here.

     *

It's pausing
over her

becomes poem.
"You'll want to

know who you
are relative

to shivers, shrieks,
& screams."

How poseless
you alone

let me yield
such verses as

caravan,
me blocked

to soften as
the clock ticked.

     *

In the stare the
predilection

talk to each
other in

different direction
different-looking

in face leapt out
locked like cousins.

I thought of
the dark

matter, how
the connection

lasts and then
to go where

& stay
as selves.

*

Is it the whirl
—the guy, the

mush—& is
it a heart?

I saw a crocodile
in the bath

& the crocodile
& I hungered.

My finger en-
tranced from

groin to
your book.

It drew a
desire-

form on
real time.

*

Not a quiet
space but a lush

one—where we
could follow where

the pure blisses
hum. So to make

... homeness, change.
Kind of alarming.

Not to grieve
or even

miss, in that
emotion

reaches this
peak, not

the lavender.
The mist was.

*

My kiss
is the bisexual

innocent one,
neither creepy

not betray-
ing, it cart-

wheels beamingly.
I'll melt you.

Risible orange
of the stimu-

lant—slaver
at long waiting.

Sung that
worry out on

a walk, the
many walks.

*

Now sound
is being &

acute: lick
of snatch, or

hump me or
her, the

meanderings, pur-
ring meanings.

Asleep in the
innuendo

fishing
for the

sound of
the pro-

forma
lilt (lust).

Warp & woof, the
ineluctable

pain & death.
When writing,

reading, talking—
folds of being.

"Its miraculate,
chanted surface."

*

If lonely,
not such a

question of
nascence

through gravity,
but this

man is as
is a man.

I wanted to write,
epistolary

(no jackal) like
I was running

toward you, it's brighter
and it burns

right into the
nightingale, fearless.

∞

From: Gary
Date: February 18
Subject: 2/18

Dear Nada,

A walk to Russ Pizza for a slice takes about five minutes
at the corner of Messerole & Manhattan three
teenage girls in dark down jackets huddle together one
wipes her nose "But I only went out with him
because he has a card ... so I could get my cigarettes"
The rest of this depressing conversation is lost to me
as an ambulance rounds the corner lights flashing siren, etc.

I focus my attention on a plane as it appears over the horizon
of buildings on my right its silhouette against
an almost completely indigo sky I like the way this airplane looks
like a secret agent almost & I almost forget the nasty things
everyone's ever said to me people sometimes imagine they're writing
everyone else's biography I don't understand this plane either
there's something graceful or elegant about its apparent stillness

Someone's left the *Daily News* on a table I order read the headline
MY LIFE IN HELL Supermodel Kate Moss Talks about Drugs
        & Alcohol
the man behind the counter sings along with the radio
"I believe I can fly I believe I can almost touch the sky" he's very
earnest I try to imagine a life in Hell with Kate Moss
what would we say to each other? what do we have in common?
drugs booze both notably underweight "Hi do you want a hit off this?"

The counter's sticky to the touch I fish $1.50 from my pocket
I guess I'll wind up in Hell someday too I won't be seated
next to Kate Moss probably Russ Pizza will be there there'll be
photographs of Kate on the walls signed "I love your pizza
I'm sorry I used your restroom to stick my finger down my throat"
only pictures of rich or famous people will grace the walls
just like everywhere else just like Greenpoint Brooklyn

The teens have moved on from Messerole & Manhattan the slice
warms the palm of my hand soon it'll warm my belly
I wonder if you would still love me if I had a belly well would you
bother to make me speechless really I'm practically dead
without you tonight not even Laurie's Polish landlady
sticks her head out to acknowledge me climbing the stairs
if I lived here I'd owe her a lot of money but I don't what a relief

I have teeth and a tongue and use them to eat the pizza
it goes without saying they won't be used for anything else tonight
tho I'll chew on my memories of you even as they're fading
will you still love me when you arrive in New York if there's no heaven
we can live out our days out by the sea or near Coney Island
I imagine we'll live wild & tangled like seaweed
you smell like the ocean and used to come quickly I do remember

I have enough to eat I live in Brooklyn these are small miracles
I'm glad I bothered to think of them even as I think of you
are you the same person you were yesterday I like to think so
tho it wouldn't be so bad if you weren't like the airplane I hear
out Laurie's window is not the same one I saw earlier nothing's perfect
if it were there'd be no room for improvement o quickly
imagine me no longer writing this to you but home

Seen from one corner of the room folding this page up standing
& walking it over to you "Here" where you sit reading something
you take your eyes from to see me standing above you
handing you this letter folded neatly but in haste wanting you
to take this from my hands how warm they are now I've eaten
will you think of lovers as you read this will you read me
as a lover reads and not as someone wanting something

Brooklyn fades Laurie's apartment disintegrates everyone's had
a bad time none of this is anything but words
from the "biting-mouth part" of your lover his nakedness
seen thru like a jungle or tangle of seaweed he being only the I
it's darkest against there is nothing to say about him

but what's been said here no account without meaning
like this world your eyes glow in amber is open all night lost by me

> Love,
> Gary

∞

From: Gary
Date: February 23
Subject: darling, there is an ocean

Miles off, and because I know you I think of sea creatures, the jelly
fish, the eels, the many different kinds of fish and crustaceans,
animals that light up, phosphorous-tipped beings, there are tons and
tons of seaweed in the ocean, floating & growing, they're a kind of
bulb, I love how certain birds seem to congregate only on the beach
where else do they live where do they go when they're not at the
beach I never see them elsewhere maybe they live on the beach but
where do they lay their eggs, isn't it amazing that birds lay eggs and
that given all the bad things that could possibly happen to those eggs
that sometimes nothing bad happens and someone, a bird, hatches,
and will grow up and mate and lay more eggs, but will certainly have
a whole bird-life of its own, what kinds of things are important for a
bird, what takes on the level of importance besides hunger and mat-
ing and finding shelter, there must be moments of self-recognition I
can't believe humans are the only beings who experience that, I
know looking at this photo of your cats Nikolai and Zoe that they are
self-aware they know who they are and kind of what they are, and
they are behaving as they do because they know they are cats and
are comfortable with each other, one is soft and the other is soft and
both know that they are as soft as the other and that the other feels
what they feel lying together, it's ridiculous to think only humans are
self-aware yet this is a perfectly acceptable scientific belief, we're so
arrogant, I mean not all of us, but humans as a species, where did we
ever get the idea we were important, I guess this is how come sometimes I get mad at the idea that anything human is important, like

poems are not inherently important, we just make them, because we can, because we have a need to make things, and a poem is at least something that won't destroy the earth, at least so long as we don't print 100,000,000,000 copies of it, which it, being a poem, cannot expect, I like the idea of failure as an aesthetic and I liked what you said about having no real style or no one style in the *Bay Guardian*, I've always felt that about myself too, do you realize how similar we are sometimes about some things about really sort of basic things, this is probably how come we clicked together like Dorothy's heels at the end of Wizard of Oz, hey I think if we never forget this about ourselves it will always be of use to us, help us get through bad moments or periods, I suspect there might be some, no matter how much we love each other, sometimes we're weak as human beings, sometimes we mess up, even in small ways, not major betrayals, but small ways that can be, over the course of years or even months, devastating to a relationship, I know for instance sometimes I go on & on too much about things and seem like I'm being condescending and probably this is a particular kind of weakness like fear that I'm not being understood, so I try to talk simply, go over every point, and that can be irritating or insulting even, I'm glad you point it out when I do that, even if for a moment I feel defensive, at some point usually not too long after I realize oh yeah, oh god, what an ass I'm being how come I'm being like that, and maybe right now when I'm like that it's just because I can't kiss you instead of talking which is what I'd rather be doing right now than writing you, I'm looking at your photo again, the new one, and I want to walk around the table and pull your hands from behind your back, and curl my fingers in yours and maybe let go of one of your hands so I can lift your head with a finger, so you'll look up at me, into my eyes, and I'll tell you Nada I really love you, please please don't say anything, just kiss me we don't have to do anything, I just want you to kiss me, oh, and then I think you would kiss me and I'd have to control my excitement to make good on my promise "we don't have to do anything" meaning of course sex, but I'd control myself not because we wouldn't want to do anything but sometimes I'd just want to kiss you and have that oh so delicious lingering feeling, and then I would walk you around the table to the chair on the left, and pull out your chair for you, and I would ask, do you want to wear your apron, and you might say no and so I would take it off you and go hang it up, and come and sit down, and we'd both be there, I would be confused because looking at the table I see I don't know what all this food is, but I would watch you to see what you ate and how you ate it, whether you used chopsticks whether or not you dipped it into some kind of sauce, and then I'd slowly learn this meal from you with you, and would be eating with you, I would tell you then a story and I would ask you first do you want a story about humans or animals and if animals should they be sea creatures or land creatures or what and you would be maybe teasing me a little when you said I want you to tell me a story only about colors and geometric shapes, but I'd probably believe that that's what you wanted and would begin ...

"Once upon a time the blue did not function as blue but was a rectangle, not a square—squares were all pink—but a rectangle, there was division between shapes and colors because someone had thought to name them, not any of them amongst themselves but an outside party, someone fully colorful and not simply geometrically shaped, it was kind of snooty to do that, like 'I'm not one color, which is why I can name you' and 'I am not one shape which is why I can name you' so there came into perceived reality triangles and orange and squares and pink and circles and green and saffron colored ovals, and rectangles and blue, which did not function as blue but to further signify rectangular"

I would pause and you would chew your bite of food, some fish perhaps, and would consider this, and look around the table for something did you forget something? No it's right here, and having found it you'd reach for it

"But there was a problem which no one foresaw, which was that of overlay—how a triangle could situate itself such on a rectangle so as to hide its triangular shape and be seen as only part of the rectangle, except for the seeming 'discoloration', well it was not a problem that came up much except say when an oval shape and circle of similar size came together green and chiffon and the circle hidden as oval, it was thought that in these moments the circle was weaker the oval stronger because the oval remained, though the green of the circle was stronger than the chiffon of the oval, so another problem, which was that some colors were seen to be stronger, depending who was laying on top of whom"

"Hey," you'd say, "what about all the space between the shapes, what's that like, is it shapeless and colorless?"

"This was another problem, was that if four rectangles situated themselves suchly, perhaps a square would be seen in the negative space they created, but the square wasn't blue, now is that a square or was a new word called for, another name, 'shadow-blue'? Some color-shapes made up their own new names, and names proliferated to explain things that were before all of this naming, just taken as fact, not considered not scrutinized, and soon everything was being scrutinized and color shapes were rearranging themselves no longer naturally as a product of moving freely through space, but in order to affect certain phenomena, which were then named"

"But," you interrupt, "is all this happening in 2-dimensional space? Or three dimensions? How are they able to communicate? Do they write or talk?"

"I'm glad you brought up the three dimensions, because you see, the color shapes began to get anxious, all this naming, and realizing that there were limits. They discover limits."

"Is this a thinly veiled analogy of our relationship?"

"Maybe. Not consciously."

"I wasn't saying that it was, I was just wondering, the thought just came to me."

"Hey, no, wait: come with me. Let's go to the roof."

We leave the table and go up to the roof. It's a beautiful night out, the city is glowing in multiple colors.

"Each color shape each shape and color, for now colors and shapes were beginning to discern themselves, began to get nervous, or anxious, and it affected them, they began to move in ways previously foreign to them, to move 'upward,' to 'curl,' so what was once flat became voluptuous"

"They were no longer shapes"

"Oh, they were shapes, just that they changed, kind of, became more complexly shaped"

"What did they do with all those names?"

"The name became quickly antiquated, no longer held one-to-one equivalent value, and I guess mimesis was sort of questioned at this time"

"And, now, they're moving into three dimensional space, they're anxious, they've become aware of their limits, and in this awareness, begin to push against them, they're no longer single colors or shapes, they're beginning to blend together, to become fully formed."

"Sometimes I wonder if we're completely sane, I wonder what the fuck we're doing, I don't understand why you love me, I don't know why I love you, there are moments when there's just this emptiness, this question, it's like a question, not a specific question, but like a question mark, or hole."

"Well, sometimes I wonder the same thing, especially after writing you all night, and then, oh, I'm alone. All my writing didn't bring you here."

"You believe it does?"

"Yeah. Kind of. I believe it can."

"Well, I'm coming there, I'm going there, I'll be there, but I'm here now. I love these words from you but they're just words."

"All words are just words. Anything is just what it is. We fill anything with belief."

"That's frightening, kind of."

"It is, but it's kind of how our minds work. There's a part of me that believes we love each other because we believe we love each other, that really we're just these two beings and that we've invested, we've filled, this relationship, or interaction with belief, with the belief that we love each other."

"Do you believe in love?"

"Yes, love isn't possible without belief."

"Are you going to stop being pretentious and finish your story?"

I open my mouth to continue the story. No words come out. No breath. It is an open mouth.

Lack of oxygen turns me blue. I recede into myself, sense suddenly the parameters of this screen, become wholly rectangular. I'm reduced to blue rectangle.

The wind picks up, I have this image of you on the roof, arms folded around yourself, cold and anxious. Your lover is a blue rectangle, moving gently in the wind. He lies at your feet, speechless.

You kick him. He's as silent as a blank sheet of blue paper. The wind picks him up, sends him over your head you look up, watch him, realizing everything you love is in that blank sheet of paper. A plane appears on the horizon. For a brief moment you focus your gaze on it. The paper, you realize, has vanished.

You stand there, incredulous. Why is he writing me this melancholy bullshit? you think. You stand there for a good three minutes, looking out over Manhattan. I have a life, I had a life, what is this bullshit melancholy nonsense. He could have written anything. Why this?

You walk back to the door, then down the stairs, and back into his apartment. It's empty. Chris is gone, otherwise you'd ask him where I went. The table is full of dirty dishes. You look into his/my room. The bed is made. Everything is in order. You walk into his/my room, take off your shoes, scan the bookshelves. You pull down Laura Riding's *Collected Poems*. You sit on the bed, open the book and read:

World's End

... No suit and no denial
Disturb the general proof.
Logic has logic, they remain
Locked in each other's arms,
Or were otherwise insane,
With all lost and nothing to prove
That even nothing can live through love.

You close your eyes realizing he's bibliomanced this hasn't thought of it prior that the universe speaks to us ceaselessly nothing happens by accident there are no accidents your eyes closed you feel me with you he becomes me and I not words or usage but the literal fact of lying back into my arms suddenly full with you as you are full with me all color & shape funnels into this moment you feel a slight twinge of guilt giving in to what's ostensibly romanticism we all live in the real world after all but so why is this so convincing you realize you don't know what love is it's just some word people made up to describe what they couldn't really describe a form of shorthand or almost dismissive gesture his arms around you now you realize his heart beats like any other animal's just as yours beats how is it animals exist no one knows no one really knows everything is speculation but what you feel you want to call love just as what he feels he also calls love because no complex of words could otherwise describe it you have things to do today you realize you become aware of everything around you and that he isn't there he's writing you you're reading what he writes you for reasons you finally don't understand and invest them with power that you realize have no intrinsic power and you sense your own power that he writes you these words he does little else but write to you but think of you as you think of him and why is he referring to himself as him you suddenly want him to acknowledge himself to say hello to really be here even though you know how ridiculous that is and that he knows it's ridiculous which must be why he's keeping up this curious fictional front like we don't know already we love each other whatever love is we don't know what it is but we can't otherwise describe it a thousand stories will be told between us and we'll still never know just what it is we're doing or feeling won't be able to describe it really to anyone else though we both know at least that much what we do feel genuinely longing and not for just anything but for each other for love for this too for whatever moment in which we both realize together that love exists & that we love we love we love & will never fade away

Gary

MARCH

From: nada
Date: March 1
Subject: a story for you

here's what i did this morning at work instead of doing my work like
i said i was gonna:

__a story for gary__
by nada q. gordon

the photos of me lie spread out on your filthy rug staring at the
underside of your cock and your fingers moving around it, your balls
contracted in imagination. one of the photos suddenly turns animated. the photo-nada pulls her hair back so it's behind her shoulders
and kind of slides off the desk she's sitting on. she puts her hands on
her hips. "gary, what are you doing?" it excites you beyond belief that
she has moved, spoken, and the way her chin is lifted, that naughty
look in her eye, uhn!
    "oh baby, how come you turnin me on so much?" your fingers
start moving more rapidly on your shaft, then start lightly rubbing
the head, and your eyes get so intense you have to close them. the
photo-nada gives you a giaconda smile. "because you're so easy," she
says, "you're so susceptible to me. i've never been more amused. and
i'm not even doing anything. when you first started beating off you
didn't even know i was gonna come to life like this did you."
    "oh man, oh baby, how do you do this to me?" your other hand
finds its way to your nipple, "ohhhh, ohhhhh, oh god."
    "listen just hold it a minute. you're like getting way ahead of me.
what if i actually did something kind of provocative?"
    "like what," you say, in between panting breaths
    "well ..." suddenly she stops looking right at you. her eyes close

for a minute. she puts her face down, her body sort of folds into a center, and then she lifts up , very slowly, her right arm, like it was a kind of calla lily growing out of her huddled body, but with a stem like a fluid snake, the hand rises above her head, the fingers massaging the air in spirals, but very slowly, you can see the slowness of her concentration. and then her left arm kind of extends to her side and that hand makes a slow spiral, the arm rises ever so slowly to get near the other arm so they can dance together, do a kind of *pas de deux* together ...

and the upward force of the two arms moving together pull up her torso, which she sways sidelong, and starts to breathe in such a way that she moves her stomach muscles in waves, but you can't quite see it because she's got on that a-line wool dress with the autumn leaves on it, it's kind of loosely cut, but you know beneath it her body is moving in a way you've never seen it move before because when she was with you she didn't dance for you, i mean she didn't have to you were all over her anyway, dancing would've been too much for you she thought and besides she was still kind of self-conscious, having just, um, just met you

and by now you are so stricken with this fluid, seductive dance she's doing, there's something ancient about it, you can really see that she's descended from desert nomads who played wild, plaintive music in minor keys on wind instruments in tents eating dates and drinking date wine while the women danced in a way that must have been something like this, anyway you are so stricken that you can't even move any more, your hand's gone still, but you're still standing over her, totally erect, your jeans and boxers somewhere at mid-buttock, which seems a little undignified, or too modern somehow for what you're witnessing

so you take off your clothes. and you kneel down, get on your hands and knees on the rug. bend your face down very close to the animated photo-nada, who is completely absorbed in her dance. now she's gone past seduction and is just loving feeling her body moving, the sets of muscles working in tandem "nada, nada, baby, sweetie, what do you want? what can i do for you?"

"ohh," she says, "just be here with me. just watch me."

"but i wanna touch you! i wanna hold you! i wanna make you moan and whimper. i want you to come on me the way you did when you were here in this room, the way you shuddered, oh oh, oh god, i'm going crazy without you."

"i know but we can't do that now. for now i'm two-dimensional and we have to both just accept that. i know it's frustrating but it's the best we can do."

you try licking the picture.

"no, baby, sorry, i can only see you. i can't feel anything." you look really giant though, it was cool to see the little bumps on your tongue so close up like that, but kind of scary too, like the giant pink sea-snail in doctor dolittle."

"but that was pretty too," you say "kind of magical."

"so's your tongue," she says, turning around and dancing from the back. you are getting kind of annoyed that she's wearing that loose-cut dress. "lookit, nada. i know you're in a cold classroom right now, but why don't you just close the door, and, wouldja just do this one thing for me, would you take off all your clothes for me?"

"gary i'm at work. and this is the middle of winter. look at the date on the picture. november! remember, this is the week you were in florida. ahem."

"oh baby, you gotta let me off the hook for that. i was confused and besides, i totally totally love you. and lookit, i'm standing here in the middle of brooklyn totally naked for you. come on. do it for me."

"but if i get naked, that could lead to all sorts of things. now i'm just dancing. i don't know what i'll do if i get naked."

"nada," you say, getting impatient, "that's kind of the point."

"i'm shy," she says, suddenly shy.

"no you're not don't give me that coy act, come on, i want you naked Now."

"oh ok. god gary, sometimes you're so insistent."

the room gets warmer. at this point photo-nada has stopped dancing, she's just staring at you and you're staring at her. you're both thinking how wonderful it is to be making eye contact after all these months, kind of wishing you were higher-tech people with video-conferencing and stuff. it really would've come in handy. when you stare at each other it feels like you're each tugging at the ropes of each other's heart, it feels like someone has let loose all the caged birds, it feels like all the great sopranos in the world are suddenly practicing the same aria together and it's making the earth hum. and in that state, still staring, photo-nada steps out of her clunky shoes, then reaches under her dress and starts pushing down her tights and underwear. now she's bare from the waist down, but you can't see cuz she's still got her dress on.

"oh nada, let me see you, please please please let me see you."

she sits up on the desk again. you can see her white legs. you realize that when she was there you hadn't really really looked at her. you see now how perfectly formed her legs are. she crosses them. you imagine how it feels to her to cross her legs in her naked-ness. you start up feeling crazy again.

she puts her hand under her dress, in between her crossed legs. "gary i'm totally wet," she says. "i'm leaving a slime trail on the desk. and i'm sweating. it's really getting hot in here." she takes out her hand, puts her finger in her mouth. "don't you kind of wish you were here?"

"UHN" you bellow, "let me see you!"

gingerly, she takes off her raspberry sweater with the frog closures, folds it with exaggerated care, and puts it on the desk beside her. she's moving really slowly. you're almost angry but you know what she's doing. then she turns around, and lifts the dress over her head, not ceremoniously at all, she just does it really quickly, in one gesture. now she's wearing only her bra. "should i leave my bra on? she asks

"no. everything off. everything."

"what do i look like to you now?" she asks, still with her back turned to you, as she unhooks her bra, the solid black one.

"welllll ... your hair is falling down your back, i can imagine what it feels like brushing against your shoulderblades, oh and when you lean your head back like that i imagine the swish of it on my body, oh my god you are the most gorgeous creature. and your ass, ok, lookit nada, i totally apologize for not being more demonstrative about this particular body part before, oh oh, oh nada would you just, could you just, maybe bend over just a little bit, just kind of bend over the desk, oh please, please ... please???"

"well, it's kind of undignified, but ok, i'll do it" and as she does she feels the coldness of the desk against her bare skin and a sexual longing so keen that right now she would probably do anything you asked. you put your face up really close to the picture, so you can see what's happening with her body in great detail, yes, there is the patch of hair on her lower back, her asshole is hairy too, you notice, and that's just so erotic to you you notice a thin line of drool is falling from your lip. and then, then between the rounded white globes of her buttocks, so willingly offered yet so completely inaccessible, there, the chestnut oyster of her sex is gleaming.

she reaches behind her back and draws a finger along it, three or four times, and then eases in her middle finger. "what are you feeling now?" she asks

"unbearable desire," you say, "nada this is a kind of torment. why are you doing this to me?"

"would you rather i put my clothes on?"

"no!"

"well ok then." she turns around, kind of leans against the desk. you can see her fully frontally naked now. her belly is pooching out a little, you think it looks cute, very "aphrodite." and her breasts look like, what, almost pre-adolescent, you imagine taking each of them completely in your mouth, completely covering them with your saliva, which right now is flowing copiously. you notice how the waist-hip ratio she was bragging about was no exaggeration, she really is beautifully proportioned. "nada," you say, "you're really beautiful."

"so? i mean what good does it do me now? i mean you're not here. i'm just performing. and i don't know what to do now. would you tell me what to do?"

"ok ... put some of those desks together and lie down on them. maybe put your clothes under you so you have a softer surface."

she does this. she's lying down so you can see her from a kind of angle, neither from the front nor the side exactly. the knee of the leg that is farther from you is angled up. you can see the exact curve of her pubic bone and the darkness of the hair there. there where you really want your mouth like right exactly now.

"oh oh, oh nada, do you know what you look like now?"

"no, what?"

"you look like one of my favorite man ray photographs. of a woman in just the pose you're in right now."

"hey i know that photo. hey gary you know what?"

"what"

"i really love your poems. they are so brilliant. did i tell you that?"

"yeah, i think you did, but sweetie, we're not talking about poetry now."

she sits up on her elbows. "why not? what if i want to talk about poetry now? can't i talk about whatever i want to talk about?"

"well, yeah, but i mean look what we're doing."

"what are we doing? i mean what do you want me to do?"

"ok just lie down. close your eyes. i want you to completely relax, just listen to my voice. i want you to take a deep breath. then exhale. yeah like that, now do it again. feel your breath filling your whole body."

"mmmmm"

"ok now i want you to imagine that your hands are my hands. i want you to feel each arm, run your fingers lightly up the underside of each arm. yeah, like that. that's right. how does that feel?"

"really divine"

"oh goooood. ok now i want you to caress your breasts, just really lightly, really sweetly, until your nipples are completely erect."

"they already are gary"

"i know i can see that. but i want you to play with them a little. yeah like that, exactly. ohhhh nada. oh god you are the love of my life."

now her hands are working on their own, you don't need to tell her what to do any more, they're moving all around on her body, over her stomach and around her hips, softly stroking her inner thighs, and she's kind of starting to writhe around on top of those desks, now and then while she's stroking the rest of her body her hand will swipe through her labia, she'll wipe the moisture up her stomach or outside of her vagina, she uses her palm to kind of spread the moisture around.

you are flat on the floor now, lying as close as you can to the picture, your cock in your constantly moving hand, your heart banging to the same rhythm, it smells dusty down there and the rug is scratchy and it annoys you so you pick up the picture and put it on your pillow and move your body to your bed "ohhh gary that's better, i didn't understand why you put me on that filthy rug in the first place." but as she says this she's panting a lot, and moaning, so that what you really hear is more like this:

"ohhh gary that's, mm mm mmm better, oh i didn't oooh understand why you uhn! uhn! uhn! put me on that hmm hmmm hmm filthy ruuuuuuug in the uhn uhn first plaaaaaace."

now she's got the first two fingers of her left hand spreading her labia at the top of her vulva. the middle finger of her right hand is moving on her clitoris, her eyes are closed, and she's lifted up her hips. "gary talk to me. i can't stand this, your not being here. it's awful, i need your lips on me now, i need you inside me, i need to feel your heart beating over me. i hate this, i'm sick of this."

"oh nada nada oh god, me too, do you think this hasn't been completely awful for me as well. but just look at you there. oh god i can't stand this either, ok, lookit i'm going to try something. look at me."

you're looking right at each other again. there is a moment of puzzled searching around in each other's irises and then, suddenly, your eyes completely lock. like you couldn't get free even if you wanted to. this stare continues for like a solid two minutes, and during that time you are both aware of a kind of cracking sound, like the earth opening up, followed by a dull roar that keeps getting louder and louder, and suddenly she starts freaking out

"oh my god, gary, something's hapening. i don't know what it is, oh my god, this is scary. am i dying? what is this, i feel like i'm going to faint"

"oh baby what is it, i'm so sorry what can i do, did i do this is it my fault? did you eat enough today? oh no, what should i do, nada are you ok?

"no! i'm not ok, this is totally weird, oh gary i'm so scared, what's happening????" and she keeps talking but the weird thing is that the roaring sound has now gotten so loud that neither of you can hear each other and not just that but you can hardly see her in the photo anymore because it's getting lighter and lighter. the last gesture you see her in she's holding out her outstretched arms saying, "garrrryyyyyyy, i love you ... helllllllpppp meeeeeee" and then she disappears in a flash of light.

the photo that was so evocative and dark and full of shapes

before is now completely white. a glossy white rectangle lying before you on your pillow. you lie your head down on it and sob. you have never felt so ineffectual. never felt such a shock of grief.

"she's gone. i loved her and now she's gone. maybe she was just an illusion after all, maybe even her visit here was a kind of illusion, some kind of virtual reality trick or something. oh god, if there is a god. or goddess, tell me this: does love exist? or is it all just some simulacrum designed to fool us into ridiculous gestures. are you just taunting us? oh nada, nada baby, i wanted you more than anything in this world, i wanted only you, and now you're gone, taken from me ..."

your tears fill the pillow, your wails fill the apartment. in a moment of practicality you think, good thing chris isn't here right now. you feel the warm wetness of your tears on your pillow turning cool in the march air in your room, you feel your body getting chilled too, you wonder what will become of you now

so you think to crawl under your blankets

just crawl under your blankets and die

so you do, not die but crawl under them i mean, and you just lie there for a few minutes, face down, your lips against what used to be a photograph of the woman you love, when suddenly

you feel a form of a woman emerging beneath you as if out of some other dimension, first just as an idea, sparkling, and then liquid, then gel, but warm, and then you can smell smells, a kind of vanilla saltiness, and then, then, there she is, beneath you, no longer "she" but "i," the real nada, not a photo nada, not an e-mail nada and not a phone nada, but the animal nada with the breath and the hair and the movement and she's i mean i'm looking right into your eyes and my arms are reaching to clasp you and you are looking at me in wonder but my eyes are smiling at you, my whole face is smiling, my whole being is smiling, i bid you enter me, your lips fasten to mine

and we lie there, finally, for as long as we like

    love

    nada

∞

From: Gary

Date: March 2

Subject: 3/2

Dear Nada,

Harvey Pekar urges R. Crumb to cash in goads You like money
don'tcha? tho Crumb's oblivious
eyes fastened on sneering Amazon Jewess in black boots
I can never have her he trembles we like to imagine
anything fulfills us if it doesn't really save
the odd genius smitten by fractals complex systems
would Dante have written the Comedy if he'd gotten Beatrice

the object of desire isn't muse unless elusive all's
courtship we talk ourselves into or out of
pride keeps us from throwing ourselves at the feet
of every beautiful stranger O
you're more lovely than Cher I thought
when I first saw you that you sneered at me may be
why I've written you so passionately

why I drink alone tonight instead of bar hopping w/Ange
D— or Laurie tho all the stars are like
little fish Courtney Love says people think she drove Kurt
to suicide because the sky was all violets she's
the one with no soul O kill me pills no one cares
mythology what the dead or elusive lover reduces us to
that or money I have nothing Chris loans me for cigarettes

I wanna be with you tear your dress off during ordinary conversation
I hope I don't have to go through this ever again
it's impossible to make clear in a poem in charcoal ochre
sinew atom blue as the screen these words pop up on
pieces of web glisten to inner spider overpilled evolve
in push of light blurred to gold ache as I ache someday you will
Chris pokes his head thru to tell me Jesse The Body Ventura

apologized for saying drunken Irish responsible for St. Paul's
confusing streets dumb fucking Viking if I were to lay out

the city now it'd be in the shape of you I guess
that would be confusing maybe we're all drunk maybe we're
all Irish I mail all my drunken blueprints
of uninhabitable cities to you & we both wake up alone
maybe we're just gutless

undressed look the same talk the same fuck like anybody else
everybody fucks it's not remarkable why mention it
it's not even discussable groupable into words I really want
what you taste and smell and think as you read this
all for nothing human mental hope
delicate viands the cure of this going & coming world's woe
mind tricked into believing or dead forever & ever & ever

am I what am I going on peacefully at your feet
caring not for ideas yellow palm leaves waving
no trees nothing to break it the surf dull & lifeless
but continuing I don't want to hurt you
guilty only of trying to think of the next sentence
it could be sweet as your forehead as accidental
or whole as certain light shimmers

against oceanic tides rare Egyptian emerald-agate tiara
a prayer in the form of a poem
copulating in the empty library of my brain other than I
whatever that is maybe inability
learned from other men merely in poverty's pall boulevards
their hard-earned monies non-crucial & w/out hope
formality merely a way of life

what if Crumb leapt at her I improvise any dream your own
a walk on broken bits as broken as tonight how can it
feel this wrong broken the fast of hands
I'd sell out in a minute but nobody's buying the milk
of the sun I'm scared I guess that's distance
or will become in mingled frame of mind shivered along lines
of sight each time my heart is broken

& tired of anyone's gun cracker barrel Big Town laughing
love, love, love to ignore me like a record player
like a French word like the bridge all dreary music
reaches for why in your white pants do you play such dreary music
I'm in love with you & nothing else has happened

did you really want this world if it really is what it is
& that's all it is & belongs to everybody

how wily silence abiding perfectly no question of being
alive tree trunks sunk in the grass there is
another world with people you are not arguing with in life
fallen upon myself my starving Irish ancestry
not private final one I forget every emotion I ever had
it could be sweet not meticulous or habit
"I wish I were a bird & not held down to anything in particular"

      Love,
      Gary

          ∞

From: nada
Date: March 3
Subject: Sonnet

Sonnet

How do I love thee? let me count the weaknesses.
I love thee to the dereliction and breakdown and helicon
My sound can reach, when feeling out of signal
For the endeavor of Belief and ideal Grade Point Average.
I love thee to the levitation of evidence's
Most quiet negative, by sundae and candor
I love thee freely, as most menageries strive for Right-to-Life;
I love thee purely, as they turn from Praline.
I love thee with the passivity put to use
In my old griffons, and with my chill's falconer.

I love thee with a love I seemed to lose
With my lost salaams,—I love thee with the breech-cloths,
Smoke detectors, tear stains, of all my lifeguards!—and if Godiva choose,
I shall but love thee better after death instinct.

∞

From: Gary
Date: March 4
Subject: 3/4

Dear Nada,
                 Brilliant wind conflicts the absorb I set sail against
red & golden coated people to obey their legs
move away from each other scoot thru bodega aisles
where I tonight skill not efficient to render
a mistake to write I'm walking lovelorn idiot savant while
you intelligently sleep effulgent head against mundane pillow
except for the beautiful brown messages you send
there'd be no Brooklyn no bodega no aisles eccentric flutter
wads of string to hold up my head
                                    divinely sick to stomach
black swaths of buildings beneath the white collect
                                              some bird
appears washed against the window
                                   as I am hurried by
shaken by another woman how proud I was of your tousled hair
as I lay beside you
maybe I just take everything too seriously
I can't go home there's too much light the worm
from D—'s mezcal floats in urine in the toilet bowl
I guess we're off to see *200 Cigarettes*
& walk out half an hour later demand our money back I did like
watching Courtney Love pretend to get drunk
it's not that I don't like being an audience to others
drunk I've never been afraid to watch anything but tonight
all the animal wants is you
                              not possible to say I love you
without smoking or where's the hand lotion

who was it said we can't say anything however unexaggerated
at least something's going on what causes this
                                        if I continue
fixating on nothing I'm bound to say everything to you
the streetlamp curves above me like an invitation
if only I had the time & inclination to observe all the parts
there'd be none left
                        or will our days overexamined be over easy
will we repeat everything like a bad poem someone
who wants too badly to write a good poem writes
I write in a feeble attempt to hide my fear Jimmy Reed
incongruently prominent on my sleeve I wanna be loved but by only
you because I never had—
                        it's merely poverty
poem placed at the feet of a steady stream of gray figures
breathing through the nose & mouth
angel warm
            hush hush
                    baby
shut your mouth Ange slides into the seat next to me at the bar
I forget what I've ordered what I've said it's all a wash
finding form for the tolling of the sea & we
so seldom look on love that it seems heinous not my line
it's just I'll become anyone for you
                        Alles ist Elend und Wucht
Ange imagines I'm listening well I am but I'm also writing you
she'll read this later wonder if I really was it's history
dust I write to charm you & therefore
never cease will wear my sleeves inside out insomniac slosh
mambo yo yo how many don't ask if your mouth is dry
it's two months since you kissed me I forget to breathe
& am too easily grabbed by the throat my cock
an anecdote's flickering lights others get hung up on
nervous thinking of the last clench of light
is it merely pornographic to write you every time I beat off
am I whorish an exhibitionist should I seek medicinal
dogma's hopeful blossoming spew or stare at blanks
pre-matin forgetting how we writhed in 69 my nose in your ass

to be gone from the world
                    poem as portable as a bedpan
heading the wrong direction or at least as unavailable as you
suppose next time we stare at each other
w/out longing sweat-covered subway cancellation ill-repute
unimpressed by Big Apple gunshot mutilation the parade
of continents beneath airplane wing
                              at least I'm fulsome
tonight my heart not like a penis someone's stepped on
on their way to see other people what's
worth saying worth saving any train passage locally I acquire
not enough shut-eye your lips the last I've kissed
how can I sleep tonight faceless w/out you while you shake
in the snow
or is that optimistic cliché
                    I don't know
shit! not even your soaked panties have arrived
why didn't you FedEx them as I asked
                         I'm home now pantiless
Tito Rodriguez makes-to-nod my head but he's not as brazen
as you you dirty girl I'm indulgent but not insane
la la la-la la la la la-la I'm pompous a man
we're neither of us young I fear when we finally sink we're done
drug induced or not come
& fuck me already otherwise I might as well live in L.A.
I wanna spank every word your face has caught upon
O be the flattered bomb that thru subway-wind plummets cohere
spermily not to this my marooned & throttled catastrophe
but to me like "a shovel strikes an amber bottle"
really take me above gravity below sunlight & the shining birds
fuck me like *soy Cubano y tu* "Bronx tambourine"
w/out dirt or "face fallen like a waffle" sink yr fangs
in my flesh w/beautiful subtitles no one will read
my hand's in my pocket it's not Pierre Reverdy but Mr. Wilson
I adjust no one who reads this will ever shake my hand again
hardly matters I seek only a paranormal licentiousness of waste
know what I mean
                    get on a fucking plane already

1,000 palm trees wag in my otherwise empty mind
it's lightning outside Chris just got home meaning I can't
jack off comfortably authority's dicta
creep towards—equinox yeah whatever big fucking deal
mambo mambo mambo yo yo no one listens but you
Tito Rodriguez is dead the heart's enemies
in mutton sleeves beg us think about it or at least
be physically together before we fuck
again
      veracity indulgence confusion pilfering
the richness of the earth is ours
it's okay with me your breath will fill
this otherwise empty fog like a balloon
                  love,
                  Gary

∞

[*Received in a letter from Nada, early March.*]

      grayling's

         mansuetude. but he would

               lunge
        her intemperate
         musky
             cantabile
     skylarking
           even encaged

             the hoyden drools
             on a bed of roses

             the escapee bethinks,
               erelong ...

      lumbar insouciance,

resonant

plenum.

∞

From: nada
Date: March 11
Subject: letter 3/11

dear gary

i think when i write i often want to start from a place of silence, to see what noises struggle up out of that silence, getting into the writing state in order to quiet self rather than mimic the noise and rhythms of hamster brain. this comes out on the page halting or as white space.

the chuo line sweeps past muse music school, the woman washing the window of the riverside pool hall, the fishing center for old guys with nothing else to do in the daytime, terraced ferroconcrete buildings narrower and more haphazard than buildings in your country, four white blossom plum trees and two pink, my face is flat against the train window, the sleeve of my down jacket rubs against the condensation on the window, at lunch the polished rice glistens each grain at the contours, muzak i actually choose the restaurant for cuz i can sit and write. when i come back it will be a sentimental journey but right now i think i hate it here, this long distance from other human beings, not my tribe, they shut me out, i hid here for so long.

soup in which hair has been cooked
a handsome man asking for a second bowl of rice
a costly hair ornament, fingered
porno ads stuck on public phones

it all comes down to here i sit in my body feeling not quite right with the location or the food i fucking hate japanese food. and then what i have put myself through to talk to you, if i were a doctor i'd scold myself. this, oh, so long neglect of basic need, sleep. the food is so salty. mercury fills it.

if it's not your rhythm, don't
go there. squirrels dart ////////
////////// ////////// trees

ramen

dozo

kaplump

will i be clean as a ring?
why are you so poor? and cocky?
i vacillate, making and just saying.
a body of hurt imbues the grasp of
language on my midsection, how
to explain this to you?

today i want to smoke.
why are you still smoking?
don't you love me? or are you
just hurtling through space.
i thought to smoke like the
peripheral vision of a cartoon,
not one of yours.
some days i feel secret, a morning glory in february, a photograph of an autumn leaf through glass (sounds mannered), a hand
gripper, a small bulging. and on those days i want you to leave me
alone. why did i say that? now i'm panicking, no! no! no! don't leave
me! i miss you i'm cranky. why do i think i need space with all this
space, i'm tired, i'm tired, i'm tired.

direct lens.

i understand the chatter of the foreign language around me. i'm
tired, it's change. here in this restaurant a plastic tub (like the ones
i'm shipping my clothes in) fitted with a pump, filled with water and
in it semi-large semi-transparent fish alive and swimming. i took a
class at sf state called grammar and rhetoric of the sentence but you
know what no matter how much i write i always feel something
intractable about my sentences (do they feel intractable to you?), or
is the thinking intractable. or am i just stupid. always striving to get
past ... given limit, nonsense ... or to get to nonsense. and to start
from nothing, no influence ("purity"). i'm not hungry, my hair's real-

ly red, surprise it's raining and cold my tights are thin today, why am i here, i love you. why do i love you? you ask. and well i just do, or else why don't i sleep why do i get all derailed. maybe i'll get me a bow and arrow. i was thinking how to protect myself in america. perhaps i will be totally agoraphobic for a while, would you understand that? because ... it's like ... i'm hatching. i'm kind of proper, i told you i prefer bach to beethoven, there is a sense in which i can be said to "mince along"

the salmon roe stud the whiteness of the cuttlefish, juicy carmine jewels

the wood grain makes a long rose vagina shape, why do i have to think with my poem, i'd rather the poem drag me along, i'll sit in in the wheelbarrow

"i want to kiss the whole manuscript" you said, and i opened my mouth

do you really love me? i promised i wouldn't ask, so as not to be like your wife. i don't care about being your wife but i don't want you to go away. like you loved her and then went away. sometimes your ego makes me sick. so does mine. like swallowing an iridescent beetle.

("oh you come up with the squishiest images, how do you do that" i don't "come up with" i don't you know think what to write, they well up maybe as a substitute for sleep)

i went into my brain and found a man there, a small man in a tattered overcoat. he made the motions of desire and i felt shocked. then loosened my screws. when he talked to me i felt my ovaries sing they sang just thinking of his talking. the marriage of the radish and the carp, the marriage of the bucket and the strung chili peppers, of the crab and the jug of rice wine.

heart hurts, gary, gary, my heart hurts. forehead in left hand. leg tightly crossing twists my spine. i can't breathe. heart hurts.

i could write all day the three red circles he killing me ridiculously pulled at the elastic

my tea's gone cold i hate this kind of tea i hate tea i hate rice i hate haiku, i especially hate haiku, i hate fucking seasons and i hate delicate refined subtle beauty and i totally fucking hate fish, i hate temples! i hate trains! i hate wacky fucking english, i hate innocence in grownups i hate courtesy

i put you in front of me at this table. it's the face of you pouting.

you know at first i felt you were so unfamiliar, didn't you feel i was unfamiliar? like didn't you at the mona lisa tell me you were in love with me or do i imagine that and but if you did i think i felt, but we've only just met! it was like i met you on the street. this part i'm writing now i'm not transcribing from my notebook, i'm just writing, as i'm writing my head goes puzzledly to one side, there's a pain in that not-connection i'm remembering. ok back to transcribing. it's the face of you pouting. why are you pouting at me gary, are you worried by the negativity of what i'm writing? you don't like it when i'm negative, do you, you think i'm going to withdraw from you but i'm not, i'm not going to do that. it's just that, these months ... will i look back, later, bemused by the difficulties? of that chaotic house with that man? of the zombie days in the drafty school building? of the hassle of possessions & transition? oh i really really want to cry. you write yourself to orgasm, i write myself to tears.

(practical question. how do you do that? you type with one hand? i mean you write, "i'm coming now". do you really mean literally "now" or you just did and now you're reporting it or you're about to and your hand goes back to work its magic. would you get your hands on me please, by the way)

self pity! what is there to like, exactly, about cherry trees ("ephemeral fading away"). if you put your penis inside me will i become you? have your memories? think your thoughts? or what? why do i want that?

women were not meant to sit at restaurant tables putting their feet worriedly against the backboard without their beloved men sitting across from them, just an imagined photo-form of their beloved men, as far away as this from their beloved men. suddenly "when you wish upon a star" comes on as muzak.

fucking stupid awful cold march rain.

love,
nada

∞

From: nada
Date: March 24

Subject: quote

> "One either does or does not catch fire."
> —H.D.

∞

From: Nada
Date: March 24
Subject: i'm still here

tomorrow i'm off to california, where i'll stay with my mom until leaving for new york on april 5. this is my last night in japan.

what did i do i went to the *sento* (public baths), wondering if they would kick newly-tattooed me out but they didn't, so i scrubbed myself and soaked in the whirlpool and ogled the women. human beings are so nice to look at when they're naked, even ugly ones. there was one oh so beautifully proportioned girl, i really wondered what it must be like to have full breasts, looking at them hanging there in their sacs of flesh. they look so squeezable and suckable but also kind of in the way and, what, temporary, like you can easily imagine their downward progress to the navel. is that part of their charm? like cherry blossoms? ephemeral and fading away, makes us appreciate the parade of life & time passing by?

i was tired after a day of serious pot hangover. i kind of forgot about that part. so spaced out. but i slept like klunk big heavy sleeping last night, and again when i got home this afternoon from selling my phone line. by the way i can use this phone line up until the last minute as you may be noticing just now. i then wandered in shibuya a little bit, ate thai food, bought you a little something and then came home and had that nap. i'm totally ready to leave. my bags are at the airport, my carryon is almost stuffed full. i sadly had to part with a few things i forgot to put in my boxes: my set of acrylic paints, my soy sauce pourer, my witch hat i wore at halloween. i suppose i can always get another witch hat.

i've been amusedly dipping into a book about kierkegaard in between all my preparations. and a national geographic article about coral reefs. i feel, gary, that there is always so much to pay attention to, so much to say. i was a little annoyed when you wrote in your last e-mail:

> Oh! I don't know what to say!!!!!!!!!!!! I think I said
> just about everything or not everything no but as
> much as anyone i guess in the last six months or so

to get such an utterance from mr. voluble! totally unacceptable. i
mean i know you were on your way out the door but come on.
    hey i love you. i want to be with you. you are the most amusing
person i have ever met, and the art of love comes out of your pores.
    nada

∞

From: Gary Sullivan
To: Subsubpoetics List
Date: March 30
Subject: Poem in Absence of Any Poem

    for Nada

Sounds to me like Nicanor Parra when what I really mean is more like
my coughing roommate's badgering me to admit in some poem
he didn't sleep with the Brooklyn "slut" you dreamed about I
        nodded assent
thoughts elsewhere specifically on the phone worried
someone I'd let down would call & berate me or beg me to do whatever

it is I was supposed to have done I realize everyone I know wants
something from me involving time or money neither of which I have
having "invested" it all in love last night fell asleep 7:30ish
early anyway & woke 11 hours later having dreamed I'd finished
every task I ever took on in life & was now vacationing along the Russian

River Larry Fagin had a TV show everyone was watching I could finally
see it 3:00–6:00 a.m. but it was purely slapstick skits ending in fisticuffs
bored of this I wandered out into a meadow where above me a huge
        balsa wood

airplane was brought down by someone's rubber band crashed into a tree
passengers leaping into chlorinated pool "they wanted to be relieved

of flight" I woke soon after thought to write it all down instead "found
myself" thinking of you "even the emanants I use have been given
        the semblance
of the living within and without the imaginary" as Alan writes
against "the common language of critique" which he claims never
        accounts
for daily human behavior for instance me lying in bed masturbating
        thinking

of one photo of you in particular taken recently perhaps not so beautiful
as others you've sent but how anyway I most remember you "the images
want to emerge" as tho we wrote any of us to render any elsewhere
like spirit world more authentic than doing breakfast dishes say shorts
cum-stained groggy pre-caffeinated Chris hacking away in other
        room checking

his e-mail an hour later I'm on the F train reading the letters of Abelard
& Heloise which Douglas suggests some think medieval forgery he
        spells it
"midevil" thick w/20th century bias it's odd to think anyone might
        prefer
one century to another academic specialists oddly dressed hunch-
        backed from
years of poring over primary secondary & tertiary texts I love that word

"tertiary" it looks like it should be a certain kind of bird maybe parrot-
green w/yellow orange red & blue markings I wonder why no theory
accounts for the odd hallucination any grouping of letters might make
manifest I'm probably just ignorant of it some French theorist no doubt
has written on this the impulse to write on everything over every-
        thing "the

primacy of writing" my co-worker Elizabeth arguing on the phone as
        I write
pisses me off can't hear myself think "tomorrow night I go out to

Long Island for the satyr" is that right she means something to do
      w/Passover
it sounded like "satyr" now she's rustling papers I'm seething she blurts
"whether I have money" most arguments reducible to economics
      like how

class consumes the Buffalo Poetics List these days it's true if I had any
I wouldn't be here at work trying to ignore Elizabeth's kvetching I'd be
w/you in an inner tube on the Russian River or at least writing
more vividly about it or about you I'd rather write about you but it
exhausts me realizing we've another five days apart after six
      months after

our whole lives spent on with & through others "where have you
been all my life!" as tho it or anything mattered
in this world the world of writing world written into existence
out of its own absence "absent-mindedly" scrawled into this
notebook I'll close now having in your absence only everything
      still to say

POSTSCRIPT

[*Written July 8, from our new apartment in Brooklyn.*]

Dear Nada,

       Think each thought through to its logical conclusion?
I think about you all the time
But as I said, not through, not towards anything at all
Like this evening, how I think not even I so persists
As when I think of you, & then I think
How I love your continuity, how beautiful you are tonight
Still hungry?
       Perhaps I'm agreeable merely because I'm naked
Or because I'm honest & not so upset as to be too delicate
As though anyone can give me a solution to all my problems
Such as myself, to whom I am speaking.
                  No, that's a lie.
That's just me. Like you I need to be oiled, & kissed
It's only Thursday, I'm 36, mostly sleepless
Except in my continual tendency not to be. It's no fun to say
Goodnight, what if we grow older? As I write this
You're in bed, asleep, where I can't find you
I wish I was hung over, my wingspread foliate, my fronds
Be small & stand in awe.
       Sometimes I get depressed
Because I smile like you. When will
You be up? Don't you want
Another beer? My weak bladder, let me, it's too hot in here
The moon on your face, it's not even August yet
What is there ever besides various nouns & there they are
Like the weather ruffled & filled & raining
Don't any ordinary person, well, frankly I am, & need

Nothing having happening.
              To do, anything. & being
Alive? Me too.

              Love,

              Gary

                        ∞

[*Written August 23, Brooklyn.*]

              dear gary,

              —essay—

              the other** as succor*
              a domestic ocelot—you
              are   my   emanant
              in a room with calendulic
              walls. stretching out
              against glabrous
              and fluff, as a panoply
              of textures we are made.
              PAT the BUNNY.
              i'm sorry for my
              undelicous omelette,
              but i do want to feed
              you. you are valiant.
              not zipless or optically
              deluded finally cured of
              pansexuality (trees). real life
              is too adorable for
              "textual operation" or mere
              "metrical experiment."
              "metrical" becomes
              "meretricious" but i meant
              "textural operation" of

hands run up and down
the length of specifically
your body. *by which
i do not mean "flan"
or "macaroni and cheese"
tho' perhaps "steamed
milk" (note how dairy
implicates itself in love).
language is u bi qui tous,
fitting against the body
as isolation gel. this
is how the lover functions
also, but with hair
and strategic object
(language) mushrooms.
i put my ram's horn
to the ground, trump-
eted, then heard your
warmth as antipode,
like we'd built tunnels,
carrying crumbs of language
to and fro. if there
are crumbs on your
face they are precious,
hermaphrodite: index
finger along chin's valley
ring finger on moustache
middle finger between lips,
the sole of my foot on your
forearm "who is this goddess"
with her ram's horn nudging
into me. "contemporary
practice," oh.

desire is a wedge
that comes between
you and what you
really want.
it is a spongey
material. loosed
in it i stumble in
japanese forests,
OK, in photos
of japanese forests,
the moss, the invisible
golden deer, the hard
devas—with thunder.
only there can
i incubate the brain
and forget the
close crumpling
this daffy lyricism's
brought me to:
"i suck." in the
cartoon i hold
"my penis" to my head
like a revolver. word
for word it's
a morality play
in which aphorisms
sanguine up out of the
"oriental" mist.
that's "idealism"
for you. suppress!!
that incubator. in red
dress with starburst
chrysanthemums,
white spike heels,
i loll around, waiting
for you to show up
on your motorcycle—
that's the moment

i realize i'm mortal
that the apples have
gone all—oh—
variegated, why you ask me
hourly if i love you?
am i going to have a seizure?
(pomegranate) like Right Now?
am i going to die? (vermillion)
i fell down again and again.
sloppy in the bodegas
clutching thin asparagus "i
totally worship you"
and my urge is lambs,
drunken lambs.
rhymes with "dithyrambs":
the very word conjures
a character with
a melonhead
and round knobknees on
stick legs, cut-offs,
a kappa hairdo.
i know you will never
read this as carefully as
(i didn't write it)
i want you to,
maybe never even ask
"what is a kappa"
or why i abhor
culture or why desire
is a wedge—are you
really listening to me?
i *will* fondle vegetables,
ceramics, assemblages.
"that's just how i am,"
resuscitating speech
in emerging measures.
the parachute is really
a goldfish bowl.

the green weed waving up.
the medium doesn't matter,
you see: air, water, gel
or whatever it is
our inner eye floats in.
just check to make sure
the syntax is OK. lately
i'm concerned about that
and about whether a chick
will appear in my omelette.

i want to buy
a certain kind
of wife. we hate the
avant garde and its nutcase
theories.*** we write something
to flutter another. the self
is a reason. the self is a stomach.
a hole, is full of blood. the body
rules the self with mirrored horns.
there are substrata of self. a
spanokopita of subjective
greenery. a panopticon
of poesy. ***not really but.
ooh the angoisse—the gleeful
intensity of opening
to crisis—smear. my
smother = the writing
sheds light on the person.
and when the light is shed
there is only a naked grub of
writing, in the corner,
shivering. this, gary, is what
it feels like to be in love.
(since you asked.)
brush the excess light
off your black jeans,
or i will put my tooth on

your shoulder, buttock
on thin wrist. writing
sheds its light on the person
at risk. it spews out light
like machines for hot
dogs, cigarettes, packs
of cracker jack with
real toys inside them.
for example, toy
elegant syntax, toy
roughness, toy irony,
animal toys couple—
dancing in an ether
of mechanical reproduction.
it's near the deep place
i swam in to come
here to you. there were
so many ventricles.
was there any choice in the
current. "the poem as
birth canal; negative
vaginal space." when
will there be a sunset
i approve of? "she is
not sad." edgy. like
a marble. highstrung,
i appeared, changed
lives, in a rubbing way.
as love is experienced
as among other things
rubbing. fierce, but not
gravestone. grotesque and
attractive as stamens,
cycles, pain. strange
pain the marked special
person in the eaves (
poison in the ears)
sloughing off

what a foetus clings
to. excuse me
for having been
born. i'm sorry,
i'm sorry i'm sorry.
"umarete sumimasen", but
that doesn't answer
your question. cochineal.
the self is red. the sun
rises in the self.
everyone has the right
to perceive. the brilliance
of the sun in the self
is a joke. joke pain.
and this loose slobbering.
joke pain popcorn.
joke pain sunny-side-up
eggs. it's private how
my finger finds your
golden hairy asshole. how
i with love fellate you.

"their sex poems
are like trophy poems."
"you guys, it's sax
you talk about."
"a propensity to go
into whatsisface-land:
'i rub against thee,
guava'" "the phone rings"
(the phone rings) "i have
weird feelings about her.
she's really in the
category of a woman
who's been overpraised."
"we'll meet again in
fifteen years." "i was being
rude to the dead. people

always want to put their dead
friends on it tho space is
limited." "you don't have to
flatter me cuz i'm staring
at your thorax."

this is really prose,
several thin sheets of it
folded into an accordion,
pinched at the middle,
then formed into florets.
"that's crap"—but it's
"expression." is there a
place for merengue
in the new formalism?
is there a place for ribbons
in the little dogma?
i don't care i'm free
except for my attachment
to you. and then there's
equilibrium. it's worse than
politics and littered
with scraps: menudo.
brains. livers unground.
GIVE ME MY TORCH
and i will carry it all the way
to key foods. in flagrant
delirium.

love ignites by
confession. it weaves
into an argument.
there is no other
rhetoric, spiral,
but these wide margins
i leave as space for you
as space for me but
i'm keeping you awake

with the light i need
to write. crenellating
with guilt i know
i need to stop before
the giant clock.

i can't sleep.

tomorrow i'll propel
again and work devour
the collard greens,
the neurasthenic birds,
in desperate dilation.
the light of anguish +
the blue worm,
low roar of something:
afro-cuban drums?
a herd of bison? or just
your breath/ instrument

the body wants to be
the rash is on the mermaid now,
and the onus. a child's
garden of verbs, a golden
treasury, gary, my little
cries ... no one else
has read the book.
my book. on the
is lost the no anterior
view, the—hey—
hey—i'm not just a woman. i'm.
i'm. i'm. rougher
than daughter, lazier
than ice, the recondite
pours forth
as pleas. but really
i only want your body.

i disturbed you.
the peacocks are
at the door now.
they are eager—
eager as peacocks.
like me, they can
scribble, having
personification—
and little claws.
wait—what?
your circumference.
your casing your girth.
everything else
is talons—
the woman without ...
talons. writing
on the circus tent flaps:
(cuneiform)
the fox is pregnant.
everyone incubates
something. fervor
of a phosphorescent skull
belonging to the same class
as platypi: a small
alligator beak, and eyes
simply white as if capped.
it is gaping. is that what
it feels like to be in love?

"trauma" sounds like
dream, the mind
stripped bare by her
picadors. you crave
pepperoccini. the
yellow-green oil.
i a kind of lowness
at the waterhole.
with dikdiks, titmice.

more. more. more.
dioramas. the shark's
slightly open mouth
i was bitten by exchange
of mental fluids.
another phosphorescent
grub in armchair,
pulleys, cause and effect
that brought us to this
b-b-b-b-bed. you are
breathing, i feel
deranged but tender,
radishes. i LOVE you
i can't live WITHOUT
you. the morning glories
take over right about here.
your protein vivid by my
side, somewhat curled.
wake up wake up
and be with me
in salad dressing, with
tarragon, dill. flaps
of portabello over your
nipples the imagination
is the sweet hippo of
consciousness
sometimes. people
open their legs in wonder—
the room fills with pronouns.
jack, what is the argument of
this poem. is it eyeballs
twisting on their stems.
is it a cone.

**you, gary

AFTERWORD

At long last, here you have it: the first full-length book by Nada Gordon and Gary Sullivan. Nada Gordon (b. 1964) was a rising star in the San Francisco literary scene in the mid-1980s, having performed her poetry, published a handful of chapbooks and occasional reviews under the name "gordon" in such venues as *Jimmy & Lucy's House of K* (this was how I first became aware of her; though at the time I had imagined "gordon" to be an older male Bay Area figure like Kush), who later "dropped out" of the scene to live in Japan. Gary Sullivan (b. 1962), on the other hand, may be most renowned for his role as humorist and provocateur, co-editing the journal *Exile*, publishing cartoons in *Rain Taxi*, as well as for his effusive and controversial remarks on the Buffalo Poetics List (for instance, his statement that the bulk of Frank O'Hara's poetry had a relatively limited emotional range). Yet, there is also a serious side to Gary, who, in addition to editing Detour Books, has previously published a collage novella in chapbook form and had work in *Writing from the New Coast*, among other places. None of these previous engagements, however, sufficiently prepare the reader for what this book has to offer.

First, if not foremost, *Swoon* offers a love-story: two writers, more than 10,000 miles apart, who have never met each other (though Gary had seen Nada read twice 15 years earlier), through voluminous e-mail writing, come to live together, both figuratively and literally. This in itself is no mean achievement, and suggests a conjurer's or hypnotist's magic. But because these two individuals conceive of love as, in Nada's words, "a grand *literary* passion," such a conception complicates the plot by suggesting that there may not be a profound, or lasting, connection between two lovers (especially if both are writers), unless there is also an attempt to connect—or at least forego the attempt to divide—life and art, the ethical and the aesthetic, the private and the public, etc.

Such an attempt, and achievement, on Gary and Nada's part,

also serves to render explicit, through dramatic embodiment, many concepts that are touted and ostensibly embraced by many "experimental" or "visionary" writers. *Swoon* documents the symbiosis that occurs between lovers "in the throes," who in the process become mutual muses in a collaborative dialogue that replaces hermeneutics with, in Susan Sontag's words, "an erotics of art." Love is not subordinated to the writing, but neither is the writing subordinated to love. Such a dynamic can suggest either a perfect symbiosis or a vicious circle, and this book evokes its share of both. Yet, even though the book offers as much of a happy ending as could be wished, this does not mean that it answers all of the questions it raises. Some of these questions are less blatantly eroticized; for instance, Nada's of March 11 (p. 280): "why do i have to think with my poem, i'd rather the poem drag me along ..." One of the most particularly relevant series of questions is asked by Gary: "Is love binary? & if so, why does triangulated desire so intrigue? Do we lack appreciation for simple things, is there some mania for the 'complex,' is the speed of binary love unequal to that of our thoughts (& therefore emotions)?" (November 28, p. 113)

Triangulated desire need not take the form of the family romance (baby makes three) or of love triangles, though those are perhaps the more common ways (though childless, both Gary and Nada are "seeing" others in the early stages of this epistolary relationship). Rather, when Nada writes on November 30 (p. 121), before they've even talked to each other on the phone, "one thing i think we should do, together, if after your week in the sun, you still feel like hanging out with me, is to go over all the pages and answer all the questions that remain unanswered," you (or at least I) have to laugh, because it becomes obvious that this would take nothing less than a lifetime to do adequately. Thus, the reader, the imagined audience, becomes the third term presiding over this "marriage" of Gary and Nada in its most mythic proportions.

To measure this achievement, one could consider it against the assumptions of two prose-books celebrated in poetry circles that consider the relation between love/desire and writing: Roland Barthes' *A Lovers' Discourse* and Anne Carson's *Eros: The Bittersweet*, both of which make a cameo appearance in *Swoon*, and both of which emphasize the polar tension between love and writing. To summarize somewhat reductively: for Carson, writing is largely an individual action which becomes threatened by the presence of an actual other, while for Barthes, writing is largely born from the frustrations the lover feels in the beloved's absence. There is some truth to both these assumptions, and there are points in which Gary and Nada succumb to such ideas, but what makes *Swoon* special is the way it provides an alternative to these either/or binary assumptions.

This alternative is hinted at early in the correspondence, before either of them can be said to be "in love" with each other. Gary tells the story of how he wrote, and even published, his first poems:

"I had a HUGE crush on Lori Lubeski! and my roommate, Brent, told me that she co-edited *If*. I couldn't even look at Lori without my heart pounding, whole body sweating, mouth dry, etc. I found it completely impossible to talk to her. So my plan was to write some poems that would impress her enough to publish them in *If* ... and if she published them, I'd have an excuse to talk to her ... I showed the results to Brent and he said "Yeah, they'll love this." We had a mini-argument about it because Brent was adamant about it being "real" poetry, that really worked as poetry, and at the time I thought that (a) I was faking it and (b) that anyway poems were ultimately worthless except as you might use them to move, physically and emotionally and otherwise move, through the world ... To me, it didn't register that something human-made might be autonomous ... I soon found out after that ... that Lori was gay. I was depressed for a long time after that. The fact that my poems were published meant nothing to me." (March 19, pp. 11–12)

Such an attitude is extremely refreshing in the context of contemporary American poetry, and Nada, for one, with her stated love of the epistolary mode (October 31, p. 54) responds to it positively. Yet, however courageous Gary's admission of the necessity of such erotic "alterial" motives, they are not sufficient. For, as Gary also puts it (Oct 26), "the only thing I enjoy reading more than your e-mails right now is your poems." Thus, for both Gary and Nada, the epistolary mode is not considered ultimately more authentic than the poetic mode, and the illusion of an "autonomous" poem is not entirely rejected in this book. Yet, the dialogue that occurs between these two literary modes allows us to emphasize moments in the poems in which a desire for communication exists while at the same time allowing us to appreciate the letters themselves as poems. In short, there is a de-hierarchizing of the relationship between poetry and letters here so that the two genres mutually illuminate each other, as lovers often will.

If Gary at first begins by conceiving his desire to write poetry as but a means to the end of "mov[ing] through the world," and to the extent that that desire was frustrated could not commit to it, Nada, too, we learn, has come to similar frustration—attempting to explain why she is not writing as much poetry, she writes: "there's a cable connected from my creativity to my teaching, and i only occasionally reconnect the cable to my writing. i feel very bad about this, but i know i am a great teacher ..." and in the same letter (October 17, p. 46): "it's just that for the past decade my writing hasn't had, i haven't sought or allowed it to have, much of a context." (p. 32) She seems at first nostalgic for the SF literary scene, until she remembers how petty much of it was. Nor does her current relationship provide her with a context for her writing, for even though her lover of 7 years is a "careerist poet," he is "unable to really be in a committed relationship (the writing always comes first)." (p. 32)

Thus, we see two writers able to provide for each other a context—one which neither of them were able to find in writing before, a context that is personal as well as poetic, erotic as well as literary. If this sounds to you too good to be true, you're not alone. In fact, as this relationship develops, there are moments in which a significant backing off occurs, a backing off which lends plausibility to more "realistic" notions (cf. Carson's and Barthes') of love. In terms of the narrative, most of the backing off comes from Nada (though there are indications that if Nada hadn't played this role so theatrically, Gary would have).

Once the intensity of the epistolary relationship is established, it has to stand the test of physical presence and the quotidian. In terms of plot, there are three particular moments, each one more intense than the previous, in which an attempt to increase intimacy threatens to decrease it: 1) the first photo Nada receives from Gary (November 13, pp. 73–78); 2) their first phone call (December 2, pp. 140–141); and 3) their first physical meeting (December 26, pp. 165–170). For the present purposes I am less interested in pursuing the psychological causes or implications of each of these events than

I am in exploring a few of the ways in which these highly dramatic instances help illuminate the relationship between epistolary e-mails and the people who stand "behind" them. Of special interest here is Nada's first e-mail after their first phone call, in which (after calling him a "goofy gigglehead") she expresses the core of her disillusionment ("you're really a much better listener in e-mail") and setting some ground rules for future phone conversations ("give me lots of time to answer questions"). Although Nada's letter here may at first seem to be somewhat cruel, her candor is exemplary and anticipates what becomes a core problem (but also opportunity) in the second half of the book: that there will still be a need for these two writers to continue to write to each other even after they consummate their love in more physical ways. This is crucial if the book is to truly undo the twin assumptions that writing is a mere means to an end to love, and that someone is ultimately more authentic in person than in writing.

This is even more dramatically pronounced at the climax of the book: their first meeting, which seems, at first, to be in every way a disaster on the human level. On the aesthetic/conceptual level, however, it is a *tour de force*. Meeting in a café, the two cannot even talk to each other. Instead they pass a notebook back and forth—the result: a stichomythia that rivals anything from Beatrice and Benedick, or Kate and Petruchio, and which could certainly be played, to great effect, on stage. One example:

Nada: It's as if by meeting you the narcissistic echo-love I'd felt in the other media was obliterated. You are truly other ...

Gary: WILL IT KILL YOU TO STEP OUTSIDE FOR THREE MINUTES?

Nada: To do what exactly? Duel?

In retrospect, this is hilarious, though I find myself getting teary-eyed when on December 28 (p. 170) Nada writes of "a quiet anguish," and they do manage to consummate their love before the new year. In this week's worth of writing alone, we may see enough "emotional range" to understand more clearly Gary's comment about O'Hara's relative limitations. From this point on, the book changes in character, as it becomes (almost?) a foregone conclusion that she will come to live with him in New York in April. Yet, though the dramatic intensity diminishes from this point, there are other things to hold our interest.

It is no accident that it is from this moment on that both Gary and Nada begin to try to write poems to each other as well as letters (before, for the most part, they were content to send each other older poems, by themselves and others), and that we become aware of aesthetic differences between them (Gary: "I like long poems, long lines"; Nada: "i like short poems/ short lines"), as well as a symbiosis on an aesthetic level (they begin, more self-consciously, and theatrically, to imitate and parody each other's dominant mode of writing).

It is also around this time that the idea of making public their correspondence is bandied about, and the question of triangulation takes on more specifically literary dimensions, as their previous lovers progressively drop out of the picture.

* * *

It seems perverse to single out particular poems in this book as well-wrought urns for literary analysis, in part because such poems get lost in the shuffle of the narrative—not only for the reader but even for the writers, though it becomes clearer that this is Gary's "problem" more than Nada's. Nada's poems are more patently lyric than Gary's; for instance, her beautiful poem "Sympathy," or even her e-mail titled "vows":

> i promise to
> listen to anything you say
> help you say what you want to say
> give you the time you need from me
> tell you when i need to be alone, and when i need you around
> tell you the truth anytime you ask and sometimes when you don't
> surprise you often
> answer your questions
> respond with all the energy and attention i have available
> take care of you as i can
> allow you to love me
> keep communication possible in any any any eventuality
> and worship the back of your neck
>   (December 23, p. 163)

If read as a poem, this e-mail is not so characterically Nada as her more imagistic minimalist pieces, but its blend of concision and straightforwardness make it a standout for me, even if the contemporary poetic climate (not to mention the writer herself) might not be so inclined to deem it publishable straight without the "chaser" of the book in which it appears. Much the same might be said of Gary's more discursive lyrics. For reasons already suggested, it is much more difficult to distinguish between Gary's "letters" and his "poems" than it is to distinguish between Nada's, yet this is precisely the aesthetic agon that occurs in the final section (January–March) between these two writers. In fact, there is some degree of comedy as both writers try to move away from their characteristic modes. For instance, on January 5, we see Gary trying on Nada's mode as if it's a pair of pants that will make her want to sleep with him, only to find the fit comically uncomfortable:

> My letters & your answers, having risen out of obscurity
> like a column of air in the larynx, now sleep
> folded in a book of poetry, some phantom
> no less than human flesh
> but beside it, as beside your glans the reddest flower
> would look gray as asphalt.
> It's the book I open now, my
> fingers blackened by our consonents, the present
> devoured by our past, though I do think it's funny
> you asked me to send you
> short lines,
> tightly inhabitable, when
> the camellia is more like what I am ...
>   (p. 193)

As the letter-poem continues, the lines get longer, more effusive, more diaristic *á la* Philip Whalen or Ted Berrigan. The formal structure of this book gives me permission to appreciate the improvisatory writer showing his work rather than worrying about what lines I might or might not cut out. It is precisely the self-proclaimed "failure" of many of Gary's poems, his belief (or stance) that "poems are not inherently important," that reveal his generous spirit, even as

Nada tries to "cure" him of the former in hopes that the latter will remain. And, even in the least "successful" of these letter-poems, Gary has many brilliant lines that may shine even brighter because they are surrounded by more distracted prosaic words rather than the "proper" allotment of white space. On an aesthetic level, then, I find myself at times agreeing with Gary against Nada, and at other times with Nada against Gary. The triangulation here (with "the reader" as the third term) thus takes on proportions which, for me, go beyond even the Brownings' epistolary love-saga by suggesting such literary antagonisms as Byron and Shelley (in the latter's "Julian and Maddalo"), Williams and Stevens, O'Hara and Ashbery, to name but a few literary friendships based on differing aesthetics (I could add Spicer and Duncan, or Graves and Riding, were it not for the disastrous turns those relationships took).

There are a variety of other genres that occur in the book's final pages I should mention—in part to undo the binary I have established in typecasting Nada as a poetic minimalist and Gary as a poetic maximalist. For Nada reveals a wider literary range in her brilliant allegorical narrative-within-a-narrative of March 1 (pp. 263–270), and Gary tries his hand at explicit pornography. (January 11, pp. 208–212) The inclusion of pornography raises some interesting aesthetic questions. For it seems, to this reader at least, that Gary feels that Nada has made a demand for him to not only write short lines but also porno. This is conjecture of course; there is nothing in the book (or even in my "privileged" knowledge as Gary's roommate during that time) to confirm any explicit request on Nada's part. But shortly after their first meeting, Gary muses, "I'm not sure if porno can be written by a person ..." and asks "Was fucking you an avoidance of words?" Only then is he able to write, "I want my words to open your legs." (pp. 199–200)

Obviously, sex has altered the significance of words for Gary, and this is a danger, since it was precisely his adeptness at words that won her over. Pornography, thus, seems to be a way to give back to words some of the power they've lost now that he has lured Nada to his lair. There are many levels of irony here. For when he writes that he wants his words to open her legs, he is wishing for what already happened, and thus not being entirely honest—for it becomes clear that now he has to want words to get in the way, and rather than opting for a "When Love Becomes Words" mode attempts to combine his erotic and writerly needs through the agency of porn. Yet it remains but one of many ways for Gary, for even after succeeding in writing pornography, he writes things like "When I/ beat off, I did try to imagine it was you/ but I still need to know/ a lot of things." (January 15, p. 215) Certainly such hilarious asides, filled with pathos, contribute to the overall sensation that these sex poems are hardly the "trophy poems" of other writers, but part of a dynamic process that raises many questions that I will honor by not attempting an answer.

* * *

This "perversely fascinating" book is valuable not just for what it may tell one about love, or of writing, or of Nada Gordon and Gary Sullivan particularly, but also for the various insights it offers into others. Nada's ruminations on the body, health maintenance, and Tokyoites, for instance, and Gary's "secret history" of the SF poetry scene of the late 80s, are all quite illuminating. The pleasures of this book are varied, more varied than any book of poems by a single author in over a decade, but at the center of it is a love that is as pure as it is theatrical, a love that is at once as heroic as that expressed in Shelley's "Epipsychidion" ("in love/ to divide is not to take away"), and yet which doesn't end in panting, trembling, expiring *per se.*

Swoon manages to revitilize the art of romance and romanticism without succumbing to the temptation to believe, as Nada's previous "lover" did, that "after sex the mystery is lost." In contrast we can experience Nada's desire "to suck out all of the knowledge and energy from your brain (not to take it from you, more like a disk copy) and swallow it, so i am fairly pregnant with it" as a perfect emblem that allows the mystery to continue, as these writers make hungry where they most satisfy.

—Chris Stroffolino, Brooklyn, November 2000

NADA GORDON was born on January 14, 1964, in Oakland, California. In 1988, she moved to Tokyo, where she lived for eleven years. Now she lives in Brooklyn. She is the author of *more hungry, Rodomontade, lip, Koi Maneuver, Anime, Foriegnn Bodie* and *Are Not our Lowing Heifers Sleeker than Night-Swollen Mushrooms?*

GARY SULLIVAN was born on July 31, 1962, in Long Beach, California. He grew up in Northern California, moved to St. Paul, Minnesota, in 1991, and then to New York in 1997. He now lives in Brooklyn. He is the editor of Detour Press and an online poetics magazine, *Readme*. He is the author of *Dead Man, How to Proceed in the Arts, The Art of Poetry* and a book of cartoons, *The New Life*.